WYOMING SHOOTOUT

A JOHN POPE WESTERN

G. WAYNE TILMAN

WOLFPACK PUBLISHING
— EST 2013 —

WOLFPACK
PUBLISHING
— EST 2013 —

Wyoming Shootout

Paperback Edition
Copyright © 2021 G. Wayne Tilman

Wolfpack Publishing
6032 Wheat Penny Avenue
Las Vegas, NV 89122

wolfpackpublishing.com

Paperback ISBN 978-1-64734-282-1
eBook ISBN 978-1-64734-287-6

WYOMING SHOOTOUT

ACKNOWLEDGEMENTS

Appreciation is expressed to Denise Kearns, Becca Payne, and Susan Stecker for their contributions as Beta readers.

CHAPTER 1

Detective John Pope was irritable. He was recovering from two serious bullet wounds sustained in the line of duty as a detective for Wells Fargo & Company. His partner, Sarah Watson, had shot his attacker.

But, the man, dying from her two bullets in the chest, aimed one last shot at Pope's beloved Sarah. Before he could press the trigger, Pope painfully extended his one good arm from where he was laying on the floor. A trigger press put a .44 slug in the back of the man's head. He finished the job, preventing something which happened all too often in the American West.

Someone would be shot in a vital spot with a commonly used round nose solid lead bullet. Yet, he would live to kill the person who shot him, and then die himself a day or two later.

Pope knew how to avoid this from training by

his former mountain man grandfather, Israel Pope, from his years as a San Francisco detective and most recently his Wells Fargo experience. The solution was to shoot to disrupt the central nervous system. To instantly unplug the gunman with a head shot or any shot to sever the spinal cord. Or, to use the ten or twelve-gauge shotguns the stage drivers used.

Bleeding out took too long when the aggressor still had a gun or knife in hand.

These thoughts were on Pope's mind as he hobbled around his grandfather's remote cabin in Marin County in early autumn 1882. It was fast approaching noon.

Pope was an action man. Being invalided was an interruption to his natural way. Being ten miles and a slow ferry ride across San Francisco Bay from his Sarah was an interruption to his happiness.

He sat on the swing on the front porch of the cabin he and his grandfather had built by hand. His blue tick hound, Scout, sprawled watchfully beside him. Pope still was wearing a sling supporting his left arm. Having his arm immobile contributed to the healing of a wound where a bullet hit his left collar bone, breaking it. The bullet then angled upward and exited the top rear of his left shoulder. Another bullet had been surgically removed from his right thigh.

Pope was fit and strong. He would heal if his patience allowed it.

His grandfather had ridden into town for supplies. And, probably to send a letter to his new lady of interest, Millie. Pope grinned at the thought of the man who had raised him. Tall, slightly longish hair, bright blue eyes and a perfect handlebar mustache and beard. Pope had to admit he was a fine-looking man, even in his mid-sixties.

Even the best investigators often miss the most obvious clues. The one Pope missed was he, at twenty-seven, looked like the old mountain man. Looked like him minus the gray hair, a beard, and a lot of knife, bullet and tomahawk scars. As of several weeks ago, he had started to catch up on the bullet scars.

Pope could feel the hair rise on the hound's back before seeing it. Man and dog understood each other. Then, he heard the low growl. Always a signal trouble was about to happen. The dog stood and faced southwest.

Four riders were coming in fast. Somehow, the dog knew they meant trouble.

"Scout, go in the house, boy!" The dog looked at him with a question in his eyes.

"This is gonna get ugly. I don't want you to catch a bullet meant for me. Go on, now!"

The hound obeyed. Pope saw a wet nose appear as the dog peeked around the door jamb. But, the nose was inside.

The horsemen drew to a stop in a cloud of dust.

One called out to him in an obvious Irish accent.

"Would you be John Pope?" the man said gruffly with more yelling than talking in a reasonable conversational tone.

"I would. Who wants to know?" Pope said. While the four were contemplating the answer to this obviously difficult question, Pope was assessing the situation.

The horses were plain brown horses with matching saddles and blankets. No saddlebags, slickers, lariats, not even a canteen. Livery horses. Ones likely to not deal well with gunfire.

The men were city men, and their caps and style were indicative of the Irish accent he heard. He had dealt with such men as a San Francisco detective.

Though holstered, their guns were in holsters designed to be hidden by city clothes, not worn on the trail. The odds were looking better and better as the seconds passed.

Pope had readied himself before they got close enough to see. He knew men galloping in meant trouble. Cowboys riding up to a ranch to ask for water for themselves or their horses would not gallop in at speed.

Pope held one revolver in his left hand, hidden inside the sling. The right-hand gun was also inside the sling, butt to the right, ready to grab.

The four men all reached for their revolvers. It happened quickly and without notice. As was usual in Pope's experience.

Pope's act of drawing the two 4 ¾ inch Colt Frontiers may have surprised the men. If they had time to notice it. He started firing both Colt's before they could comprehend what had happened.

There was a difference between thugs and gunfighters, Pope knew. And, these appeared to be thugs.

But the fight could still end badly for Pope. Even blind squirrels find acorns sometimes.

Pope had thumbed and squeezed a left hand shot and it hit one of the men in the midriff. The man screamed and bent at the waist before falling off his horse. Horses began to scream and buck.

Pope did not notice. His attention was already on the next threat and he cocked and fired his right-hand Colt by rote.

The two hundred grain lead bullet struck the next shooter in the head. His head snapped back, and he fell of his horse. He hit the ground with a thud and did not move. Before he hit the ground, Pope had already simultaneously cocked and fired both revolvers at the two remaining men as they shot at him. One man hit Pope in the left bicep. Pope felt an intense burn as he touched off his left Colt, missing. He fired the right one at the same time. The right gun did not miss.

From the corner of his eye, he saw a sixty-pound fur blur as Scout flew through the air and knocked the remaining rider off his horse. Even Pope grimaced at the sound of bones cracking. He heard Scout snarling as he bit and clawed the man. Clearly, it had not been dog bones breaking.

He raised himself painfully from the swing. He saw blood on the sling over his shoulder wound from the gunfight in San Francisco and on the upper sleeve from the new one. Pope picked up the cane his grandfather had fashioned for him from a cottonwood branch.

Pope limped over to the fallen men, having to hold his cane and gun in the same hand. The gun dangled by a finger in the trigger guard. He could drop the cane and spin the gun up into shooting position in a split second. He left drops of blood in the dust as he limped between the porch and the bodies.

"Scout! Back off, boy!" The man kicked the dog away and drew a wicked looking dagger. So, Pope shot him.

The gut shot man was rolling in the dust groaning as he held his stomach. Nobody else moved.

Pope had to question the man before he passed out from pain or died. Pope knew the man was going to do both. Very soon.

He nudged the three dead men with the toe of the moccasins he wore around the cabin and often hunting. None of the three stirred. Eyes open, mouths open, they were deader than hell, he thought.

The gut shot man looked at him with malevolence.

Pope guessed his own face was not transmitting any sweetness as he glared back.

"Patrick Riordan sent you, didn't he?" Pope said.

"Go to hell," the man replied.

"Not to rub it in, but a guy with a cane and one arm in a sling just killed four of you without breaking a sweat. So, don't be smart with me. I'm not in the mood for it."

"I count three dead," the man said.

Pope laughed.

"You need to count yourself, partner. You are in for a painful, awful death. No way you are going to make it to any doctor before dying. So, tell me if Riordan sent you. Clear your conscience before you meet your maker."

"Pope, why don't you…" but Pope poked him in the ribs with the cottonwood cane before he could finish. The man screamed out with pain.

"Damn! You warn't fair!" he exclaimed.

"Life's a bitch, ain't it?" Pope commented. "Now, you were saying about Riordan?"

"All I'm saying laddie is you will be following me to hell soon after I go. And, the woman detective. Well, she will be fun for the rest of the boys before they kill her!"

Pope heard a horse approaching. He saw his grandfather in the distance. He was glad, because he needed to have another person hear this man's deathbed statements about Patrick Riordan, the Irish gang leader in San Francisco.

The mountain man swung down off his pinto and glanced around his front yard.

"Been busy, huh, boy?" he said rhetorically. Before Pope could answer, Israel said. "How bad you hit?"

"I haven't had a chance to look. I'm hoping the one in the arm is only a crease. The shoulder is where jerking my guns out pulled some stitches loose," he said.

Looking back at the wounded man, Pope said for his grandfather to hear, "So, Riordan says his boys are going to have fun with the lady detective? When is this going to occur?" Pope said.

"Too soon for you to stop it!"

"Who's gonna do this for Riordan?" Pope said, not really expecting an answer.

"Paddy and his boys are gonna have before fun killing her and you can't do squat!"

"Paddy O'Rourke?" Pope said, deliberately making up a name.

"Paddy O'Brien, you dumb shite!"

"Anything else you expect to get from this one?" Israel Pope said his grandson.

"Not really," Pope replied.

The next sound was the crack of a seven and a half inch barrel .45 Colt as Israel put the man out of everyone's misery.

"I thought he was going to throw the sissy little sticker at me," the former mountain man grinned. Israel had noticed the other man's dagger on the ground ten feet away. Pope shrugged. "Yep. I thought the same thing," he said.

"Grandpa, we have to get to San Francisco and look after Sarah! I will probably not be able to ride, so I guess the slower buckboard is the only choice. What do you think about dropping me at the ferry pier, swinging by the sheriff's office in San Rafael and tell him what happened. Then, sending a wire to Wells Fargo Chief Detective Jim Hume telling him his only female detective has a Riordan thug named Paddy O'Brien coming for her. And, I'm on the way!"

"A solid plan, boy. Then, I'll hie on over to San Francisco and back your play!"

Grandfather and grandson grinned at each other as they had done for the almost two decades since the older man took over rearing Pope. His young grandson had been left an orphan by an Indian raid which killed his parents and little sister.

While Israel Pope hitched the buckboard for them, John Pope washed the crease the bullet cut across his bicep. It was a glancing hit and did not penetrate. But, he thought, *it sure hurts like hell!* He smeared homemade black walnut salve on, wrapped a bandage around it, and tied it with one hand and his teeth.

Pope hobbled over to his room, changed and tossed

some clothes and ammunition into a carpet bag. He added more jerky for Scout to his own supply of the trail food and put cold well water into a canteen. He knew he would be needing to rehydrate and replace some of the liquid he had leaked into the dust outside.

With a light bag and carbine in his right hand, he limped outside.

Pope reckoned he and Scout would make it to San Francisco by dinner time, depending on the ferry schedule. Israel Pope would drop him at the Sausalito ferry first, then go on to the sheriff's office in San Raphael to make their report. He had unsaddled the four livery horses and put them in the small corral with feed and water. The bodies lying around and scattered guns were enough of a crime scene to validate the report.

The older man was a legend. He knew the sheriffs in Marin where the cabin and woodland was and in Alameda, where his ranch was. His word would not be questioned. Nor would the actions of his detective grandson. Pope's prowess with handgun, rifle or shotgun had spread across the West as he brought outlaws to justice for Wells Fargo. His actions this morning would only serve to increase his reputation as the top gun for Wells Fargo.

His grandfather helped him onto the buckboard. They nodded at each other and the mountain man shook the reins.

The detective and dog were both dropped at the ferry dock. Pope bought a ticket and sat on a bench. He was now wearing a dress shirt, tie, dark suit and black derby hat. His suit coat bulged out on the side. Because of the wounds, he could not wear his usual in-town shoulder holsters, so he strapped on the gunbelt he wore on the trail.

In many respects, he thought, he *was* on the trail. The trail of Paddy O'Brien and whoever was following him to harm Detective Sarah Watson. Pope would show no quarter. He would cast aside Wells Fargo's policy of apprehension wherever possible.

It was very simple. Set out to harm Sarah Watson and you die. It was as obvious as could be.

The ferry pitched and rolled in the rough gray waters of San Francisco Bay. They skirted Alcatraz Island and headed into the city piers. Pope usually enjoyed the ferry ride but, not today. Today, he was worried for Sarah and was weak from the loss of blood.

By now, the telegram to Chief Detective Jim Hume about O'Brien seeking to harm his former Pinkerton detective should have arrived. Wherever Sarah was, Hume would find her and surround her with the finest and deadliest detectives and shotgun messengers to be found anywhere. Paddy O'Brien may already be no more than a blot on history, Pope thought.

The ferry docked. Pope slung both the carbine case and the carpet bag over his shoulder and limped off the gangway onto the pier. Scout was right beside him, distrustful of the assortment of humanity surrounding them.

Since it was a weekday, Pope told the driver of the hansom cab he had flagged to head for Wells Fargo headquarters as fast as he could. Unless out investigating, Sarah would be in the office

They sped through the streets, Scout's head was out the open window, sniffing the city smells, and warning off anyone who would harm his master.

CHAPTER 2

Jim Hume, the fifty-six year old legendary Wells Fargo chief detective, read the telegram quickly and summoned Detective Sarah Watson from the bull pen.

She walked in smiling but turned immediately serious when she saw her boss' face as he held a telegram.

"Sarah, Riordan has had four men attack the Pope cabin up in Marin. Israel wasn't there, but it seems he didn't need to be."

Her heart sank.

"Because," Hume continued, "Pope killed all four according to this wire from the Marin sheriff, though it seems his grandfather sped one along after Pope shot him."

"Is John..." she began.

"He caught a crease on the arm. We'll have the details shortly when he and Israel arrive. The important thing is Riordan, the man you arrested for the kidnapping of Mattie Lane, sent them and Riordan has a man named Paddy O'Brien and his men after you. We are not going to let them get near you. They better hope the Popes don't see them first. Riordan wants retribution. Well, he sure as hell is going to get it. At the end of a Wells Fargo shotgun!"

Sarah had never heard Hume curse, nor had she heard such vehemence from the normally calm, deliberate man. Hume, with his friend private detective Harry Morse and Sarah's former boss, Allan J. Pinkerton, were the three most famous detectives in America. Probably, the world.

She unconsciously patted her suit coat and felt the .44 Russian caliber Smith & Wesson underneath. Hume saw the subtle movement and smiled but said nothing.

"I am going to bring the San Francisco police in on this one, Sarah. We are going to put a protective ring around you until O'Brien is either caught or makes his play. Due to the deathbed—so to speak—words of one of the men Pope shot, I will also contact the district attorney about Riordan sending out a hit team on the two of you. I want more charges against him when he gets to court next month."

They discussed the kidnapping of a Wells Fargo executive's daughter. It was a case where Sarah suspected that the perpetrators were not sophisticated enough to demand bearer bonds or pick such a specific target. After the shootout where Pope was injured, but the victim was returned safe, Hume had given Sarah the go-ahead to follow up on her suspicions. Those suspicions had resulted in the arrest of a prominent San Francisco citizen for both masterminding the kidnapping and running an organized crime ring downtown. Now, it was apparent the arrestee, Patrick Riordan, was guiding retribution against the Wells Fargo detectives from his jail cell while awaiting trial on numerous felonies.

Hume's secretary tapped on the door and stuck her head in.

"Detective Pope has arrived. He's not looking so good, sir. Should I show him in?"

"Yes, please. And please bring us a pot of coffee. And, scare up some pastries of some sort if you can. Is the senior in?" he asked, referring to Senior Detective John Thacker. The secretary nodded and went to get him.

The two men came in together. Pope was white-faced and drawn and was limping on the cottonwood cane. Sarah immediately rose to go to him but stopped short. Hume was aware they had a relationship, but ordered it be kept invisible to coworkers. To the world and the company, they were very effective partners and nothing more.

Hume looked at Pope with great concern as the latter painfully lowered himself into a chair. The jostling around on the buckboard, ferry and hansom cab from the docks had started him bleeding again. To save ruining a perfectly good suit, he took a handkerchief and placed it between his shirt and lapel and applied pressure. As covert as he tried to be, he was unable to hide his action from the three top investigators who noticed virtually everything.

"John, are you bleeding?" Hume said.

"Only slightly, sir. I will have it checked as soon as I have made my report and am sure Sarah will be safe from these ruffians."

"My telegram from the Marin sheriff says four Irishmen rode to your grandfather's cabin and, in the ensuing firefight, you killed them all. He said one identified Riordan as having sent them and one Paddy O'Brien has been assigned to harm Detective Watson," Hume said.

"It's about the sum of it, sir. My grandfather had to finish off one after I shot him. The man went for a knife as a last act. Grandpa also heard him identify both Riordan and O'Brien before the man died," Pope added.

"I take it was a 'clean' shoot?" Hume said.

"As clean as four men against one man and a blue tick hound could be," Pope said, petting Scout on the head as he sat panting beside his master.

"I'd like to hear how the two of you pulled this one

off, but later. We need to formulate a safety plan for Detective Watson first. Thacker, some ideas?"

"I will put some men on the street near the docks to see if we can get a location for O'Brien. I think two men outside wherever Sarah lives and two inside with shotguns until the situation is resolved," Thacker said.

"I need to be there, too," Pope said. "Grandpa is coming shortly. Maybe the two of us can handle the inside guard duty. Plus, Sarah demonstrated her lethality several weeks ago, so we'll really have three inside."

Thacker and Hume knew Israel Pope and were both on scene shortly after Sarah shot the lead kidnapper in the chest several weeks before. Both had seen the legendary older man in action.

Pope whispered something to Sarah, who had moved next to him. She withdrew a clean handkerchief from her sleeve and handed it to him. He folded it and withdrew one hand from beneath the sling and his coat. It held a bloody handkerchief which he replaced with hers.

"Pope, I want you to get to the hospital down the street immediately. You are no good to Sarah if you bleed to death. Thacker, get a carriage with a top to help hide your identities. And, a shotgun messenger fully armed. I will send Israel to Sarah's address, Pope, as soon as he arrives," Hume said.

"As soon as I get patched up, I need to go to the

docks and put some markers out for locating O'Brien. Also, boss, how about the boys you rewarded for speaking up about Riordan?"

"I didn't want to bother you about this during your recovery, but they were all found dead last week. Throats slit. SFPD is investigating. I will leave here when you do, but I'll go see Detective Sergeant Howell. He's heading the boys' murder investigation and the attack on you and threat against Sarah will likely be associated. Maybe it was O'Brien who knifed the boys."

They quickly finished the coffee. All three men stuck a scone in their pockets and all left. They knew it would probably be dinner.

Sarah and Thacker each picked up a short-barreled shotgun and box of shells at the company armory. An unarmed messenger boy was summoned to carry Pope's carbine and carpet bag down to the carriage.

He leaned on Sarah going down the steps to the ground floor. It was about as close as he could get to her under the circumstances. She stopped at her desk and retrieved another handkerchief to replace the one he had already soaked. The bullet had made a mess of his shoulder and today's activities had worsened it.

The large carriage made good time to the hospital. Hume had taken a smaller buggy to the police department.

The carriage waited at the front of the hospital.

Thacker and Sarah, both with a shotgun in hand, helped Pope in.

The same surgeon who had treated Pope three weeks ago revisited the shoulder wound and replaced several stiches. He washed and applied a different ointment to the four-inch crease wound on Pope's bicep before redressing it with a wrapped bandage.

The surgeon wanted to admit Pope for another day or two, but the detective told him he did not be time to be sick. "Do you have time to be dead, detective?" the doctor said.

"I have some things I have to do. They cannot wait. I will have to deal with healing and dying later. No time now, doc," Pope told him as he limped out the door, the wound in his right thigh unchecked. The doctor just stood watching him leave, shaking his head.

It was almost dark by the time the three people and one dog were dropped at the rooming house where Pope and Sarah had adjoining rooms. Their proximity was unknown to anyone other than Hume and Israel and they wanted to keep it their secret for now.

Thacker took Sarah's key and went in and cleared her rooms.

Nobody was hiding in wait for her. He retrieved a chair to take to the front door and position in the bushes until the shotgun messenger arrived.

"Grandpa will be coming along soon, so don't y'all shoot each other," Pope warned as he munched the scone from Hume's office.

Sarah's rooms were an actual apartment with a fireplace and kitchen area. The bedroom and a study were separate. An adjoining door led to Pope's original two rooms with only a stove for heating and cooking. There were several privies out back and a place to temporarily tie, feed and water horses. Pope reckoned his grandfather would put the buckboard and horse there.

"I suspect Hume will swing by here before midnight, maybe with Howell from the police department," Thacker said. Possibly Hume's only real friend, Harry Morse, knew the chief detective better than Thacker did. "You watch, the boss will have Harry on this case before it's all said and done!" Thacker predicted.

"There's not a bull in SFPD who knows the Irish gangs better than Harry does," Pope agreed, referring to his former detective peers.

Sarah had been remarkably quiet. She did not like to be guarded like some incapable woman. She could shoot as well as any man. Except for the two Popes and maybe John Wesley Hardin, she added to herself. During training, she had amazed Pinkerton himself with her marksmanship. She was sure Hume had shared her shooting the kidnapper with her former employer. They periodically exchanged telegrams, as they had when Hume was contemplating hiring her.

As soon as Thacker left with the chair to take up position, Sarah rushed to Pope. She did not know where she could hug him with a shoulder wound, an arm wound and an opposite leg wound. So, she leaned up and gave him her famous smile which always melted his resolve and kissed him passionately. He collapsed into a stuffed chair and she held the kiss all the way down.

"Don't you ever get shot without me there to look after you again!" she said fiercely. He nodded. He lay back in the chair. It was pretty comfortable. He had sat in it many nights and weekends. His apartment only had the ladder back chairs with his dining table. But tonight this one felt comfortable. Really comfortable. He fell asleep at the second "comfortable."

Sarah knew his wounds were tightly bound and the shoulder stitches repaired. Waking him and helping him over to her bed would make him more comfortable and not injure him further. She eased off his boots and jacket and guns. She hung the latter on a bedpost and put his derby on top. She covered him with her blanket, and he was asleep again within minutes.

Sarah straightened the rooms. She knew Thacker would be back up, maybe the shotgun messenger on guard duty for food, Hume, the detective sergeant, Israel, and maybe Harry Morse. More company in one day than she ever had. She worried about the appearance of Pope in her bed but chalked it off to operational necessity.

Sarah slipped her jacket off and checked her holstered Smith & Wesson's. They were the same double action design. Her primary was a .44 Russian caliber and the smaller frame backup was .38 S&W caliber. She went to her cupboard and got a box of cartridges for each and placed them next to the shotgun shells from the Wells Fargo armory. The Remington double, with its mule-ear hammers, was propped in a corner, ready for immediate action.

She wanted to loosen the damn bun holding her long black hair, kick off her shoes and lay armed beside Pope as he slept but she knew she could not. Forget the appearances, she was currently one of her own bodyguards. More importantly, she had to protect Pope if there was an attack. And she would protect him like an angry she grizzly protecting her cub - with fast and devastating violence.

An hour later, Scout growled low at the sound of footsteps on the stairs up to the second floor where they were. Then, he stopped growling and started wiggling with glee. There were only two people who could cause him to be so happy. One was asleep ten feet away. It had to be Israel.

"Missy, it's me!" came a familiar deep voice.

Taking no chances, Sarah opened the door, .44 in hand at her side.

"How's our boy?" Israel Pope said. Sarah liked the 'our' instead of 'my.'"

"He's asleep. We took him by the hospital and the doc replaced the broken stitches. You should have heard the doctor complaining about the black walnut salve."

"Ha, it's kept me alive after a bear clawing, a tomahawk wound and more'n you can imagine," the older man said with conviction.

He walked into the bedroom and checked his grandson.

Israel came back and looked fondly at the beautiful, raven-haired woman.

"If your hair was down, like I've seen it before, you'd look like my second wife."

"Second wife, Israel?" Sarah said.

"I married again after my son's Ma was killed in a raid."

"You mean after Pope's grandmother was killed?"

"Yes."

"Did Pope know her?"

"He didn't know either one of my wives, Sarah. It was his loss. Both were fine women. One white, one Cheyenne. Both killed by Crow war parties. Our boy don't know about the second one. Mebbe one day I'll tell you two the story, but not yet."

This was the most personal thing about his history he had shared with Sarah. Like his grandson, he kept a lot to himself.

"Clint Fuller, the top shotgun messenger has arrived. He was with us when you shot the kidnapper, Lang. A good man, Sarah." She nodded agreement. Fuller was a legend at Wells Fargo like Israel Pope was in the West.

"Do you and Thacker and Fuller want coffee?" she said. "Or sandwiches?"

"Food and coffee carries scents. Guards need to get spelled and come up here to partake. I'll go down and let them know, though," he said, walking out the door.

She made five sandwiches with cheese and bologna and wrapped them in butcher paper. Setting out five mugs for the coffee or water, she answered the tap on the door.

It was Fuller, who she knew.

"Miss Sarah, how are you? And how's Pope?" he asked.

"I am fine, Clint. Pope is not quite fine. He's asleep now," she pointed at him through the open door. Fuller nodded.

"Thanks, for coming. I can't think of anyone I'd rather have here protecting us," she said. "Grab a sandwich and some coffee or water."

"Thanks, it'll be dinner." He ate quickly like he would on the top seat of a Concord stage-coach at speed and left. Clint Fuller was a man of few words, but a lot of talent. Talent with any gun ever made.

Thacker came up next for a food break. Sarah forgot she had not eaten either. Not even one of Hume's scones. She joined Thacker.

"Those Irish gangs have real good intelligence operations," the senior detective noted.

"Apparently, John. Almost nobody knew about the Pope cabin up in Marin County. I hope they didn't burn the ranch in Alameda. I just thought about the ranch. Maybe we should wire the sheriff to check it."

"Good idea, Sarah. Mention it to Hume when he gets here," Thacker suggested.

He went downstairs after eating and Israel returned.

"There are sandwiches, Israel," Sarah offered.

"I might eat one," he said, smiling.

"What are you so tickled about?"

"I was thinking of the old days, roaming. Things were sparse of the plains. Still are. I'd kill a buffalo and eat the tongue, liver and most of the hump. It was a lot of meat. But it lasted me a week. All I had to do is drink enough water."

"Did all the meat give you a stomachache?" she said.

"Nope. Never. I guess I was doing like those camels in Egypt do with water."

Sarah should have known to not be surprised at things Israel knew. But she was still caught off guard.

Around eleven, Hume, Morse and San Francisco detective Howell arrived.

Using good tradecraft, they noted and winked at

the two watchers hidden on chairs in the bushes by the door and walked in.

Israel and Scout heard them at the same time. Israel drew the cavalry model Colt. Sarah, gun in hand but out of sight, opened the door.

The three detectives, all from different agencies walked in.

Hume nodded approvingly as he saw both sheath the two revolvers.

"How's Pope doing?" he asked.

"The hospital fixed him up. The doctor wanted him to stay a day or two, but he refused. He's asleep now. I think today took a lot more out of him than he'll admit," Sarah said.

"Let me go see if he's up yet," Israel said, walking towards the bedroom.

He leaned over an awakened his grandson. While still leaning he whispered "There's a lot of badges in the next room. You shot the fourth man. He was dying. I just helped him get to hell quicker. It might be best to not credit him to me. I kinda arrived after the party was over. Too many questions, right?"

The two locked eyes. With an imperceptible change in Pope's pupil signaled he heard and agree. A small grin sealed the deal.

"Luckily for us, his stubbornness makes him an even better detective," Hume said and the other two agreed. Howell had been his boss while Pope was a detective at San Francisco Police Department.

The subject of their words walked in slowly. He had a stag-handled Colt stuck in his waistband as he shakily entered the room. He leaned heavily on the cane.

"Pope, I'm going to get you a fancy cane like Bat Masterson has over in Dodge City," Morse said.

"Thanks, Harry. This one is special. It was made to my exact height."

"And, carved with this little pen knife," Israel grinned, producing his massive Bowie knife.

Howell studied the big knife, then said, "How many credits does it have?"

"I lost count, sergeant. Somewhere upwards of ten. Maybe fifteen. The 1840's and 50's were real active for me," Israel replied.

"While things are quiet, this might be a good time for you to tell us exactly how you killed four attackers. And only got a scratch this morning, John," Hume suggested.

Pope told them in report style vernacular instead of story style. His telling of the events was factual and included only what he thought they needed to know. Israel, who knew the whole story, sat listening as stoically as his grandson was in the telling.

They chatted for a while. At close to eleven thirty, the group heard noise outside.

"Throw up your hands, and don't move!" Thacker

yelled.

The order was followed by the blast of a big ten-gauge shotgun and a scream.

Hume pulled his gun and motioned for Pope and Israel to guard Sarah as he, Morse and Sergeant Howell went downstairs, guns out.

They found four men kneeling on their knees, hands up. One man was writhing on the ground, missing most of the lower part of his right leg.

Fuller had reloaded and was watching the others while Thacker fashioned a tourniquet above the man's right knee.

Upon arriving on scene, Howell summoned help with his police whistle. Facing away from the detective sergeant, Hume rolled his eyes and Thacker saw him and suppressed a smile. Hume's message was the blast of a big bore shotgun in downtown San Francisco ought to attract police attention quicker than a whistle.

Howell knew it was both protocol and a message police might already be on scene.

Two uniformed officers responded within minutes. Howell sent one to get an ambulance wagon to respond from the hospital and had the other begin taking a report from Fuller. The other four were field interviewed one at a time in the hall. Hume, Thacker, Morse and Howell peppered them with questions and threats.

Before being taken to jail, the group had what they wanted.

They had made separate statements Riordan ordered the killing of Detective Sarah Watson. They had statements O'Brien was their leader. O'Brien was there and arrested but refused to talk. Hume suspected Howell would soften him up in jail and get a full statement. Either way, he knew Riordan would be charged with two counts of attempted murder by hire and moved to solitary confinement where he could not give orders to have anyone else harmed.

Hume explained this to the Pope's and Sarah. He then headed home for several hours of sleep. Sarah thanked all involved and opened the adjoining door to Pope's rooms. Israel and Scout slept there, door open. At Sarah's insistence, Pope resumed his position in her bed and she took the chair. Within an hour, she snuggled up to the sleeping detective and dozed off contentedly.

CHAPTER 3

For the next several weeks, Sarah went to the office daily. She had a few small cases requiring travel within the Bay area but was home by evening each night.

Pope walked farther and farther each day during his recovery. He spent an hour a day practicing his draw. He practiced from belt and shoulder holsters equally.

Israel returned to the cabin in Marin County. The Alameda sheriff responded to Hume's telegram. Pope's ranch was untouched.

Sarah met with the prosecutor and prepared to testify against Riordan. Israel Pope returned to testify at the trial, which his grandson attended as an observer.

Riordan received a total of thirty years imprisonment for an assortment of crimes. His kidnapping and attempted murders for hire were the keystones of the case against him.

Detective Sergeant Howell was concerned about who would take over the gang. Riordan operated within certain limits on most of his organized crime enterprises. He avoided prostitution and drug trafficking. Howell was not too sure if the young hoodlums under him had any limits.

After the trial, Hume called Pope and Sarah aside.

"Detective Pope, when do you think you will be ready for full duty, including travel?" he asked.

"I am ready now, sir. I will move a little slower and more deliberately for a little longer. I have been practicing my draw. I believe I am much faster now than ever before," Pope said.

"Sarah, are you ready to hit the rails with Pope?" She nodded affirmatively.

"Meet me in my office early tomorrow morning. I will brief you on a case I want you two to take. We have had two train robberies and three stage robberies in Wyoming. Two Wells Fargo employees wounded, and three civilians killed. Come ready to board a train after the briefing. And remember to bring warm clothes. October in Cheyenne is different from October here."

They parted.

"What kind of coat did you bring from Chicago before relocating to Arizona Territory where we met?" Pope said.

"A heavy wool dressy coat."

"Sounds like we may both need to get heavy trail coats. I have spent most of my adult life in California. So, I am not equipped for the plains or mountains of the middle part of the country either. Let's go shopping before heading home," Pope suggested.

They bought similar style, but not matching steerhide coats with shearling lining. Pope's was dark gray and Sarah's tan. She bought heavier riding skirts and boots as well as earmuffs and a heavy wool shawl.

"Once we get there, I will probably buy a heavy caliber rifle," Pope noted.

"We don't know how civilized Wyoming Territory is or what's there. I'd say buy the rifle now," Sarah suggested.

They walked to C.D. Ladd's in the 500 block of Kearny Street. Ladd's had a new .45-70 caliber lever action Marlin Model of 1881 and highly recommended it. Pope bought it, a scabbard and four boxes of ammunition. Despite the load, Pope insisted on walking back to their rooms. He considered it part of his recovery regimen.

They packed for an unknown time span in Wyoming. Pope left his original 1873 Winchester carbine at home. Sarah took his short shotgun with its combination saddle scabbard and carrying case. She had seen the effectiveness of buckshot close-up the night O'Brien attacked.

The next morning, they were sitting in Hume's

office at seven. He reiterated what he told them the day before.

"This gang seems pretty well organized. It may be as many as twenty men. The train and stage robberies stopped a week ago. They netted twenty-three thousand dollars in gold and bills. It's like the gang made their money and left. Local law enforcement and the marshals have no clue. They wore masks. There were no good descriptions.

I want the two of you to find out who they are. Then, where they went. Work with the Laramie County sheriff and the US Marshal in Cheyenne. Don't get confused. Cheyenne is in Laramie County, but Laramie is in Albany County. It's the next county over. We have an office in Cheyenne and a sub-office in Laramie. Once you get solid suspects, introduce yourselves to the lawmen and lead them to the outlaws. Pope, there could be up to twenty men. Do *not* go after them alone. This is a direct order! Sarah, if he tries, shoot him in the other leg.

I suspect you two will winter in Wyoming. It will be cold, so plan accordingly.

I have approved two travel drafts at the cashier's window. They are also holding train tickets to Cheyenne. It will take several days for you to get there. You will have to be undercover most of the time. Work out your cover identities after you get there and determine the situation. I will expect regular and frequent wires by way of the Cheyenne Wells Fargo office. I am not sure you can trust anyone else. This is going to be a tough one. I wish you both Godspeed." Hume said.

The chief detective stood, signaling the end of the meeting. He shook hands with both.

They went to the cashier's window and picked up tickets and drafts, which they endorsed and cashed.

Luggage and armaments collected, Pope flagged a hansom cab and they headed to the train station. An hour later, they were eastbound on a train to their first transfer, Salt Lake City.

The train ride was a romantic getaway for two people who had been apart for weeks. They had a formal lunch in the dining car. Pope added money to upgrade their company ticket. It provided adjoining roomettes instead of seats. They talked, read and enjoyed scenery new to both.

They noticed it was getting cold outside very quickly as they headed across the country. The trip over the Rockies was spectacular. They transferred at Denver for the quick hundred-mile trip due north to Cheyenne.

As always for detectives responding to a crime to investigate, they reported to the Cheyenne Wells Fargo office first. It was a small office. The manager was fairly new and young. His name was Byron McCarthy.

He was expecting them at this time because of a

wire from Hume.

"Welcome to Cheyenne, detectives. I suspect this will be a thorny one. This gang robbed three trains and five of our Concord stages. Two of our men, one driver, or jehu, and one shotgun messenger were wounded. Both will recover fine. Three civilians were killed during the train robberies. Our only corporate liability so far is to the stage passengers and for the twenty-three thousand treasure."

"We are five days late for even the last one. I suspect any tracks will be obliterated by the wind. Have you had rain?" Pope said wondering if there had been mud which might have made for longer lasting hoofprints.

"Naw, dry and windy. I suspect some snow soon though," McCarthy said.

"Let's take the stage robberies first," Sarah began. "Did they all occur on the same road?"

"Yes. The first two were on the route up towards Rapid City, South Dakota. One was between here and the Lodgepole Creek station. It was about fourteen miles north. The second was between there and the LaGrange station on Bear Creek. Another thirty-five or so miles further on. The jehu was wounded at the second robbery," McCarthy said.

"Is he recovering here in town?" Pope said.

"Yes. He's over at County Hospital."

"I have to tell you, Cheyenne is a far more sophisticated city than either of us expected," Sarah said.

"We even have a really nice Opera House. And, of course, everything is decided at the Cheyenne Club, where the money boys sit around with good whiskey and cigars and decide all our fates."

"If you will give us the name of the jehu who got shot driving the stage, we will go by the hospital and question him before lunchtime," Pope said. McCarthy wrote it down and passed a slip of paper to Sarah, who was sitting closer.

"Now the train robberies," Sarah said.

"They were in a different direction. Both happened on the line westbound towards Laramie City. The first, where the shotgun messenger was wounded, was near the Willow Springs and Fort Sanders area. The fort is closed now, but it is a good marker for the track location where they stopped the train."

"How did they stop it," Pope said.

"They piled spare railroad ties which were being stored by the track. Made a virtual wall of them six feet high and six feet deep. The engineer said it was more than enough to stop the train. He did not have a lot of time and laid hard on the air brakes. They slid, steel on steel, right up against it. The rapid stop was what killed two passengers. One struck his head on a seat top in front of him and one was thrown out of an open window where he was smoking."

"Where is the shotgun messenger?" Sarah said.

"He's in the hospital over in Laramie. They moved

the ties and steamed on in after the robbery," McCarthy said, recovering the slip of paper from her and adding the name.

"So, the robbers didn't kill all three passengers?" Sarah said.

"No, they shot one who pulled a gun during the second train robbery," McCarthy said.

"Where was the second train robbery?" Pope said.

"It was fifteen miles this side of Laramie."

"Sounds like about thirty-five miles from here?" Pope said.

"Just about," McCarthy said.

"The jehu who was shot," Sarah said. "Did he draw on them or otherwise provoke the robbers?"

"Nope. They just shot him in cold blood. He told me he was pretty sure the robber meant to kill him, but his horse moved and threw his shot off," McCarthy said.

"What about the train messenger guarding the treasure for Wells Fargo" Sarah said.

"He challenged them with his ten-bore and one shot him in the arm before he could bring it into action."

"Which came first, the stage robberies or the train robberies," Pope said.

"They were interspersed. Which is why I wondered if it was two related gangs."

Pope walked over to a Wyoming Territory map framed on the wall behind McCarthy's desk.

"Byron, a way we usually try to estimate the robber's base of operations is to take a map of the area and draw a circle around the robberies. Often the center is a logical base for the miscreants. Here, we have a top half of a circle with the territory line being the bottom boundary. However, the left quarter of our circle only extends thirty-five miles west, while the right one goes at least fifty-miles. It looks like if we adjust the center, it bases them in the middle of nowhere. I don't see any towns fifteen or so miles east of Cheyenne. How about ranches?"

"No, it's pretty barren territory. The conductors I talked to and our drivers and messengers all said these men looked and rode like cowboys. If you forget the fifteen-mile discrepancy and put the middle in Cheyenne, it doesn't make sense. Twenty or so cowboys living in town and having to board their horses would be noticed," McCarthy said.

"Twenty is a lot to rob either a train or a stage. Where did the number come from?"

"I have notes from where I questioned everybody I could before the two of you arrived. I will give them to you. It appeared to me we had several groups doing the robberies. Maybe there was one leader each time," McCarthy said.

"I wonder if there are two different gangs. One in the east one in the west," Pope said.

"I thought about the possibility, but a famous detective I know once told me there is no such thing as a coincidence," Sarah said.

"Mr. Pinkerton?" McCarthy said.

"Mr. Pope," Sarah said.

Pope was already scanning the reports McCarthy had prepared.

"Byron, it looks like the robberies were pretty quick in succession once they started. Now, they have either stopped or are taking a break. Nothing for five days," Pope said.

"True, Pope. Or they made all the money they needed to finance something else."

"Buy a ranch?" Sarah said.

"Mebbe."

"If you are right and there are twenty robbers, and the top one or two get a bigger piece, there's not a lot left for the rest," Pope said.

"I guess I'm not as firm on the twenty number as I thought after thinking things through with the two of you," McCarthy admitted. "I based it on taking statements and reconciling them. Mebbe the witnesses were not real accurate."

"Wouldn't be the first time," Pope said. "You did a fine job with your report. Chief Detective Hume wants us undercover on this. He said the only one we could really trust was you. You've saved us a lot of interviews we'd have to make if we weren't going undercover. Sounds like there is some question about the sheriff and the US Marshal?" Pope said.

"The sheriff is good. I'd stake my job on it. The US Marshal is a political appointee who was a wholesale grocer. The chief deputy is his nephew. Neither one knows which end of a gun goes 'bang'."

"I think we will go to the hospital here and talk with the jehu after we find a hotel and move our gear in," Pope said.

"Go ahead and leave your gear here. We've grown to be a large under-staffed office in too small a space. However, I have a really good young messenger I like to keep busy. He can put your stuff in a cart and deliver it to the hotel.

I'd recommend the Western Hotel. About everything you will need in town is within a block or two of 16th or 17th Streets and their intersection with Third.

There are some saloons having separate restaurants where ladies can eat and some just restaurants.

While ladies cannot go in saloons yet, they can vote and hold office in Wyoming Territory, including being magistrates," McCarthy said.

"How far is the hotel?" Sarah said, impressed with how forward Wyoming was.

"About a block out the door and to the left," McCarthy responded.

"How about I'll get some rooms and you sketch the map portions where the robberies occurred. I'll come back and give Byron the alias'. You and we will talk with the wounded man here and get some lunch. After, we will secure horses for tomorrow and head west to the train robbery sites. I'd like to look around where the robbers waited, then executed their plans. I suspect the trains here are too busy to stop and wait for a detective to make sketches and think."

"I am pretty sure you are right. The Union Pacific runs hard and fast down the tracks to California from here. Their schedule is tight," McCarthy said.

"We will go undercover now, except for you and questioning the two injured employees.

There will be times we need to flash badges to get people to talk. Doing so will break cover, but always for an urgent reason. So, don't be surprised.

I am conflicted as to whether to contact the sheriff yet. On one hand, I'd like for a deputy to lead us to the robbery sites instead of trying to find them ourselves. On the other hand, Chief Detective Hume told us to stay undercover until time to get a posse and warrants," Pope said.

McCarthy was thoughtful for a moment.

"As I said, Pope, I completely trust the sheriff. He has a senior deputy in charge of investigating all of the robberies, though the farthest one west is just over the county line. He worked out some sort of agreement on it with the Albany County sheriff. I grew up here. I have known Chief Deputy Horatio Akin all my life. You can trust him."

"How about this. You contact the sheriff and ask if Deputy Akin can lead us to the robbery sites over the next several days. The eastbound trip will require camping unless you know of a place to stay," Pope said.

"No, there really is not any. You should go on to Laramie on the westbound trip and spend the night. I will tell the sheriff Wells Fargo will cover Horatio's expenses," McCarthy said.

"Then, we will leave our stuff for your messenger to deliver and will head to the County Hospital to see the jehu," Pope checked the note, "Isaac Berenson. We will check in with you first thing in the morning to see how it goes with the sheriff."

McCarthy nodded and the two detectives left to walk to the hospital.

They arrived within very few minutes and inquired about his room. He was in room 124 with another patient. Having a second person was not what they had hoped. It impaired their undercover status.

The two walked to the room.

There were two men within. One was a lank man with a mustache and Van Dyke beard. He was about forty. He had his right arm in a sling and was eating lunch with one hand. The other man's tray was on a table and he was sleeping. He had snow white hair and was easily in his eighties.

"Mr. Berenson?" Sarah asked.

"I'm Berenson," the first man said.

Sarah and Pope both showed him their badges. Sarah held a finger to her lips to indicate they should keep the conversation soft.

"We are investigating the robberies and are undercover," Sarah said.

"I am Detective Sarah Watkins from San Francisco. This is my partner, Detective John Pope, also from Wells Fargo headquarters."

"I've heard of both of you. The lady detective and the gunfighter."

"If you are up to it, we'd like to ask you a couple of questions," she said.

"Shore. I sure don't have anything else to do right now."

"How many men did you see?" Sarah said.

"Six, I think. One had the drop on me and fired before I could do anything. The shotgun messenger was brand spanking new. When we saw these fellers, I told him to not do anything stupid. There was too many for the two of us to shoot it out with."

"Did the man just shoot you without provocation?" Pope said.

"Yep. He just hauled off and shot me. I think he recognized me."

"Did he seem familiar to you?" Sarah said.

"He did. But I couldn't place him then or now. He looked like a cowboy. But I used to drive a twenty-mule team before becoming a jehu. I figure we must have been mule skinners together."

"How long ago were you a mule skinner?" Sarah said.

"From my late teens to about four years ago."

"Where did you do this?" Pope said.

"Pretty much Utah and New Mexico."

"Did you have any run-ins with any of the people you drove with?" Sarah said.

"One feller. He was a Reb. About three years older than me. Didn't like some of our Negro drivers. We got in a fight. Helluva fist fight. Then, he pulled an Arkansas toothpick on me. One of my compadres broke a stick over his head. We had the sheriff haul him off. Never saw him again."

"Will you describe him, Mr. Berenson?" Sarah said.

"Very average. Mebbe five-seven, one hundred forty. Brown hair and a beard. Medium length."

"Any memorable characteristics," Pope said. "Like scars, limp, anything?"

"Nope."

"How Southern was his accent?"

"Pretty much hillbilly. Not like educated Southern."

"Did you get the impression your shooter was the boss?" Sarah said.

"Not really. I fell over and played possum. I couldn't tell who ran the robbery."

"Do you remember his name?" Sarah asked.

"He went by Cletus. I'm not sure any of us knew

his last name."

"Do you remember his gun?" Pope said.

"Yeah. Which is why I'm alive! It was a Colt 1849 pocket .31. It was converted to .32 rimfire. Brass frame with nickel plating. If it had been a .44, I'd probably be dead."

"You're pretty sure of the caliber?" Sarah asked.

Berenson reached over to the bedside table somewhat painfully and picked something up and handed it to Sarah. She looked at it and handed it to Pope.

It was a small conical bullet in the same condition it came out of the barrel. It did not have any deformation due to a low powder charge and accordingly low energy. It hit at .32" diameter and stayed .32" diameter.

Pope handed it back to the jehu.

"It helps. Though the 1849 was the most popular revolver Colt ever made, I doubt many were converted and are carried out here. Would you trust your life to something this underpowered?" Pope said.

"Hell no! But, I shore am glad he did!"

"Me, too, my friend. Get some rest. Hold on to the lucky bullet. I am pretty sure we are going to need it for evidence at the trial when we get these outlaws. And keep this mum. We weren't here, alright?"

Horatio winked and they quietly left.

"You know who carries one of those little popguns?" Pope said.

"The boss."

"Yep. America's greatest detective."

"John?"

"Yes, dearest."

"At least it goes bang, unlike the one I used to carry."

"True. But your new ones go bang quite nicely," he said.

"Because they were picked out for me by my partner. My forever partner."

"Don't you forget the forever part."

"I won't. Now, let's eat or my stomach will start growling like Scout when he senses trouble."

"He's in his glory now, riding around in the buckboard with Grandpa talking to him like a fellow mountain man," Pope said.

The walked to the Western Hotel. John P. Smith and his sister, Sarah W. Brown had adjoining rooms there. Their luggage had already arrived, and they ate in the hotel's café.

Afterwards, Pope walked over to the IXL Livery at 16th & Thomas Streets and hired two horses for the next several days. The trip east would require camping. Pope bought several blankets, tarps, canteens, and some cook gear. They would get trail food after they returned from Laramie.

The partners retired to their respective rooms. But, not for long.

CHAPTER 4

Pope and Sarah had an early breakfast the next morning and went straight to the Cheyenne Wells Fargo office. Laramie County chief deputy Horatio Akin had just arrived.

The three Wells Fargo people and the deputy discussed the westward trip. Since the two detectives had to get and load up their livery horses, they agreed to meet outside of town in an hour.

Pope asked Sarah to go to nearby P. Bergerant's Gunsmith & Firearms Shop. It was a long shot, but he wondered if the gun shop knew of anyone with a conversion 1849 Colt.

Pope brought the horses back to the hotel and packed trail gear behind the saddle's cantle. They planned to stay at a hotel in Laramie, but he thought it prudent to carry the gear just in case. He also included lunch and trail food.

Sarah went into the gun shop and looked around. When the other customer had left, she approached the proprietor.

She knew she had to break cover and showed her badge and asked, "Do you know of a medium-sized cowboy with a country Southern accent and carrying a Colt 1849 Pocket converted to .32?"

The man went to the counter, reached in and took one out. Just as described.

"Feller like you described traded this on a .45 Colt last week. Said it was too puny for his liking."

"Did you happen to get his name?"

"Nope. Squirrelly feller. Would have lied if I'd asked," the proprietor said.

"But he had the country Southern accent and was average in most respects?" Sarah said.

"He was. Brown hair and beard. Some gray showing. Probably mid-forties. Sounded like an ole Appalachian Mountain boy to me. I served with some during the war," he said, referring to the War Between the States. She assumed he was a Confederate, since most Appalachian mountaineers fought for the South.

"How much for this revolver and five cartridges?" Sarah said.

"You sure you want a little popper like this? I would have thought a detective, even a lady one, would carry something more powerful."

"I do. This is to test for evidence."

"What?" he asked.

"My boss has been experimenting with matching bullets used in crimes with guns confiscated from the suspects. Seems you can tell a lot about the grooves in bullets fired from the same gun."

"I'll be! I've been around guns for forty years and never heard such," he said.

"It will stand up in some courts. Not in others. It's a new science, so it will take a while to get recognized everywhere."

"Well, the gun is five bucks. I'll throw in a cylinder of cartridges. Is five enough to test?" he said.

"Oh, I believe so," she smiled. "If not, I'll come back."

She handed him a five-dollar bill.

"You do it, little lady. I will be right here. I always am," he said.

Sarah walked a block back to the Wells Fargo office. Pope was tying two horses to the hitching rail out front.

"Learn anything?" he asked.

She palmed the little gun and covertly handed it to him.

"Just traded in on a .45 last week by an average-looking man with a country Southern accent."

"Guess we ought to borrow the pistol bullet from the jehu in the hospital, huh?" he said.

"I guess."

"Did you happen to get any cartridges to test bullets against his?"

She just gave him an arch look of reproval. One he had not seen before and would endeavor to not see again.

"Sometimes, because you are so beautiful, I lose track of how smart you are. Sorry," he said.

"Fair recovery, but not sufficient."

"What would make it alright?" he asked.

"I'm working on it."

******

The three rode for almost two hours beside the westbound Union Pacific tracks. Deputy Akin, held up his hand.

"We are at the first robbery site," he said.

All dismounted and dropped reins.

The robbery was too long ago to find tracks they could use. Pope walked off into the woods and studied, while Sarah sketched the crime scene. She walked off and marked distances on her drawing. They could see the railroad ties used to stop the train. The conductor, fireman and a couple of passengers had broken down the barrier and just dragged the heavy creosoted ties off the tracks. They were still there. Sarah added the ties and their positions to her sketch.

In the woods south of the tracks, Pope saw a

number of broken small branches. They were about horse shoulder high. While there were no hoofprints remaining, the underbrush was still in disarray. He saw a cigar butt laying on some pine tags.

"Damn fool could have burnt the woods down," he thought aloud. He collected it and put it in one of the several small paper evidence sacks he carried in his pockets on investigations.

Pope walked out of the woods and approached Akin and Sarah.

"I found where they waited. One was smoking a cigar. I collected the butt. It won't do much good unless we arrest someone with a matching ring and leverage it with a few untruths."

"I have our crime scene sketches," Sarah said.

"I'm just learning this detective stuff," Akin said, "but, we better get going. The next stop is about four hours further on."

They ate turkey sandwiches Pope brought from the hotel café and had water from their canteens in the saddle. They were too tightly scheduled for a lunch stop.

The three arrived at the second train robbery site at three in the afternoon. Akin had not responded after the robbery because it was outside his jurisdiction. He had gotten a wire from the Albany County sheriff with directions. The directions were helped by the robbery site being an un-manned watering station for steam engines.

This time, Pope did the sketches and Sarah took Akin on a search for clues on the ground. There were no woods nearby. Sarah thought the robbers must have hidden behind the water tank and flue arm which swung over to the engine to put water in. They found some horsehair on some of the rough timbers of the supports where horses had been crowded in together.

They also found and retained another cigar stub. The paper ring on it matched the one Pope found at the first crime scene. Any cigarette stubs had long since broken up and blown away.

The two detectives got a sense from McCarthy's report, and corroborated by Akin, the robbers had become more efficient this robbery. They chose a site where the train was going to stop anyway. And nobody was harmed.

By the time they finished, it was dusk. They still had an hour and a half to ride to get to Laramie for the night.

At Laramie, the two detectives took rooms in their Cheyenne aliases. There was no need for Akin to use an alias.

They found a small restaurant open for dinner. Due to the late hour, they were the only customers. They were able to speak low, but with privacy whenever the manager and the waiter were behind the closed kitchen door. It was apparent they were not only father and son but cook and bottle washer.

"Well, what do we have?" Akin asked.

"Not much," Pope said. "We have two crime scenes with the evidence where horses were hidden, but no clue as to how many without hoofprints. Probably, at least one of the robbers was the same man smoking the same brand cigar. But not necessarily."

"They either got smarter for the second robbery or luckier," Sarah said. "They didn't have to build a blockage to stop the train and they did not either shoot anybody or almost cause a train wreck by blocking the track too close to a blind curve like in the first one."

"What can be concluded from those facts?" Akin said.

"Probably nothing," Pope said.

"Was our trip a waste of time and Wells Fargo's money?" the deputy asked.

"Not necessarily. We had to investigate. The one clue which would solve the case might have been here. And we got the cigar stubs which might be of use. We also made sketches to use in court. So, we did due diligence," Sarah said.

"Due diligence?"

"Another way of saying we did our jobs."

"Now, what? Ride to the stage scenes on the other side of Cheyenne? I've been to both of those closer to the robberies. Didn't see much," Akin said.

"Even though it's even later now, Horatio, you might see more. Your way of looking for and at things has changed. Plus, we need our sketches. Before we go, we have to interview the wounded shotgun messenger in the hospital here in Laramie," Pope said.

They ate. Akin went outside to smoke in the fresh air. The detectives went to their rooms.

After breakfast the next morning, they walked over to the hospital and called on the Wells Fargo employee.

******

They introduced themselves and Pope asked the man "How are you?"

"No permanent damage. I took a small bullet in the fleshy part of my right arm. It passed through. I'd be out of here, but it got infected, so the sawbones kept me. He said if it got gangrene, he might have to live up to the 'sawbones' name."

"You said 'small bullet,'" Pope said. "Describe the gun to us."

"An older pocket revolver. Not one of those Montgomery Ward specials for a buck fifty. A real Colt. Just old."

Keeping his face expressionless, Pope said "Describe the shooter."

"Just an average-looking man. Average in height, build and hair. He had brown hair and a small beard."

"Anything memorable about the average man," Pope said.

"Yep. He had a strong Southern accent. But like he was from 'way back in the sticks."

"Anybody smoke a cigar?" Sarah said.

"Yeah. One man did. Stood back in the back and watched. He may have been the boss. Never said anything. He was the only one without his gun out."

"How about thinking hard and giving us everything you can on him? How tall? Build? Was he dressed like the rest? Hair color? Beard, mustache or clean shaven?" Pope said.

"He was maybe five foot eight or nine inches. Shorter than you. More like the deputy, but maybe one seventy. Wore a dark suit, but sure looked trail-worn. Hard to tell whether it was black, dark gray or dark blue it was so dusty. Black hair and a mustache. Typical handlebar. Can't say the accent like with the shooter. This one did not say a word. You said you picked up a cigar stub?" The wounded messenger said.

"Two, actually," Sarah said. "Both were the same band, La Rosa Española. We have one bullet to study and the two cigar butts to follow up on," Pope said.

They wished the wounded man well with his infection and took their leave.

On the street, Pope stopped a well-dressed businessman and inquired where he might find a good cigar.

"You can find a pretty good cigar in any general merchandise. But, for a great cigar, go to Smith Tobacconist's. The man pointed across the street, four shops down to the right.

They angled across the street.

Pope walked into the tobacconist's. Pope skipped the undercover identity. He flashed his badge, knowing it would prompt a better response from an honest citizen.

"Howdy. I'm trying to identify someone who smokes cigars with "La Rosa Española" on the band. Do you sell them?" he asked.

"I do. They are premium cigars. Three dollars each. Made by Seidenberg & Co., down in Key West, Florida. They are made out of Cuban tobacco seeds grown elsewhere."

"Three dollars! I bet you don't get much call of those!" Pope said.

"Oh, I sell a lot of expensive ones. These La Rosas, though, have a taste some purist cigar smokers don't like. Some flavor in the wrapper," the tobacconist said.

"Anybody buy these?"

"I sold a whole box about three weeks ago. Glad to get them off the shelf before they got stale."

"Tell me about the man who bought them," Pope said.

"Just an average looking fellow. Medium height, muscular build, maybe mid-forties."

"Hair and eye color? Beard?"

"I don't rightly remember. Dark brown or black hair and beard. Maybe some silver flecked in," he said.

"Any sort of accent?"

"Not as I remember. He didn't talk much. Just asked for them by name and bought a box for seventy-five dollars."

"How'd he pay?" Pope asked.

"With four shiny twenty-dollar gold coins. I gave him five dollars change in bills."

This interested Pope, in view of the coins stolen in all the robberies. "Could you see any other gold coins on him?" he asked.

"Yes, he had some more in the leather bag he used for his coins. When he opened it up, gold is all I saw."

Pope asked the man if there was anything else, he could remember.

"Now's I think about it, he had a black horse with matching saddle tied up at the hitching post out front. He had saddlebags and a bedroll on it. I saw him mount up after putting all but one of the cigars in his left saddlebag," he said.

Pope thanked the man and joined Sarah and Akin and told them what he had learned.

"The picture of Cigar Man is he buys seventy-five dollar boxes of cigars, sticks with a particular variety, does not talk much, and rides a black horse with a black saddle. And at least the day he went shopping in Laramie, had long trail gear on his horse. His suit was dusty from on the trail somewhere. Mr. Appalachia is average height with a brown beard and hair, strong rural Southern accent and a Colt 1849 pocket converted to cartridge. Until recently, when he gunned up to a bigger Colt."

"Sounds about right to me, Sarah." Pope asked Akin if it seemed right to him.

"Me, too," he said.

"Okay," Pope began, "I have one other clue to add to Cigar Man. He's missing a molar on the right side of his mouth halfway back."

The other two looked at him as if he was crazy.

Sarah stopped on the dusty wooden sidewalk and put her hands on her hips, staring at him.

"Okay. Talk."

"I studied the two butts last night with my magnifying glass. He chomps down with an upper and lower molar. But there is a space about a tooth wide not compressed on the butt. It's on the top right between the upper and lower molar indentations. There's a fainter molar imprint directly below it. The protruding part is on the left. Which indicates to me the missing tooth is on the right."

"If we get a suspect," Sarah said, "he ought to have a missing tooth on the top right of his mouth more or less halfway back, right?"

"Right! Circumstantial, but every bit of evidence we can put on him helps him get a longer sentence. And don't forget he is probably the ringleader. Get him and we'll recover more stolen treasure than from any other of the robbers," he said, adding "And, maybe the names of the others."

"One thing I'd like to establish," Sarah began, "is whether we are dealing with one gang or two."

"You've pointed out a definite goal," Pope said. "A goal to which, at this point, we have no clue. If we follow our base of operations strategy, we'd draw two circles. One with the center point between the two train robberies, and one between the stage robberies. If we did it, even the point of intersection between the two circles would be twenty miles or so north of Cheyenne about where the Lodgepole Creek is. Horatio, is there anything there? A village? A ranch?" Pope asked.

"I don't know about a thing on the west side north of the trail from Cheyenne to Laramie," the deputy said. "On the east side, there are two. They are the Davis and Goodman Ranches. I grew up with the sons of the ranchers. There's no way in hell old man Davis or Goodman would put up with outlaws working on their ranches. Both are Bible-thumpers and hold their sons to a real high standard."

"It almost makes me think the leader, Cigar Man or

not, pulled together a robbery team and is not based anywhere. They robbed two trains and three stages and quit. Maybe left the area. It's not like they had posse's hot on their tails either."

"This makes me come back to the idea they got together on these robberies to raise money to do something else," Sarah said.

"But, what?" Akin asked. "Buy a ranch, build a saloon, what?"

"The answer to your questions, Horatio, is probably the solution to the cases," Pope said.

"The first stage robberies were about fourteen miles due east of Cheyenne. Want to ride to them and set up camp? Then, tomorrow morning, we could sketch them, look for clues and begin the trip up to the Willow Spring station where the last one was," Sarah said.

"I agree. One thing we should find along the way here will be campsites. Campsites are usually rich with clues," Pope said, though more hopeful than convinced.

"If we strike out on the east side with the stage robbery crime scenes, maybe we should go with Horatio to the two ranches on the west," Sarah suggested. Both men agreed.

******

They rode to Lodgepole Creek, the scene of two off the stage robberies. There was a bridge with a stand of cottonwoods just past the northern end. Akin told the two detectives the robbers had waited on horseback in the woods until the stage cleared the bridge, then struck. It was too dark to search the scene, so Pope lit his Dietz police lantern long enough for them to collect fire-wood and set up a simple camp. While the other two got the fire going, Pope did his usual security circle a quarter of a mile out from the campsite. There were no threats. He whistled low before coming in. He was surprised and pleased when someone answered him. He found it was Sarah. Wait until he shared it with his grandfather, he thought!

They sizzled some ham steaks on a grill erected over the coals. A coffee pot sat on grill along with some store-bought cornpones warming on the corner farthest away from the heat. Local honey from Laramie served as desert poured over the cornpones. Pope thought to himself, "I have had worse trail meals and some nights with no meals. This is what grandpa would complement as 'passable fare.'"

The next morning's meal was similar, but with bacon replacing ham. They cleaned the dishes with sand and put them away. In turn, Pope got out his investigative kit and Sarah her sketchbook.

Their job was simplified by having two robberies at the same place. Pope made a vague sketch of the site and split it into three sections, one for each to search.

While Sarah and Akin began their searches, Pope did a detailed sketch of the whole crime scene. He then began scouring his area.

The first thing was what they did not find. Key West cigar butts. Akin found five .44-40 brass casings and a .56-56 Spencer case about fifty feet from the northern end of the bridge over Lodgepole Creek.

"These fit with what the driver and shotgun messenger said," Akin told the two detectives. "They came riding out of the woods yonder and a couple were firing their rifles up in the air." Sarah took them and placed them in a paper evidence sack and marked them with a dark pencil as to description, location found and date.

After the search, they sat and talked before heading north towards the LaGrange stage station scene on Bear Creek.

"I don't think we can conclude Cigar Man wasn't here. We pretty much know Appalachia was here for at least one robbery and probably at a train robbery because of using the little .32. Maybe Cigar Man was not here, or maybe he was just out of cigars. While I'd like to find something to put the possible leader at both train and stage robberies, we cannot do it here. Maybe a cigar butt will turn up at LaGrange," Pope said.

They packed their gear and rode on, darkness causing them to stop short of their destination to make camp. They rode into the LaGrange crime scene the next morning.

The scattering of rifle brass was similar, to the first scene. They found another Spencer empty case and a .32-20. The latter was a good small game cartridge.

Good guns, like Winchesters, Colts and Smith & Wesson's and a few others were expensive. Some folks carried lesser calibers if they were able to get a good gun and it happened to be chambered for a caliber they would not otherwise choose. Pope knew it from experience. Carrying a .32-20 was not the sign of anything except it was the caliber a man owned. Further, Pope knew the caliber and hence, the rifle, were brand spanking new in 1882.

Again, they found no cigar butts or any other evidence except for a smashed green wooden treasure chest with black iron strapping. It had been broken open by having the padlock shot off. The chest was empty. They packed it for evidence just out of habit. It would not evidence anything but having a Wells Fargo stage robbed at the location.

He and Sarah added these facts to their notes on the case. The three headed back to Cheyenne after interviewing the manager at the stage station. He added no new facts.

They camped one more night before arriving at Cheyenne. The sheriff could not spare Akin, his best deputy, any longer. Akin gave them letters of introduction to ranchers Davis and Goodman. He also gave them directions to their ranches.

The sheriff, Akin, and several other deputies stood outside the office as Pope conducted his ballistics test.

He loaded the .32 conversion Colt Sarah had purchased in town. She had the honor of shooting it diagonally into the watering trough near the office. The five feet of water slowed the small bullet enough to cause it to bounce off the far end of the trough and land on the bottom. Pope rolled up his sleeves and fished it out.

All watching, the detective balanced the recovered bullet and the one surgically removed from the jehu on the hitching post.

The sun was bright enough for Pope's magnifying glass to show detail.

The rifling striations in the bullet were identical. The bullet shot into jehu Berenson was fired from the gun traded in almost two weeks later in Cheyenne by Appalachia Man. Pope used his pencil as a pointer to show how he determined it to the sheriff and Akin.

"This is a new science. Our boss, Chief Detective Jim Hume has led the way in developing it and using it in trials," Sarah explained. "Even my former company, Pinkerton, is behind Wells Fargo in this method of investigation," she added.

The two ranches were twenty-five miles from Cheyenne as the crow flies. There were no hotels in the area, so they would have to camp. Sarah went to the café and a general merchandise for more food supplies and a tarp. Pope went to the livery to extend the rental on the two horses for several weeks. Sarah walked back to P. Bergerant's Gunsmith & Firearms Shop and purchased two more boxes of .45-70 loads for Pope's new Marlin carbine. He needed to regulate the sights to see where the gun hit at different distances. It looked like it was going to be a long winter.

✶✶✶✶✶✶

Just before they rode out, Horatio Akin stopped them.

"There's been a development up where you are going. Not sure if it is related, but you may be able to use it," he said.

"What happened?" Pope asked.

"There's a small ranch between the two you are going to call on. Was owned by an original area pioneer and his wife. She died last week. Yesterday, rustlers hit and the old man returned fire and died. No way of knowing if the rustlers are related to the train or stage robberies, but we could use your investigative expertise at the scene. The sheriff is sending me over to the Cheyenne Club to have a sit-down with the judge. He suggested the two of you come along."

They agreed and joined Akin on the short walk over to the posh club. It was where most of the area decisions were made by the local power mongers. On the way, he told them Herman Goodman, owner of the ranch named after him was there. He and his son brought the news of the murder. It was his son with whom Horatio Akin had gone through school.

They arrived at Seventeenth Street and Warren Avenue quickly.

As they stood on the dirt street and looked at the three-story brick building, they got a hint of what the inside might be like.

"Can a woman go in?" Sarah asked.

"You can go with a gentleman to a ball or to lunch or dinner in the dining room. You can't play tennis, billiards, or enjoy the reading or smoking rooms."

"Which is actually pretty open-minded," Sarah observed, quite serious in view of the times.

"Wyoming Territory has let women vote for years now. We have a woman magistrate even," Akin said. "Any woman who is a citizen or has applied for citizenship can vote."

Sarah already knew this from McCarthy, but smiled, nodded and said nothing.

The walked up the outside steps. The rocking chairs had been moved off the porch in preparation for a snowy winter. There was a multistory skylight. The floors were polished hardwood, covered with Oriental carpeting. It rivaled the best clubs in London, Paris, New York or San Francisco. A fire earlier in the year had prompted some renovations. Renovations include additional rooms. A number of members with outlying ranches lived at the Club instead of a rougher life on the plains.

Rancher Herman Goodman had a room there. He and any of his sons in town used it instead of a hotel.

"We will see the judge, the sheriff, and Mr. Goodman in a private dining room for an early lunch," Akin said.

"I'm glad we all are not trail worn," Pope noted.

"Ranchers ride in here in all sorts of condition but get cleaned up once they arrive. We are fine. I have been here before with the sheriff. We both have suits on and Detective Watson has an outfit which seems appropriate to me."

"Horatio, how can this little city support building such an opulent place," Sarah asked.

"Because it is the most wealthy city in America per person, right now," he said.

"How?" Pope asked.

"Because of having addresses at the Club, many wealthy ranchers out in the plains are counted as citizens. Many are investors from Europe, especially England. Some are from as far away as Russia. Folks like me are more of the exception, money-wise," he said.

Pope had on a recently brushed dark gray suit. The jacket was cut longer to cover the twin Colts. He seldom wore the shoulder holsters anymore, except in town. Same for his bowler hat. The black Boss of the Plains Stetson was his normal headwear outside large urban areas.

Sarah had on a what appeared to be a long maroon skirt, matching jacket and white silk blouse. The skirt was actually riding pants cut to drape like a skirt for the increasing number of women who eschewed the silliness of sidesaddle riding. Her jacket also covered two guns. The larger on the right was a new model S&W in the large, popular .44 Russian caliber. Its smaller frame .38 rode on her left. Neither was apparent under most circumstances, like with Pope. The pair's guns were readily presentable.

"Judge Roper, Sheriff Sharples, and Mr. Goodman, these folks are Wells Fargo Detectives John Pope and Sarah Watson."

The gentlemen stood and Sarah presented her hand. They shook with her and then with Pope.

"Please be seated, detectives," the judge said. "Seth is the sheriff and, he, Herman," he said nodding to the rancher, "and I have been looking forward to meeting you both. We also have some information which may assist your investigations of the recent robberies.

I am given to understand you two have some fame as partners. Detective Watson, you are one of the few lady detectives anywhere. And, a favorite of your former boss, Allan Pinkerton. Allan and I knew each other during the war. I hold him in great esteem.

Detective Pope, you are the grandson of the legendary mountain man and scout, Israel Pope, a former San Francisco detective and have quite the reputation solving cases by either clues or those Colts beneath your jacket," the judge said. "The San Francisco paper, which we take here at the Club, recounts a recent matter in Marin County. It said you were recovering from wounds and a group of horsemen rode up on you and attempted to assassinate you. Would you share the result of the attempt with us?"

"I was unable to take them into custody and they all pulled on me. I had to defend myself from certain death."

"Were there any survivors?" the judge asked.

"Yes, sir. Me."

"How many shooters?"

"Four, your honor. One lived long enough to tell me who sent them. We had solved a kidnapping and the brain behind it organized the retribution against Detective Watson and me from jail."

"And, Detective Watson, did they come for you? If so, what happened?"

"They did. Detective Pope and his grandfather were upstairs guarding me. The Wells Fargo agents downstairs stopped them."

"Interesting!" the judge exclaimed. "I am surprised Ned Buntline or somebody has not started writing dime novels about you two."

"Notoriety would make being a detective much more difficult, sir," Pope said.

The judge touched a small bell near his hand and a waiter appeared with menus.

"Let's eat first and then talk about the Eb Carson spread up near Herman and how it may tie in," the judge said.

The meal equaled and exceeded anything Pope or Sarah had enjoyed in San Francisco.

"Now, let us get to the matter at hand. Yesterday, rustlers raided a small ranch adjacent to mine," Herman Goodman said. "They murdered the owner, Eb Carson. Eb's wife had died of natural causes a month or so ago. He had a couple cowhands, but they were in a far pasture with a small herd. They rode back as soon as they heard gunfire, but the rustlers were riding off with the herd of about one hundred-fifty beeves. They fired at the rustlers with their revolvers, but the distance was too great. Two men were not enough to go after the six they counted riding away from them.

When they got to the ranch, Eb was still alive. He verified it was six riders. The one who shot him was a medium-sized man with what the cowboy described as a 'hillbilly' accent. Since most of the cattle were gone, the two riders brought Eb into Cheyenne by buckboard. He died along the way."

"Mr. Goodman, is the body still at the doctor's?

Sarah and I would like to take possession of the bullet if possible," Pope asked.

Goodman looked over at the sheriff, who nodded and said, "These detectives can tie a bullet back to a particular gun in a lot of cases. I saw them do it today. It was convincing enough to likely hold up in court," he said, looking at the judge.

The judge said "Get them the bullet, Seth. They or we can hold it until they get a gun to match."

"Gentlemen, we would like to ride out and see the crime scene at the ranch. The man with the 'hillbilly' accent ties back to a suspect in the robberies of both trains and stages in this area. In each case, he was the shooter. We also have some clues about the potential leader of the gang. If we can find the same clues at the scene, we can safely conclude the gang has moved from stage and train robberies to rustling.

I have an idea. It is one I am springing on my partner as well as you. What if we went to the Carson ranch and ran it for a few months? Since this happened yesterday, I might be able to cut some sign and trail the rustlers. If we capture the leader or the Southern fellow, we would have our tie-in and add murder to their charges," Pope suggested.

"Detective Pope, do you have the background to run a small ranch?" the judge asked.

"I believe so. I was raised on one in California. It was just my grandpa and me, so I did everything related to running a ranch. We had cattle and horses as well as a food garden. I hired out as a cowboy for neighboring ranches frequently to help with branding and moving herds to market."

"Eb did not have any relatives. I don't know about his wife, it's too soon for the sheriff's inquiries to be answered. What cover would you use?" Goodman asked.

"A married couple asked by the court to take over the ranch until next of kin can be found and make a decision about its fate. We would move the smaller herd to the main pasture. The one where the big herd was rustled yesterday. Try to make it a target. Put up a small fight, maybe wound one man to get him to talk. But, mainly, let them go and cut sign on the rustlers once they think there's nobody pursuing them."

"You a pretty good tracker, Detective Pope?" Sheriff Sharples asked.

"Israel Pope taught me from age ten on. I'm still not as good as the old scout, but I'm fairly competent," Pope said modestly.

"What's your plan once you find them?" Sharples asked.

"Send one of the cowboys to you to form a posse and bring them in for trial. All I ask is for Sarah and me to question them about the train and stage robberies. Once those are solved and any stolen money is recovered our job is over. And, yours is just beginning. We will have any ballistic help you want once the slug which killed the old rancher is recovered by the doc."

"Would you winter there?" Goodman asked.

"I honestly don't know yet," Pope said. "It depends on a lot of things like weather, the progress of the case, what any descendants want done with the ranch..."

"Men, I am leaning towards letting the detectives run the ranch. It keeps it solvent for the descendants, if any. And, it is the best chance we have of bringing these miscreants to justice," Judge Roper said.

The rancher, sheriff and deputy all nodded agreement.

"Horatio, do you know what kind of supplies, this Eb gentleman laid in for the winter?" Sarah asked.

"No, Ma'am. Not for sure. One of the cowboys hinted they'd been eating low on the hog, so I took it to mean things are pretty lean."

"Is there a buckboard?" Pope asked.

"There's an old broken down one. I wouldn't trust it much."

"We'll buy a buckboard and a mule and get enough supplies for several months for four. How long does it take to get out there? Will we be able to come back here in January to re-supply?" Pope asked.

"Probably not because of weather, not distance. The good news is there are a couple of good merchantiles offering food put up in Mason jars, so get several cases of those. Maybe get six, not several. Meat won't be a problem unless they steal every head of cattle. I'd put about three in the stable. Eb was winding down and had more room than livestock, so it should work," Goodman said.

Thanks. We will do it. Guess we have some shopping to do. Sheriff, will you or Horatio work on getting us the slug from Eb?" Sarah asked.

"We'll do it. If y'all are leaving today, I might get Horatio and a couple deputies to bring it to you in a few days. I'm thinking travel should be at least two people for safety. Mebbe more." Pope nodded. With the long range of his new Marlin .45-70, he was not too worried about him and Sarah taking a buckboard out there. They could keep a group of riders at bay well beyond the range of revolver caliber carbines like Winchester 73's.

"How long is the ride out to the ranch by buckboard?" Sarah asked.

"Probably half a day. I'd order up my supplies for loading in the morning. My son is in town on business. The four of us can ride out tomorrow. Safety in numbers and all," Goodman offered.

"Sounds like a plan. When would you like to meet and where?"

"How about here at ten in the morning. You'd have plenty of time to get the buckboard loaded and be ready to go."

"Perfect, assuming we can find and buy a buckboard and horse or mule to pull it today," Pope said.

"Finding a rig shouldn't be a problem here in Cheyenne. Go over to JM Newman Livery at Third and Seventeenth. He has a couple wagons and both horses and mules. Personally, I'd choose a mule," the sheriff said. Pope nodded his agreement.

The men stood, signifying the end of the meeting.

"Can we contribute to lunch, Judge?" Pope asked.

"Nope, son. Our pleasure. Just be safe and get me some suspects to try in court."

They went the livery and bought a used, but serviceable buckboard and mule for pickup in the morning. He ordered four bags of feed for the ranch's horses and their mule. The next trip was to a mercantile, where they purchased six cases of vegetables in Mason jars, eight sides of bacon, a fifty pound bag each of rice, flour, and beans, a sack of salt and one of sugar and miscellaneous small quantities of items, including first aid supplies. The next stop was the gunsmith for more boxes of revolver cartridges, more buckshot, and more boxes of cartridges for the Marlin. Pope had packed his Bowie knife and bought a dagger for Sarah. They were ready, except for paying for everything.

Back at the Wells Fargo office, they requested funds be wired to allow issuance of drafts to cover their purchases.

Since it was only spitting light snow, they took a walk around Cheyenne.

CHAPTER 5

The mule was already harnessed to the buckboard when they arrived at the livery at eight the next morning. They went to the mercantile where their supplies were loaded, then on to the hotel for their luggage, long guns and ammunition. The .45-70 and shotgun were put just behind the seat in easy reach. A box of cartridges for each rested below the seat. Checking out of the hotel, they drove to the Cheyenne Club where Goodman and his son had just come out of the door and were having their horses brought around.

"Looks like it's gonna be a gray, windy day to be riding into the snow," Goodman said.

"I told Pa he should have started his ranching somewhere warm, like Arizona," Byron Goodman, the son, grinned.

They stopped for a quick trail lunch. Goodman

had the Club pack a lunch for four and he put it in the buckboard. Pope knew it was the best meal they would get for the next several months.

"Mr. Goodman, what do you know about the two cowboys Eb has?" Pope asked.

"Let me jump in here, Pa," the younger Goodman said.

"They are both about twenty-five and decent sorts. The tall one is Willy Havers and the short one is Roscoe Thomas. Both are good riders and know cattle."

"Can they shoot?" Sarah asked.

"I never knew many cowboys who could shoot anything but a rifle or shotgun. They both have Colts, but I never saw them shoot with them," he answered.

"Do they have rifles?" Pope asked.

"I believe so."

He looked at Sarah. "I should have gotten a couple of used Winchesters," he said.

"Mr. Goodman, if I fire a .45-70 three times in succession from Eb's place, will you be able to hear it at your ranch?"

"I doubt it. Mebbe if the day was clear and the wind blowing just right. But, likely not. You thinking for a signal?" he asked.

"I was. It was a long shot," Pope admitted. "Gentlemen, I left my '73 in San Francisco and brought the new model Marlin .45-70. I will fire it about ten times today to see where it prints at various ranges. So, if you hear ten heavy shots maybe a few minutes spaced, don't worry."

******

They arrived at the ranch. The two cowboys had already shown the presence of mind to move the smaller herd down to the pasture by the house as Pope had planned to have them do.

"Mr. Goodman, please introduce us as a couple. We will use the names 'John and Sarah Smith,'" Sarah asked as she slipped on a plain, thin gold wedding band, as might befit a wife of a small-time rancher.

"Do you have to be a couple often?" Byron asked.

"Once so far. We had to stay at an executive's house after a kidnapping and we were not sure until later his household staff was not involved. We are partners and best friends, so it's natural for us," Sarah said.

The two cowboys came out of a small bunkhouse, setting a carbine and a shotgun against the door frame. They smiled as they saw the Goodman's.

"Hi, boys. Meet the Smiths. They are going to run the ranch until the judge determines what Eb's wife's family wants to do with it. Don't y'all worry. You always have a job at my spread. The Smiths are good folks. They and you should focus first and foremost on protecting what cattle are left from another raid. I'm right glad to see you moved the rest of the cattle down here. My son and I are going to head home so's you can get a chance to get to know one another. They'll be here most, if not all, of the winter," the older Goodman said.

They rode off and Pope and Sarah got to know the cowboys better and liked them. They were glad to see food in quantity on the buckboard. And, to see Pope carrying a new .45-70 and Sarah carrying a sawed-off double barrel shotgun and propping them on the opposite side of the door frame from their long guns.

Pope saw them look at each other as he propped his heavy carbine.

"I keep my friend's close and my guns closer," he said. Though spoken in a friendly, light-hearted manner, the look in his eyes told them more than the words. Pope was a gunman. These cowboys recognized it right off.

The ranch house was not a cabin. It was a professionally constructed home. It obviously had not been swept and dusted since the wife died. Sarah set out to do those tasks while Pope and the cowboys moved supplies into a storeroom. He was glad to see Eb put a water pump inside the house near the cooking area. Water inside was a lifesaver if they got into a siege situation. There was both a wide cooking fireplace with iron swing arms to hold pots and a woodstove.

The ironware and dishes appeared clean, though he knew his partner would use boiling water and wipe the ironware down and wash the dishes in a small sink adjacent to the pump.

"What time do you boys want to have dinner?" Sarah asked. "Usually just before sundown," Willy answered. "There's a dinner bell in case we're out in the stable where Roscoe is putting the mule or checking the cattle in the pasture out to the side," he said as he pointed the bell out.

Pope walked out to the side with the Marlin and motioned the cowboys to follow him.

"I just bought this and have no idea where it shoots with the sights on factory setting," he explained, handing the big carbine to Roscoe. Pope walked to around twenty-five, fifty, one hundred and two hundred yards and at each distance selected a rock or chunk of dirt to use as a target.

He loaded four rounds and aimed at the first target, a rock.

The bullet went several inches high. The fifty-yard shot was two inches too high. The hundred yard one was dead on and blew the rock into dust. At two hundred yards, he used Tennessee elevation and aimed two feet above the rock target. The rock was obliterated. Now Pope knew a man target was easy with the standard sight elevation at any distance up to two hundred yards. The big slug was deadly at any range. It just had to hit something. Beyond a couple hundred yards, the amount he would have to aim over became too much for the snap shooting required on a moving or riding target.

Though the almost the same length as his Winchester carbine, the Marlin was several pounds heavier and much more powerful. He cleaned the black powder residue and fully loaded the rifle.

Sarah had the ranch house in order. The only thing she had to do was wash the sheets and substitute the new blankets they had bought. The sheets might be a chore since the air was getting colder. She boiled some water and added a mixture of soda crystals, borax, and several bars of soap, chopped. She retained the resultant liquid soap for laundry use.

She got sheets from the two cowboys and added them to their wash. Sarah included some of her and Pope's clothes. She hung them on a line outside, where they flapped noisily in the stiff breeze. Whether they would dry in the frigid weather was in question.

Pope familiarized himself with the workings of the ranch with the two cowboys.

"Do y'all think there's enough browse in the pasture for this size heard of beefs?" he asked.

"For a while, but some hay bales would sure help. Eb was planning to plant alfalfa in the spring," Willy answered.

"Do you think the Goodman's have some bales we

could buy?" Pope asked.

"Naw, they use all they got. We'd have to take the buckboard into Cheyenne for hay and mebbe some salt blocks."

"If you left first thing in the morning, could you get back by night?"

Willy said, "We done it a couple times, so yes."

"Why don't you plan on both going tomorrow. Let me know what it might cost and think whether there's anything else you need," Pope said.

"We'll do it and will take plenty of ammo. Now—mind you—if the rustlers see us riding off, they will think the place is unprotected and come for the herd," Roscoe said.

"I'm banking on it," Pope smiled.

"You really ain't a rancher are you?"

Pope thought for a minute. He decided to be straight with these men.

"I grew up on a ranch, but now I'm a Wells Fargo detective. So is my wife. We think this gang of rustlers robbed some stages and trains in the past months. Rustling is not Wells Fargo business, but the other two sure are. If we bring the gang down, it will help everybody."

"Just you?" Willy asked.

"Haha. You have not seen Sarah shoot. She just killed a kidnapper in San Francisco. And, it was not her first shooting or fighting scrape."

"I didn't know there was any female detectives."

"She was one with Pinkertons. She's the first for Wells Fargo, but with the track record she has, I expect she won't be the last," Pope said proudly.

"Boss?" Willy asked.

"Yes, Willy."

"Could we get some pay? We ain't been paid for two months."

"Absolutely, but having been a cowboy, I'd like to ask you to leave most of it here in your bunkhouse, unless you need to buy clothes or something."

"We get twenty-five dollars a month. How 'bout we only take ten dollars apiece with us for tobacco and some hard candy sticks and stuff."

"You do what you think is right," Pope said.

Pope inspected the cattle. They had new browse in the pasture near to the house, but he saw ribs, not something a rancher wanted to see going into winter. The boys were right. They needed a supplement of hay bales. Most ranches had some milk cows, chickens, maybe a pig or two. This one did not, which crimped the food situation. It was something he would change if the ranch was his.

This would have been a good case to have both his grandfather and his dog, Scout, on. Being back in Wyoming would have brought back memories for Israel Pope, since the last Rocky Mountain Rendezvous of the mountain men was about three hundred miles northwest. And Israel had been there, one of the youngest mountain men.

The site was at the point where the Green River joined with Horse Creek. The Gros Ventre Range is on the north and the Wind River Mountains to the east. Six rendezvous were held there between 1833 and 1840. A young Israel Pope attended the final one.

Sarah, who knew she was an equal detective with Pope, took the wife and homemaker role seriously. She prepared lunch and rang the bell. They ate on the covered porch. It was cold, but out of the direct wind. She made a stew out of vegetables and meat brought from Cheyenne. Soon, they would have to slaughter a cow for beef. The meal was good and all ate heavily. With the impending threat of rustlers, the four were always unsure of the timing of the next meal.

"Boys, I think we ought to break the night into three-hour shifts and mount a guard until we take this gang down," Pope said. The bunkhouse has a good view of the pasture. The covered porch there might make a good place to squat in a coat and blanket out of the wind. A rifle or shotgun would be handy to have sitting beside you. Since you are going to Cheyenne in the morning, I will be glad to take the last watch so's not to interrupt your last hours of sleep."

They agreed with the plan. Sarah changed it by suggesting it be split into four watches of three hours each, with her taking the final one. The cowboy started to disagree, but Pope knew better and shut them up with a look and wink.

After lunch, Pope saddled one of the horses in the ranch's remuda and rode around the ranch. It was small by local standards. The land was a rolling hundred acres of prairie. A creek ran through it. There was a stand of cottonwoods a half mile from the house. Some red oaks grew further on.

Pope noticed the woodpile was not going to last even halfway through the winter, so felling a couple of red oaks and dragging them to saw and split would be necessary.

He knew the ranch had been homesteaded early enough for Indian raids to be a valid worry. The stands of trees there when the place was being settled were cut down. The reason was to provide less hiding spaces near the house. There were a few lindens in the yard. They did not provide much cover for raiders, but still gave shade in the summer. After circling what he thought would be the circumference of the property, he returned and checked in the stable. He found what he sought. It was a thirty-foot logging chain and a well-oiled bucksaw and two axes. The axes, too, were rust-free and sharp.

"A man should have pride in his tools, be they knife, gun or other," Israel Pope always said. Pope knew Israel would approve of the late Eb Carson.

He and Willy rode out to the stand of oaks with

the chain and an axe. He took the buckboard with the mule and Willy rode his quarter horse.

Wearing leather gloves to protect his shooting hands, Pope felled the tree in short order. Willy cut the limbs off. They chained the tree to the back of the buckboard. The mule, Joshua, had no problem dragging it back to the area near the woodpile.

They spent the rest of the day buck sawing the tree. Roscoe split the green oak as logs became available. It would need seasoning, so he placed it at the far end of the woodpile.

All three earned their beef stew, this time with fresh cornbread and honey. They drank a whole iron pot of coffee and Roscoe took the first watch at nine o'clock.

Pope's instinct kicked in. The only one he mentioned it to was Sarah.

"Why are you awake? I can hear you thinking," she said next to him in bed.

"I feel we are being watched."

"What are you going to do about it?"

"I don't know. It's what I've been thinking about," he said. "If Willy on watch is sharp, he might hear me slip out. If he's goosey, he might shoot me. My normal procedure would be to wake you and get you to gun up while I take a look around."

"Can you get his attention? Without getting shot, I mean," she asked.

"Not sure. We don't have any pebbles I can throw at him."

"We have the next best thing. Beans! I put some in to soak hours ago. But I forgot to put the bag back on the shelf in the root cellar."

"You are simply the best wife I never had. Maybe we should hitch up for real," he speculated.

"Hold the proposal for a more romantic moment, please."

"Are you saying 'no?'" he asked.

"Don't be silly, I love you and would marry you in a minute if we did not have two pretty good careers in the way. But, if somebody is watching us, it overrides proposals."

"Right. Gun up. I'll get a couple of beans," he said.

He pulled on pants, a heavy coat, and moccasins. Then, his gunbelt. With a loaded .45-70 Marlin lever action and some extra cartridges in his coat pocket, he eased towards the kitchen area.

Finding the bag, he shifted the big carbine to his left hand and put four beans in his right.

Sarah was right behind him, barefooted in a little shift, but wearing a winter coat. She had the mule ear hammers on the scattergun at half cock for safety.

They eased out the door silently. The night was still and there was no moon. It was dark as pitch. Sarah sat on the step up to the house.

Pope slipped from linden tree to linden until he

got within thirty feet of Willy. He drew back his right arm and hurled a pinto bean through the night. It hit on the grass and did not make a sound.

The next one hit Willy on the knee.

"Holy…" he began until he heard a "sssh!" slightly audible above the wind.

He looked around and saw a figure wave at him from behind a linden.

"Pope," the figure said no louder than before. Willy nodded and Pope eased out, ready to drop if Willy started shooting.

"Sarah's on the porch with a ten-gauge. We think somebody is watching us," Pope said from the shadows.

"Pope, how do I know it's you?" Willy asked.

"My grandfather's name is Israel. I paid you and Roscoe back wages. Don't forget to get salt blocks later today."

"Alright, I believe you!"

"I'm going to scout around in my moccasins. Just don't shoot me," Pope said.

"I won't. Where in hell did you get a pebble to throw at me?"

"Pinto bean."

"Well, then. I get it."

"I may throw another when I get back," Pope said.

"I'll be ready."

Pope slipped off, heading behind the house. He

blew air out of his nose and sucked in fresh, cold air. Clear now, he sniffed the breeze.

He could smell Willy had been smoking. Hopefully not on guard duty. His sniffs picked up the aroma of Sarah's hair. Pope was not sure whether it was real or just wishful thinking.

From the area around the corral and stables, he smelled horses. So far, no odor of man. He figured a range of one hundred yards, crept out the distance and began to circle the house.

Pope went silently and slowly.

Halfway around his circle put him one hundred yards across from the front door of the ranch house. He saw a horse another fifty yards outside the circle. In the dark, it appeared to be just standing there. Pope assumed it was hobbled.

The man had to be laying on the ground between the horse and the house, looking.

After five minutes, Pope saw a movement. This man was good. It took him five minutes to move perceptively. And five seconds to raise a rifle as Pope heard the bunk house door open as Roscoe came out for guard duty.

Pope snapped the big Marlin up and pressed the trigger.

The watcher jumped and dropped his rifle. He picked it up and ran, zig-zagging towards his horse. He mounted and jammed the rifle into a saddle sheath.

In his excitement, the man spurred the animal before remembering the hobble.

Pope was sprinting towards him as the man sat. He was temporarily dumbfounded.

He raised a Colt at Pope.

The detective fired and levered for another shot. The man dropped the Colt and slid off to remove the hobble. Hobble removed, he galloped off.

Pope's snap-shot blew the man's Stetson off and he heard him yell "Sombitch!"

The accent sounded Southern. Very Southern. Was this the shooter from the robberies? Or was it just a coincidence? The rider disappeared quickly in the blackness of the Wyoming night.

Pope collected the Colt and the hat. The hat had a little blood inside the crown. He must have slightly creased the man.

Pope walked back, calling out to identify himself.

"I have a Colt to check out and a hat with a little blood where I must have creased the top of the shooter's head. Next time, I'll aim a few inches lower," Pope said as he walked back to where Sarah and the two cowboys stood.

Sarah had lit his police Dietz lantern and they focused the side beam on the Colt. It was a .45, so they had another gun to match against a bullet from a crime. It was the same caliber used to murder the ranch's owner, Eb Carson.

And, given a capture, a suspect with a crease in his scalp to match against the gun. Evidence was mounting. Custody remained elusive.

Pope saddled a horse from the corral and rode after the watcher, who had a ten minute head start. Pope cantered to the other man's gallop. He did not want to be seen after him, nor did he want to take on the gang by himself. He did not have a canteen or his Dietz lantern.

Pope got off the horse and studied tracks every few minutes. When the moon was behind a cloud, he used a Lucifer to light the tracks. The distance between tracks was lessening. The man was slowing down.

Pope followed more carefully. They had come almost five miles by his best reckoning. They may be approaching the rustlers' camp.

He pulled the horse up abruptly, having heard voices. There were no trees to use to tie his horse, so he dropped the reins and trusted it.

Pope crept forward, rifle in hand.

He saw the camp ahead and could not get an exact count on its occupants. It looked like around nine men. Some were asleep, some were milling around.

The detective returned to his horse and walked it out of hearing.

He arrived back at the ranch by three AM.

Sarah was up waiting and was making coffee. The aroma of brewing coffee awakened Willy and

Roscoe. All four had a mug of steaming coffee and the cowboys harnessed the mule and hooked up the buckboard.

The two cowboys got an early start on the hay trip.

Pope insisted Sarah go back to bed after they left. This time, he prevailed.

******

After daylight, Pope stayed outside splitting wood and watching. Again, he thought how beneficial Scout would have been. The hound could sense an intruder much farther away than the detective.

By noon, the detective was tired and sore. One thing was certain. His bullet wounds had healed. The soreness was muscles, not wounds.

He figured they were about a quarter of the way done adding additional firewood for the winter.

Sarah called to him and he joined her for a meal of cheese sandwiches and coffee.

"Not quite the Cheyenne Club," she joked.

"I don't care. Any meal is perfect with you present."

"You were serious with the proposal, weren't you?" she asked.

"I was and am. Of course, you were right. We cannot do it until one of us decides to turn in the badge and become a Wells Fargo office manager," he said.

"Or mother," she added.

She broke out into peals of laughter at the look on his face.

"I'm just saying! No worries at all!"

He looked relieved. They were in the middle of a major investigation. One which was not going very well and looked like they were in for the long haul.

Sarah smiled sweetly at him. She could always pull his strings. She did not do it often. But she did it often enough to remind him she could do it at will.

"I wish we had the .45 bullet removed from Eb so we could compare it to the Colt we just had drop into our possession," Pope said.

"Me, too. It may be spring before we can get it to compare."

"Maybe, Mr. Goodman will miss the Cheyenne Club and ride back in. He could bring it back. If we see him before April, we can ask," Pope said.

"I'm not used to this stuff of planning by seasons instead of hours. I love the rolling plains for a while, but I am not sure this is where I want to settle," Sarah said.

"Where would be your choice, my Sarah?"

"Maybe around Prescott. Mountains and warmer weather. I understand there's some pretty country in Colorado, too. But, colder than most of Arizona Territory."

"Northern California is nice, too," Pope said. "One day, we will own a ranch not far from San

Francisco and a cabin getaway north of the Bay. I hope it's a long time off though," Pope said thinking of his grandfather's hope for him to ranch the land he would leave to Pope.

"I hope so, too, honey. By then, it might be too populous for us. I think I'd like a lot of rolling land near mountains, water and a small city for doctors and supplies and all," she said.

"An area like you describe is worth seeking out. I am with you," Pope said.

They finished lunch deep in thoughts. If there was a relief watcher, he saw the two cowboys leave. The man Pope exchanged shots with would have had no way of knowing how many people were at the ranch, unless he set up his observation post before darkness. If he did, he was not much of a planner. He was laying on a knoll with no blanket or tarp and no canteen. His horse was a way away. Too far to walk to get basic needs like water, food and the like.

"All things being equal, this might be the day the herd in front of us gets raided. We have to be especially vigilant, Sarah," he said.

"We are always vigilant, John."

Their thoughts were prophetic.

Six men rode in fast, guns sheathed. They apparently did not expect a reception at the ranch.

Under the circumstances, with no guns out, Pope could not exercise the range and power advantage of the .45-70. What if they were some of Goodman's cowboys or Davis.'

As they got close, Pope walked out with the carbine and both six-guns prominent.

"Can I help you men?" he asked.

They were clearly surprised.

One pulled for a holstered revolver.

A shot from the .45-70 blew through him and he fell off the horse. Pope dropped the Marlin and drew both Colts. Another man drew and Sarah put a load of double-ought buckshot in his chest. Two down.

The four remaining spun their horses and left their dead companions where they laid. Pope thought about picking up the rifle and dropping another couple as they rode off, but backshooting was not his way. He let them go.

"What's your plan?" Sarah asked.

"Wait until the boys get back and night trail these fellas tonight. I found out last night where they are cooped up."

He walked over and checked the two on the ground. Both were dead. He removed a few dollars and wallets. No names. Their guns were a Colt Navy conversion and a Smith & Wesson like Sarah's .44. He collected them and gave her the second man's gun and cartridges.

"Here, now you have a matching revolver for two big gun events. And, you can't have too much

ammo," he grinned as he handed her the Smith &
Wesson and cartridges.

"These men came to rustle, not to fight. Canteens
and lariats, but no rifles, saddlebags or bedrolls. I figure they are no more than five or ten miles from here."

"Are they hiding out on Goodman's or Davis'
ranch?" she asked.

"I don't think so. Willy told me there is a strip due
north of here which, like this place, does not belong
to either. They rode up through this strip. When I followed the watcher, the trail led me straight north to
their camp., We will send the boys back to Cheyenne
again tomorrow with the two bodies and to bring
back a posse," Pope said.

The two cowboys arrived a couple hours later to
find two bodies rolled in old blankets from the bunkhouse and tied with rope.

Pope relayed the story as he helped them unload
the hay bales and put all but one in the stable for
winter storage.

They took one out, broke it open and spread it
around the small pasture to supplement the tastier
grass growing there.

Neither groused over another trip to Cheyenne.
Driving a buckboard beat working a ranch any day.
They grew even more impressed at the woman de-
tective's shooting rate.

They had some things for Pope. One was the .45

bullet dug out of Eb Carson to compare with the captured Colt. Another secret item was from a local bakery. A cake for Sarah's birthday. The last was a locket. Pope had sent twenty dollars to spend on a present and told them to have the jeweler pick the item for them. He was pleased at the result. He hoped she would be, too.

Sarah fixed dinner, thinking Pope had forgotten this, her first birthday with him.

"What a great dinner!" he said.

"You mean left over beef stew?" Sarah asked.

"I mean really good beef stew. Don't you think, boys?" Both nodded sincerely.

"All we really need is dessert," Pope said, nodding to Willy who slipped outside. It had turned too cold to eat dinner on the porch.

He returned with the birthday cake, the first Sarah had in years.

Her surprise turned to tears, which confused the male audience.

Pope hugged her.

"Did I do something wrong?" he asked.

"No, silly. Don't you know women cry when we're happy?"

"No, I guess I don't. Maybe a present will make you smile." He handed her a small box with the pendant on a gold chain. She opened it and said, "I love it!" and cried harder.

After, in bed, Pope gently asked her again about the crying.

"I cried because you and the boys touched my heart. Nobody has had a birthday party for me since I was a little girl. I love you so much!"

"I love you, too, Sarah. How long ago were you ten? Fifteen years ago?" he asked.

"Wrong by five years. I'm thirty today. Three years older than you and I don't even know when your birthday is."

"Neither do I," he admitted. "All I know is I was ten when my parents and little sister were killed by a war party. My grandfather came and got me. We talked and he took me on a quest to find the party. We did. And we killed them all. Every single one of them."

"Dear God, Pope! How did you feel about it? Did Israel kill most of them?" she asked.

"We killed about the same number. He saw to it. He said it was important for me to get even and to get the hate out of my system. I did it and never looked back. My parents never held much store by birthdays. As far as most of my memories go, they started with the day my grandpa picked me up in Kansas and we hit the retribution trail. Nobody could have been a better or more loving parent than him. Nobody, Sarah."

"Pope, I have to tell you something. Something which might affect where you and I go from here."

"I doubt it, but go ahead and spill it, Sarah."

"I cannot conceive children. I had a fever when I was fifteen and it made me infertile."

"You would have been a wonderful mother. Maybe, if you want, we can adopt some children someday. But, you will still be the only wife I will ever want, so it won't affect our relationship one way or the other, I promise, Sarah."

She hugged him tightly and cried softly into his chest. This time, he knew it was tears of joy.

******

Pope helped Willy and Roscoe load the two bodies onto the buckboard early the next morning.

"I have seen the outlaw camp from a distance, so I pretty much know where it is. I'm comfortable enough for the sheriff to call up a posse and come this way. He may or not want the US Marshal to participate. His call. I will just be a posse member as far as anyone other than you two and the sheriff are concerned. He may solicit some men from the two adjourning ranches. Again, it's his call.

Tell Sheriff Sharples if he wants to camp the men here, to give the Wells Fargo office this letter. It authorizes them to give him a draft to cover some camp gear and food for a couple nights for the posse. His county seat being one of the richest places around, he might not need it. I think coming up here this afternoon and searching out the outlaw camp early tomorrow would be smart. They may decide to winter somewhere else. We don't want to miss this chance at them. They are down two men anyway."

"We'll do her, boss," Willy said, and they left in the mule-drawn buckboard once again. Pope and Sarah were once again alone to face the gang if they returned unexpectedly.

The two cowboys returned by four o'clock with Sheriff Sharples and six possemen. Sharples said Akin had come but diverted over to the Goodman ranch to try to get Goodman's son and a few of their cowboys for the posse.

As they were setting up camp, Deputy Akin rode in. He said four Goodman cowboys and son Bob would join them at daybreak. Those men made for fourteen possemen with Pope. He planned to leave his two cowboys at the ranch with Sarah in case the rustlers circled around and hit the ranch while he and the posse were gone. Sharples concluded with his strategy.

"Thanks for offering to pay towards feeding the men. My budget is pretty good, so I did not take advantage of Wells Fargo's offer. Maybe next time," the sheriff told Pope.

Pope proposed, using his Dietz police lantern, having either the sheriff or chief deputy Horatio Akin ride with him a half mile in advance of the posse. He would track the rustlers. If they came up on the camp unexpectedly in the dark, which he said he did not expect to do, they would make the shoot or slip away decision on the spot. In the dark, most of the prairie looked the same.

"Your posse, Sheriff. Just think of me as a tracker or scout," Pope said.

"Pope, I am a detective. I think it's enough to have Willy and Roscoe looking after the ranch. I want to ride with the posse. We will have fifteen of us. We don't know if the Wells Fargo manager's original estimate of twenty outlaws was right or wrong. Too many of us beats too few," Sarah said.

The sheriff nodded his agreement. This lady detective had now killed two outlaws. She apparently was no slouch with a shotgun or revolver. And, likely to be more disciplined in a firefight than most of his out of work cowboy and shopkeeper possemen.

Sheriff Seth Sharples was quite aware most cowboys were lousy shots with anything but a rifle or shotgun. Some were not even accurate with those.

Pope considered her not only his partner, but an equal. Sarah joined the posse. Both were sworn-in with the Goodman part of the posse.

"Men, we don't know if we are facing four or twenty. Here's what we are going to do. Deputy Akin and Detective Pope are going to ride a half mile ahead and pick the trail. When they come on the outlaw camp, they are going to try to get as much information as possible and ride back to us. We will work a strategy. It might be to flank them from both sides, or just go straight in. We will wait 'til we see the lay of the land. If the two trackers ride up on them too quick and shots are exchanged, we will ride like hell to join the fray.

Now, this is real important, so I want you to listen careful-like. If you are going to be shooting from your horses, spread out. Don't shoot any of us in front of you. Especially me! It can happen real easy. Same if we flank them. Make sure you don't shoot a fellow posseman on the other flank! Detective Pope, you got anything you want to add?"

"Thanks, Sheriff. I believe you covered it all. I would only emphasize what the sheriff said about watching where you shoot. Don't shoot a good man. Only shoot a bad one," Pope said.

It was a cold dark morning and dawn was still almost two hours off.

Pope and Akin rode off. When they got about a half mile ahead, the posse moved out. The sheriff and Sarah rode in front.

Pope decided he did not need the Dietz lantern. He knew where he was going. They rode at a walk for over an hour.

It was a black, windy day on the prairie. Pope would stop periodically and sniff. He was attempting to catch the smell of a wood fire, or coffee, or bacon. Anything revealing the presence of men.

An hour and a half into the ride, Pope stopped.

"Wood smoke!" he said to Akin in a low voice which would not carry as far as whispers did.

"I cannot smell it," the deputy said.

"It takes training and experience. It took me a long time. But it's up ahead and not far. Walk your horse back to the posse. I'll tie this horse off and walk forward and scout. With luck, only the cook is awake, but the coffee will get everybody going shortly, I bet."

Akin turned his horse as Pope dismounted and tied his to a branch. He did not know this particular horse well enough to just drop the reins and certainly did not want to hobble it. He saw how jumping on a hobbled horse almost got the rustler watching him killed.

There was a thin line of trees along the slight trail. Pope moved to the right and skirted the trees as he reconnoitered the camp.

One man was tending the fire and another was getting coffee beans, bacon and flour ready. Pope counted six still sleeping. Eight in total. He heard cattle lowing in the distance. There would be a cowboy or two watching them, he thought. Maybe ten in total now. Before the sheriff announced, somebody would have to move around the camp and get ready to simultaneously take custody of the ones watching the herd.

He quietly ran back to his horse and met the posse.

"Two cooking, six sleeping, and I am guessing another two tending the stolen cattle. They are grazing in a bowl a couple hundred yards beyond the camp. Just to the left.

I was thinking of sneaking around there and getting ready to take them when I hear you announce your presence."

"Sounds good. Boys, angle any shots to the right as much as possible so as not to hit the detective!" Sharples said.

"Sheriff, I think I can be in position in five minutes, then you go ahead and announce your presence to the ones in camp," Pope said. Sarah looked at him in the dark and flashed her famous smile.

He rode out in a wide circle to the right, drawing the rifle from its scabbard as he rode.

When Sheriff Sharples drew his Sharps rifle and Sarah her double barrel shotgun, the deputy and his possemen followed suit. They remained quiet as the sheriff tried to see his watch.

Finally, he dismounted and stood behind his horse and struck a Lucifer on the heel of his boot. Under the light of the match, he saw four minutes had passed.

Sharples remounted and nodded to Sarah. He waited, then began to ride forward.

The sheriff, using sweeping arm movements, moved half his posse to the right and half to the left when a hundred yards from the camp. They had a semi-circle flanking around the camp.

"Hello, the camp! This is Laramie County Sheriff Sharples with a posse. You are surrounded! Stand and throw up your hands. Any man with a gun in his hand dies on the spot!"

Nobody was stupid. At least yet. All complied and the posse moved in.

Over a hundred yards away, the two cowboys tending the stolen herd had been chatting. They heard the sheriff. They froze, then realized their only option was to ride like hell in the other direction.

Immediately after coming to their conclusion, they heard a lever action operated.

"It's a .45-70 men. And I can drop both of you where you sit on your horses. Unbuckle your gun belts and let them fall to the ground," Pope said.

"Now, dismount and move away from where your guns dropped. One of you moves towards the rifle butts I see on your saddles and you both die."

They complied. Pope drew his left Colt as he sheathed the rifle. He covered them as he draped their gunbelts over his saddle horn.

"Now, slowly lead your horses back to the camp," he ordered.

The sheriff had the rustlers lined up in a clearing a short distance away from the camp. Akin was supervising the possemen in searching the suspects. Sarah watched his back.

Pope added his two to the number.

Pope saw a quick eye movement by Sarah and then she drew and fired her .44 Russian. The third man from the end bent in the middle and tumbled forward.

He dropped a Remington .41 Derringer as he fell.

The sheriff walked over and picked up the gun and handed it to Sarah.

"Nice work!" he said. He bent and checked the man on the ground.

"Dead," he said.

A short rustler who had been running his mouth throughout the process spoke up.

"Pretty bitch, I could tame you, iffen you didn't have your big gun. I could tame you real fast!"

Pope walked over to him.

The rustler had his shirt buttoned up to his neck and was wearing a bandana as a tie. It was knotted at the top button.

Pope's hand flew out and he grasped knot and shirt and pulled the man in to within a foot of his chest.

"If she took off her guns, she could beat your ass in less than a minute. You'd never know what hit you!" he said in a low growl to the man, face-to-face.

Pope then flexed his big right arm and the man slowly lifted. Only the toes of his boots touched the dirt. The man kicked at Pope.

Pope extended his arm until it was almost

straight up. The man's feet were well above the ground. Pope slowly turned his fist halfway around and shoved. The man flew several feet through the air. He landed in a pile of horse manure. Even the astounded rustlers watching broke out in laughter at their companion's expense.

Without looking back, Pope walked over to the camp and began to search for some of the stolen money. A quiet, but smiling Sarah joined him searching.

They thought they hit a bonanza when they found a green Wells Fargo strong box.

It only had four thousand dollars in it when opened and counted.

"Twenty-three thousand was the total treasure taken. Where is the other nineteen thousand?" Pope asked.

"Maybe some has been distributed to the individual rustlers?" Sarah speculated.

"Probably, but not enough to add up to the full amount. You know what else?" he asked.

"I do. Where's Cigar Man. And Appalachia? Nobody here seems to fit."

He turned to the sheriff who had walked up.

"Sheriff, any of those prisoners have a bullet crease on the top of the head? I shot the hat off one the other day and it had blood in it. It's his .45 I confiscated. Sarah and I will compare a bullet fired from it with the one which killed Eb Carson. If they match, you have a murder solved."

It was a disappointment, but the rest of the searches did not turn up a box of the Key West-rolled cigars. And none of the men had the strong Appalachia accent. The watcher Pope creased was identified. His accent was Southern, but not a strong one.

"He's not the robbery shooter. We'll see soon enough if he's Eb Carson's murderer, though," Pope said.

He assigned the two cowboys to watch the ranch. The rancher's son, Bob Goodwin, with several men from his ranch, cut the Goodwin cattle out of the stolen herd. They headed their cattle home.

Pope and Sarah rode into Cheyenne with the lawmen and their prisoners.

"We'll put the nippers on one at a time and bring a man out of the cells and to a room to question him. Want to start with the one with the new part in his hair you gave him?" Akin asked.

"Good idea. But, first let's have you and the sheriff watch Sarah and me perform the ballistics test. We'll see if his gun killed Eb Carson. Then, if the prosecutor agrees, you can charge him with capital murder in the commission of a felony after the questioning."

"I'll go over and talk with the territorial district attorney for this county. Horatio can stand in for me to observe the test," Sheriff Sharples said. He walked up to the prosecutor's office and the other three walked outside to the watering trough.

Again, Pope aimed so the bullet had almost seven feet of water to pass through, before bumping off the end of the trough.

Everyone stood back and Pope fired two shots with the cartridges they found in the gun when the shooter dropped it.

Pope collected the two bullets and they went into the conference room where the interviews would take place.

Pope put his investigative bag on the table. He got his leather notebook, pen, magnifying glass and a sheet of plain white paper out.

He placed the paper on the table and drew three two-inch circles. One to the left, two further over to the right.

He wrote "murder bullet" under the left and "test bullets" and the date under the right-hand circles.

Pope then placed the respective bullets in their circles.

He put the murder bullet on a blank space and one of the new ones next to it. Using the magnifying glass, he studied the striations from the revolver barrel's rifling on each.

They were identical. He pointed to the matching striations with his pen.

Pope repeated with the second new bullet. Same result.

The sheriff had walked in and leaned over to observe.

"Sheriff, you have a murder suspect. I will testify I shot him, he got away but left his gun. We then followed him to where he was arrested. I will then be pleased to explain to the judge and or the jury the ballistic process proving his left behind gun was the murder weapon. Let them make the final decision," Pope said.

"The prosecutor said if you find the bullets match, I can charge him with murder. Along with rustling. He will likely hang," the sheriff said.

"One other question for the prosecutor before we talk with this man. If he helps us and tells where the rest of the money went, can the prosecutor maybe request life instead of hanging? It would give us something to bargain with," Sarah asked.

"I will ask and let you know before we talk to him. You all and Horatio get started on the interviews. I suspect you will have a day or two's worth of questioning to do," Sharples responded.

The sheriff was correct. The three, sometimes joined by the sheriff, took a break for lunch. They had only fully interviewed one of the rustlers. These men were looking at five to seven years for rustling alone. The stage and train robberies could double it.

The only incentive would be dropping one charge or the other.

Sarah sent a crypto-coded telegram to Hume. She explained what they had and asked if the company had to have train and or stage convictions, or just long-term convictions on the perpetrators, regardless of charge.

Hume responded back he had spoken with his management. They wanted as much of the treasure recovered as possible. If the questioning resulted in a greater recovery, they did not care what the charges were. Incarceration for any reason would suffice.

The second suspect to be questioned was the man with the big mouth. He was known as "Shorty," for apparent reasons.

"Mr. Haldeman," Sarah started, "you are facing charges of armed robbery of a train, of a stage and commission of cattle theft resulting in murder," she lied.

"We might be able to get the last charge—the one which would stretch your neck—dropped. If we did, you may get by with five to seven years in the Laramie Federal Penitentiary. The reason you would go to a federal prison is because Wyoming is a US Territory and not yet a state.

I will also suggest you answer our questions without being a smart Aleck. Your answers and how you give them will be part of the evidence against you. Understand?" she said.

Shorty shook his head. Pope asked the first question.

"Mr. Haldeman, which train and stage robberies were you on?"

"The first stage robbery where there was no shooting."

"Where did it occur?" Pope continued knowing the best interrogation question was one where you already knew the answer.

"By the creek northeast of Cheyenne."

"What was the total take?"

"About fifteen hundred bucks," he said. Pope knew the answer was very close to his information.

"Did you participate in any other stage robbery?"

"The one where Cletus shot the driver. It was after the first train robbery"

"Tell me about train robberies. Were you on both?"

"No. We did a train robbery near Cheyenne and got our share of the money. Then, we did another stage robbery. We were hot. But Cletus shot the driver for no reason. He was crazy. Half the gang, including me, took our share and kicked out the leader and Cletus. They took about half with them. We headed up here and started to look for cattle to appropriate. We was gonna get ourselves a ranch over to Nebraska. Move the cattle over after the winter. You messed up our plans."

"Are you aware of other train robberies?"

"Nope."

"Tell me Cletus's name and describe him to us,"

Sarah asked.

"Cletus Hazeltine. He was from the Caddo Mountains in Arkansas. A hick, but a killer hick. He'd as soon shoot you as look at you. This bunch you got is cowboys. We ain't killers. So we separated from the crazies."

"How about the man who drew a Derringer on my partner?" Pope asked.

"He was just stupid. I guess he panicked. He wasn't so stupid most of the time."

"You mentioned the leader. Who is he?"

"Name of Rufus Black. Older man."

"How old?" Akin asked.

"Mebbe forty-five or fifty," Shorty said.

"Did he smoke?" Pope asked.

"He didn't roll no cigarettes. He just smoked cigars."

"Was he missing a tooth, right here?" Pope asked, pointing to an upper right molar in his own mouth.

"I don't know."

"Did he plan the robberies?"

"Yep."

"You name and describe the men who left with Rufus and Cletus after the gang split up. I will copy down what you say," Pope said.

He did. Pope and Sarah took pages of notes. The notes described men, horses, and weapons. They now had two lists of suspects, the ones how kicked Black and Hazeltine out and the ones who left with him.

"We're almost done for now," Sarah started. "Did Rufus or Cletus say where the gang was going?"

"Nope. They was close-mouthed after we decided to split up."

"Where was Rufus from before he got here?" Pope asked.

"He come here from Kansas City. But he said he couldn't go back. He never said where he was born. Talked a lot about New Mexico," Shorty said.

"When did the split off gang with Rufus leave your group?" Pope asked.

"About four days ago."

"Which way did they head?" Akin asked.

"Due north."

"Alright. We will make sure the prosecutor knows you have cooperated and will request they drop the murder charge," the senior deputy said.

"You telling me true?" he asked.

"We will make those requests. The prosecutor has to decide, but he seems to be open to our suggestions, based on cooperation," Sarah said and Akin agreed.

A deputy took Shorty back to his cell and the three stepped outside so Akin could smoke.

"Man! Look at the sky! And feel how the temperature has dropped. It feels like a blizzard is coming in," Akin said.

"Well, if they left from north of here, they must

already be in the thick of the storm. I don't have the feeling they have the type of gear to build a dugout and weather a blizzard and the rest of the winter. I'm worried even we don't have enough firewood and supplies at the Carson ranch," Pope said.

"Are there any homesteaders north of where we arrested the gang? Maybe several days north? Sarah asked.

"Not as I know of," Akin replied.

"How deep does the snow get up there?" Pope asked.

"It seldom gets more than two feet in the eastern half of the state. Move west of center and it gets real serious," Akin said.

"So, the shooting part of the gang could still ride through it?" Sarah asked.

"Yep, but they'd play havoc finding a decent camp and have to be pretty good woodsmen to construct a shelter, kill game and find usable firewood. They may have a woodsman in the gang. Or they may just be found out there frozen and dead with their horses. Remember, we asked one of the rustlers what kind of gear the ones who left had. He said canteens, coats, a bedroll and saddlebags. No axe, tarps, food, or feed for their animals if things got real bad. They could literally freeze to death out there."

"So, you would not suggest we track them?" Pope asked.

"Let's see what the blizzard gives us. I suspect your

grandfather could track them in this weather, given planning and supplies. If he taught you like he seems to have, you could probably trail them and survive, even if the people you were after didn't."

"Thanks for the vote of confidence," Pope said. He looked at Sarah who shook her head "no" and made a gun with her hand and pretended to shoot him in the leg with it.

Akin gathered what their earlier conversation must have been and smiled. Beautiful or not, he would not want to cross Sarah Watson. He had just seen her draw, fire and kill a man. She did it far faster than he could. He was pretty sure she took half the time he needed to do the same thing.

The snow continued to come down lightly and the weather got colder.

Late in the afternoon, Pope and Sarah met with both the sheriff and Akin.

"I'm thinking they only have a four-day jump on us. They don't know we are on to them and bad weather seems to be setting in. Sarah and I are thinking about going to the ranch and picking up the mule. We could use him as a pack animal with some serious camping gear on a sawbuck packsaddle. I saw one in the stable there. We will pick up a tent, cook gear and food, and axe. We could take both dry fuel for fires, a small keg of water and feed for the mule and horses.

I suspect they are hunkered down. We have a one-time opportunity to locate them. Whether we engage with them depends on the situation on scene. It might include their condition when and if we find them, or how we perceive their aggression. If we get into weather which is too rough, we will have the gear to settle in and wait. Or turn around and come back to the ranch. Sheriff, do you think it's doable?" Pope said.

"Pope, I see your point, but only if the weather doesn't get worse. If this thing becomes a big blizzard, it would be foolhardy to start out in it. Two good detectives dying isn't worth the chance of catching six or seven bad men. I think we should revisit it tomorrow morning. I agree, the outlaws are probably hunkered down wondering where their next meal is coming from right now.

In the meantime, I'd like for the four of us to continue interrogating these prisoners. And y'all ought to plan on getting some rooms at a hotel tonight." Sharple looked at Sarah who nodded in full agreement.

Pope nodded his acceptance of the wisdom the local lawmen proffered. It was just so hard to sit when there were fugitives, perhaps within a day's reach. But, nobody knew how bad the storm was going to be yet. Another night should not make a significant difference.

They continued to work their way through the interrogations. The rest of the men corroborated what Shorty had said. All four of the questioners agreed the ones in custody were rustlers, not shooters. The man who pulled the Derringer was an aberration. He panicked. The rest just wanted to steal cattle and got hoodwinked into the stage and train robberies. Once they realized the other gang with which they combined forces was violent, they kicked the others out.

In the accounting, Pope and Sarah began to see the larger part of the stolen treasure was stolen by the violent gang after the break-up. The four thousand dollars recovered was half of the take until then.

Subtracting their four thousand from the total of twenty-three proved the others were still in possession of nineteen thousand dollars. The detectives and their local law enforcement counterparts surmised there was nowhere to spend the money. It should be retrievable as long as they apprehended them before they reached a place to spend it, such as a town or trading post.

They walked back outside for Horatio Akin to roll a cigarette. The wind was so strong, he had to roll and light it inside.

"This storm is not letting up, John," Sarah said. "We'd better try to get some rooms like the sheriff said, before they are all sold out."

He agreed and they walked down the street to the Western Hotel, leaning against the strong wind and blowing snow.

They took the last two rooms. They only had trail

gear with their horses. Their long guns were still at the Sheriff's Office. They would retrieve those before returning for the night. A change of clothes for tomorrow would be nice, but shops were starting to close an hour early.

They walked back and told Akin they had found rooms and were going to get dinner while they still could.

Ramsey's Restaurant was still open. They had steaks and potatoes and coffee before returning to the office to pick up their long guns.

People were starting to crowd into the hotel due to the inclemency of the weather. There were many new people in the fast-growing city of Cheyenne. They had not experienced a winter there and feared the worst.

The two moved into their rooms then met in Pope's room. They thought, if they had to be summoned by the sheriff or Wells Fargo, it would be where the knock on the door came. Pope would just crack the door, keeping Sarah out of sight.

The room was still fairly chilly. Sarah got an additional blanket from the wardrobe and placed it on the bed. Stripping down to her shift, she crawled in and soon the top of her dark hair was the only proof the long lump under the covers was her. Pope followed suit and soon there was just one big lump in the covers.

Soon, there was a light snoring under the covers. Pope chuckled to himself at his sleeping beauty partner's snores. An elbow in the ribs proved she was not fully asleep.

She obviously did not appreciate any recognition of her snoring. Still laughing to himself, he rolled over. Soon, she was pressed against his back sleeping soundly. And very happily.

******

A look out of the window at dawn showed the storm had passed and less than a foot of snow was on the streets of Cheyenne. They were not sure of the conditions further north in the plains.

"Want to go to your room and we can conveniently meet to go downstairs for breakfast?" Pope asked.

"Not yet," she said as she kissed her partner. "Maybe in a half hour."

Roughly half an hour later, she rolled over and said, "Aren't you glad we didn't go running off in the blizzard?"

"I am."

"You know, you should listen to your forever partner," she suggested.

"Umhmm."

"Pretty noncommittal," she said.

"No, it was a positive response. I just didn't use

words."

She punched him in the shoulder lightly.

"Now, I'm hungry," she said. He was sleeping already. She shook him awake and they went downstairs for breakfast.

After, they checked out of the hotel and advised at the Sheriff's Office they were heading to the ranch.

They arrived at the EB Carson ranch midday. The road was worn by Indians, bison, and settlers. The horses did not have a hard time transiting it. They packed the sawbuck pack saddle on the mule, spoke with Willy and Roscoe and headed north.

Pope did not expect to find any tracks or people the first day.

Towards dusk, they found a likely camping place. It was his favorite kind. Off the road, on a rise, and by a stand of trees. The latter always a good find in the prairie.

He did his half mile circle to make sure the rustlers nor other hostiles were in the immediate area.

Sarah gathered wood to save the fuel they had brought. She broke longer limbs with the axe and took a trowel to make a fire pit. Pope taught her it used less fuel. More importantly, it emitted less smoke to give away their position.

She used the big Bowie from his saddlebag to shave a dry twig and make a fuzz stick. One Lucifer had her fire going in the larger pit. It drew air in through the tunnel from the smaller hole.

By the time Pope got back and pronounced their site seemed safe, she was getting bacon out and getting ready to mix water and cornmeal for fry bread in the iron skillet after the bacon grease lubricated it.

While she did the cooking, Pope put the iron coffee pot on and set up the tarp as a lean-to. He moved saddles, long guns and their bedrolls under it.

Pope and Sarah were never happier than when they were together. They were very compatible trail and camp partners and enjoyed the meal.

They spoke for a while, then turned in. It had been a long day with a lot of riding. Both were asleep quickly. Pope arose once to stoke the fire. He was up before dawn and put coffee on. Breakfast would be reheated left over bacon and cornbread.

As the sun rose, they were several miles into the ride north. They rode all day, seeing nothing. The camp and meal were just as the one before.

Pope built a reflector behind the campfire to reflect heat into their lean-to. He cut the thick branches longer to be able to push the unburnt ends into the fire. It would allow stoking the fire without getting up.

They were covered by blankets and a waterproof tarp. Luckily, no precipitation was falling. They slept well and prepared to hit the trail early. Pope studied the map.

"Sarah if we continue due north to the North Platte

River, we can stop at the old trapper's post and stage station at Deer Creek. It has a telegraph. We could wire Ft. Federman. It's on the N. Platte about maybe thirty miles from where we'll be. We can ask if men meeting the description of our fugitives have ridden in to get out of the storm. We'll swing through there either way. It's a straight shot on what the map shows to be a bigger road than this trail will ever be. It goes directly to Cheyenne. We can regroup our thoughts there and see when we have to testify," Pope said.

"You know what bothers me?" Sarah asked.

Without waiting for him to respond, she said "Why would Cigar Man and the one from Appalachia head north if New Mexico was where he wanted to go? I mean, it's exactly the wrong way to ride!" she said.

"It's been worrying me, too. He headed without gear into an oncoming storm and in a direction, which wouldn't put him anywhere near a train of a big enough city to disappear in. Colorado was a lot closer. He could get a room in a sleazy part of Denver and nobody would pay him any attention. I'm beginning to think he's just plain stupid. There was no call for him to panic. To this day, he has no idea we're on his trail. There's no way he could know. He's got eighteen or nineteen-thousand dollars in bills and gold coins."

"It's perplexing. The trappers canoed the North Platte or hiked the Oregon, Mormon, or Bozeman Trails. There's no riverboat service.

If he wanted to set up a camp along the faint trail where we are riding, why didn't he take axes and a wagon and supplies? He sure had enough money."

Without answers, they rode along.

Midday, they came upon a camp. There were three bodies. One was lying on the ground. Two were propped against trees, blankets wrapped around them for warmth.

The detectives dismounted to investigate the ghastly sight.

"This could be half his men," Sarah said.

Though shivering uncontrollably and starting to turn a bluish tinge, the two against the trees were alive.

"My non-medical guess is he froze to death a few days ago. Nobody here looks like the cigar smoker," Pope said, checking the prone one.

"Nor the Appalachian," Sarah added.

"Their guns are still here. We better confiscate those and see if we can help these two survive," Pope said.

Sarah found some rotten wood which was somewhat dry on the bottom. Instead of wasting valuable time to make a fuzz stick or pick up and sort dry kindling, she ripped a couple pages out of her notebook and balled them up. Within minutes, she had a fire going and was brewing hot coffee for the two men well on the way to death by freezing.

Pope was busy doing what the men should have done. He took the saddle blankets from their three rigs. He moved the two together near the new fire and rewrapped the blankets around them and then covered them with saddle blankets and one of his and Sarah's tarps. He put their hats on their heads for additional warmth. Western men should have known better how to survive. And these were supposedly cowboys who tended herds in the cold. As they warmed, the teeth chatter subsided. Sarah made them drink their coffee warm instead of hot.

Soon, he felt they were out of danger of death. He began to speak with them as Sarah warmed cornbread and fried bacon for them.

Within several hours, the two men were able to speak a little. Their names coincided with three on the list of names Shorty provided during questioning.

"We had a discussion about whether to ride on or weather the storm. Rufus decided not to have a shootout over the money and he, Cletus and two others rode out. I think they were going to Deer Creek, then east past the fort. Rufus had originally told us when we were all going together, we'd head south to Denver. He said it would be a good place to hide."

Each man had two hundred fifty dollars on his person. Pope put the money in an evidence bag.

"So, we have recovered a total of four thousand five hundred dollars out of nineteen thousand," Sarah said as she entered the figure in her own notebook.

"Yes. For purposes of our investigative notes, I have no idea where in the prairie we are until we hit the North Platte River. Once there, we can estimate the distance south to here by the time it took to traverse it."

"In other words, we are going to back into a wild-ass guess?" Sarah said with a mischievous grin.

"Exactly!" Pope said. "We have to estimate the location. We can't say 'found three fugitives somewhere,'" Pope said.

"What are we going to do with the men?" Sarah asked.

"As soon as they are ready to ride, we will have them put the corpse on his horse and we will escort them into Deer Creek. We will wire for the army to send a patrol to take them back to the brig. All of which will be after we see about Rufus, Cletus and the other two."

"'See about' usually means killing, doesn't it?" Sarah asked.

"We'll see," Pope shrugged.

Each of the detectives had a pair of nippers. The prisoners, who had recovered enough to represent a danger, spent the night handcuffed to each other. They had some spare feed for the men's horses and Sarah melted snow in the coffee pot for water for the animals.

All had more coffee and a little more of the diminishing food, then turned in.

Pope and Sarah took turns sleeping.

They rode on the next morning, half expecting to find the bodies of Cigar Man, Appalachia, and one or two others along the way. They hit the south bank of the North Platte River at Deer Creek first.

They entered the little village, guns loose in their jacket pockets. There was a good chance they might encounter their fugitives.

The first place they went was the stage station. It was a Wells Fargo station. The telegraph was there. Before they wired the army, the detectives wanted to see if the rest of the fugitives were in Deer Creek.

The identified themselves to the manager.

"We are on the trail of some train and stage robbers and murderers. Has an older man and maybe three others ridden in the last three of four days?" Pope asked.

"We had some riders come in about three days ago. Cold and hungry. They went to the saloon and ate and drank themselves silly. Two are probably still there. The older one and another rode on the next morning," the manager said.

"The older man who left. Did he smoke a cigar a lot?" Sarah asked.

"Yep. A real sweet-smelling one. Then, chewed on it so's it would not go to waste."

"How about the other man who left with him? Anything real memorable about him?" Pope asked.

"He talked like a real hillbilly," the man said giving Pope exactly the answer he wanted. "He was short on temper. I was over at the saloon the first night. I thought he was going to shoot a fellow over cards. But the older one brought him under control with a couple of words," the station manager said.

"Is there a lawman in Deer Creek?"

"No. Nearest law is down the river at Ft. Federman in the form of the army. Ain't no civilian law up here yet. 'Cept maybe you all. You got badges. It's more than anybody else has."

"Thanks. Would you walk over to the saloon and identify the other two to us? We will arrest them," Sarah asked.

"I will walk over and point them out through the door and watch from outside. I don't want to be in the gunfight."

"Are you sure there will be one?" Pope asked.

"Pretty sure."

"Can we leave our two prisoners handcuffed to the hitching rail and our heavy coats here? We need you to walk us over now and point out the two fugitives." Pope said.

The man nodded and the two detectives transferred their revolvers into holsters and checked the loads of all four guns. Both repined their badges on the fronts of their lapels.

"How do you want to do this?" Sarah asked.

"How about you do the talking and I'll back you up from about eight feet to your right rear?" Pope suggested.

"I'll surprise them as a lady detective and you will shoot whoever needs it if they get out of hand?" she asked.

"Alright. Though, I'm sure you will hold your own when the shooting starts."

"Thank you, my forever partner. Let's do it!"

The manager led them over to the saloon. It was really cold without the heavy coats.

Both kept their hands in their jacket pockets to stay warm and flexible for gun handling.

The manager pointed out the two gang members from the door, then ducked out of sight.

"We don't allow no women in here," the barkeep yelled as Sarah paraded in, Pope flanking her to the side.

She pointed to the badge on her lapel.

"I don't care..." the barkeep began.

"Shut the hell up or you will regret it for the rest of a very short life," Pope told him. His voice was so deadly sounding it even gave Sarah a thrill.

"You two men sitting at the table. We are Wells Fargo detectives. You are under arrest for murder, train robbery, stage robbery and cattle rustling!"

They had enough alcohol to cloud reasoning, though not hamper alacrity.

One rose and began to draw.

Sarah drew her .44 revolver and shot him twice in the torso.

The other one jumped up from his chair and pulled. Pope drew and killed him before he stood to full height.

There was shock and silence in a saloon which had seen death and mayhem before.

The barkeep and a couple men dragged the bodies out the door to keep blood from soaking into his luxurious sawdust floor.

Pope checked the men while Sarah watched his back.

"You men, and barkeep. Did anyone hear the older man with the cigar or the one with the strong Appalachian accent say where they were going?" Sarah asked.

"Them fellas you just shot was joshing with them the first night."

"Joshing how," Sarah asked the somewhat inebriated man.

"About how in heck they was coming 'way up here to get over to Denver? The reasoning beat their friends and the rest of us."

"The cigar-smoking man and the one with the Southern accent were talking about going to Denver?"

"Yep. They was going to follow the Oregon Trail east into Nebraska, then down to Colorado. They said they had to pick up some stuff at the trading post here in the village."

"What kind of stuff," she asked.

"Camping stuff. They bought some already-cooked food right here."

She turned to the barkeep.

"The trading post is attached to this saloon. Do you know what they bought?" she asked.

"Biscuits, cornpone, a bunch of beer sausages, some already-cooked beans, an axe and some tarpaulins," he said.

They recovered several hundred dollars. Whiskey was apparently not cheap in Deer Creek.

Pope composed a quick report to Hume and converted it to Wells Fargo cypher from his code book. He sent a non-coded wire to the commanding officer at Ft. Federman. He advised they would be there tomorrow at the latest. Both were tapped in before they left.

They followed the Oregon Trail east from Deer Creek to the fort. They left the two prisoners in the brig for pickup and transport by the US Marshal. They also took the bodies to the fort.

"Let the Marshal decide what to do with them also," Pope said.

The commanding officer gave them a receipt for

"Two men, described below, arrested by Wells Fargo detectives for train robbery, stage robbery, cattle rustling and accessory to murder of one EB Carson, northwest of Cheyenne, Wyoming Territory. Three corpses, male, two killed resisting arrest by below-named Wells Fargo detectives. One froze to death on the trail before apprehension. Said corpse identified by their gang members as noted below. Same charges for deceased outlaws."

Sarah mailed the receipt to Hume in San Francisco.

Now unencumbered again, they decided not to directly trail Black and Hazeltine. If they were trying to take a circuitous route to Denver, the detectives would go straight to the city. Which meant returning to Cheyenne and heading due south.

Several days later, they rode into Cheyenne. They reported to the Wells Fargo office, stabled their horses and the mule and advised the sheriff what had transpired.

The next morning, they boarded the Union Pacific train in Cheyenne for the short ride south.

"I believe we will get to Denver before our cigar-smoking friend and his murderous sidekick," Pope told Sarah.

"If we don't find him there, I'm not sure what we will do," she said.

"While I've not had a fugitive elude me yet, this could be the one. Every other detective I've spoken with has had multiple cases they could not solve and people they could not catch. Look at Black Bart. Both Hume and Morse, two of the greatest detectives in history have chased him for seven years. They don't have a clue who he is, Sarah. Not a single clue. These two could be our dead-end cases. I hope not."

"The same is true of Pinkerton's. Look at John Wilkes Booth. Few who are

knowledgable about him really think the man killed at Garrett's tobacco barn was really him. He and the inability to catch the James Brothers have wracked at Allan Pinkerton for years. And, due to his condition, I think he will carry both frustrations to his death," Sarah said.

"So, we'll keep doing our best until the boss tells us to give it up and take on another case...or five," Pope said. His partner nodded her agreement as the train rolled on towards Denver.

Neither detective knew the Wells Fargo manager in Denver. His name was Marcus Howard.

"We are pursuing two fugitives wanted for robbing Wells Fargo on trains and stages, shooting two Wells Fargo employees, murdering a rancher and cattle rustling. We have brought the gang to justice, except for these two. They are the most important and elusive. Rufus Black is the leader and Cletus Hazeltine is the shooter. We have bullets tying to his previous and current revolver and three shootings."

"Why Denver, detectives?" the manager asked.

"We have interview testimony from several gang members he and Hazeltine planned to come here by a circuitous route to avoid Cheyenne. We think we may have beaten him by a day or two," Sarah said.

"I am curious. I take the Cheyenne newspaper. Did the two of you take these ruffians on alone?"

"We had a Laramie County posse with us for one instance. We were alone for the others," Sarah responded.

The manager nodded. The paper had been specific. He was interested in how the two characterized their actions. He knew the woman had outdrawn one herself. They did not seem to exude any braggadocio.

"How are you going to proceed and find these two?" he asked.

"First, we will solicit your suggestions. Then, visit with Denver Police Chief, the Arapahoe County sheriff, then the US Marshal for their help. These two would be a good arrest for any Colorado lawman," Pope said.

"First off, avoid the current police chief. He works very closely with Soapy Smith. Same for the sheriff. I don't know about the marshal. We have a bad situation here in Denver. A couple of crime bosses run the city. They have for several years."

"Who is Soapy Smith?" Sarah asked.

"Jefferson Randolph Smith runs gambling, prostitution and protection in Denver. He started with a con game with money hidden inside the wrappers of bars of soap. Hence his name. He would gather a crowd and sell specific bars to his henchmen in the crowd. They would find a dollar bill or a five and yell out. The crowd would get excited and Soapy would say "the one with the hundred-dollar bill is still in the basket! How many will buy a bar to find it? Generally, every bar would be sold. If the hundred dollar bill was found, you can rest assured it was by one of his men.

He owns three saloons and more brothels. He also has some front businesses. He has even used fake telegraph services in the past. He'd take money for a fee and often to 'transfer.' The telegraph is not hooked to a wire. The telegrams don't leave his premises. There are few complaints because folks don't realize their money or wires never went through."

"Maybe we should talk with him," Pope said.

"You could try. He's got connections, a temper, and a fast gun though."

"Such attributes have not hindered us in the past," Pope stated matter of factly.

"You might want to have Hume wire the governor to run an outside investigation of your deaths just in case. The local one would make Smith come out a hero. I guarantee it," the manager said.

"Let's wire Hume. But, instead, let's ask for a five-hundred dollar bribe to Smith for information leading to the apprehension of both," Sarah suggested.

"If I went into his place, I'd take a letter copy of the reward instead of cash," he said.

"Let's wire the chief detective now. We can write up the reward notice while we are waiting."

"You are pretty confidant."

"If my figures are correct, we will have recovered a gross of almost eighteen-thousand of the total treasure taken of twenty-three thousand *after* the reward," Pope said.

The manager took out his cypher book and converted the telegram he had jotted down into code. He signed it "J. Pope S. Watson" in code.

They adjourned to two desks which were temporarily assigned to them. Pope and Sarah planned the strategy they would use to convince Smith to accept the offer of the reward.

Hume always arrived early to his office. By mid-morning, he was at peak operation.

It did not surprise either detective to receive a reply by ten AM.

"Pope offer two fifty. Stop. Three if reqd. Stop. Hume."

Sarah had left the amount blank and added two hundred fifty dollars to it. They took the document down the street to a printer and had him set and run forty copies of a typical Wells Fargo wanted poster. They would take one to Soapy Smith. If he did not bite, they would post the other thirty-nine around town. They would especially post it near saloons, brothels and cigar stores. They would be places Black and Hazeltine would frequent.

Howard gave Pope some places to look for Smith. Sarah went, but was going to serve as backup outside. This time, she did not plan to breach a saloon door.

Soapy Smith was in the third of his saloons they checked.

He was a medium height man about thirty years old. He had dark hair, a dark vested suit, and a heavy dark mustache. He looked like the businessman he was. Once one looked closely into his eyes, he would see dishonesty and violence. They showed a man who would con or knife someone as soon as he would look at them. The fact Pope did not see guns in the suit suggested he would be unable to pull quickly if needed. Pope spotted the butt of a Remington double derringer protruding from his left vest pocket. The observation suggested he was left-handed. If the little Remington was his everyday carry, he was only dangerous for the first five feet or so, Pope opined.

Pope brushed aside some thugs and walked up to their boss.

"Who the hell are you? Walking in here like it's you who owns the place instead of me," he said to Pope.

"I am John Pope. I work for Wells Fargo. I have a deal for you. The thugs were in my way of offering it to you. Want to hear it?"

"You're already spouting off. Pray continue."

Pope handed him one copy of the wanted poster.

"I understand you are in touch with everything happening in Denver. If you know these two men, or can locate them, it would be worth two-hundred fifty dollars to me."

"Apiece?" the con man countered.

"Together. They are not worth two-fifty apiece."

"So, all I got to do it ask around, find out where they are and let you know?"

"Yep. But I have to arrest them, too."

"What if they kill you?" Smith asked.

"Very unlikely. The gunman of the two used to pack a .32. Not the type fellow I'd be worried about."

"He could get lucky. Or the other one, while you was focusing on the gunsel."

"Occupational hazard for a Wells Fargo detective, Mr. Smith. I've come up against better than these two. I had the wanted poster run because I am tired of riding around in cold weather looking for them."

"Wal, if you get too cold, I have some places you can drop by and warm right up."

"I understand you do," Pope said, smiling, but with no intention on acting on the invitation.

"I might ask around," Smith said.

"I'd appreciate you asking around. We are set to distribute hundreds of these wanted posters in two days. It would be much better for me to deal with one man with sources than a bunch of yahoos with an itching for ten months' worth of cowboying money," Pope said.

He nodded at Smith and turned, walking out the door to Sarah.

"Everything alright out here?" he asked.

"I was just offered twenty dollars for five minutes."

"I thought the Minute Men were just during the American Revolution. I guess there are still a few around," he said.

"You know twenty bucks for five minutes is two-hundred forty dollars an hour?"

"Considering it, are you?" he asked just before she slugged him in the chest in front of a bunch of drunks. It gave them far more enjoyment than Pope. Sarah could punch really hard, mad or not. He was barely months into healing from two gunshot wounds, which she realized as she hit him, though too late to pull her punch.

He did not say a word to her or even look accusingly. He just stared at her. He saw a tear in the corner of one eye. Sarah interlaced her arm in his and said, "Let's go home, partner."

"Where is home?" he asked.

"The Windsor Hotel at 18th and Larimer," she responded as they walked. "Or, under a tarp on the trail, or a dead man's ranch house. Wherever *you* are, silly."

******

They went into the Wells Fargo office the following morning after a quick breakfast at the hotel.

There was nothing from Soapy Smith yet. They figured they would give Smith until at least late afternoon before writing him off and hitting the streets with posters and questions.

Before lunch, the chief of police showed up at the Wells Fargo office. He was a man in his mid-fifties with a florid complexion and a pot belly. He wore an expensively cut suit in a really ugly plaid material. He wore his star prominently on the left lapel.

"Howard, where are those damned detectives?"

Both rose.

Pope walked over to him and looked down.

"There is a lady present. I would appreciate it if you tone down your cursing, Chief."

"Who are you to tell me what to do?" the self-important politician asked.

"I am someone you don't want to mess with," Pope said quietly in his deep voice.

"I am scared to death," the sheriff said mockingly.

"Maybe you are smarter than you look after all. You should be scared. Now, how can we help you?"

"What gives you the right to come into my town and start looking for people?" he asked.

"It's what we do all over the United States. We

arrest and bring to justice people who rob Wells Fargo and our customers. The two we are after are wanted for murder, train robbery, stage robbery and cattle rustling. We are looking for results not credit. You should be glad we are doing your work for you," Pope said.

With a "humph!" the portly lawman turned on his heels and strode out of the office.

"Well, certainly a conversation which went exceedingly well, I'd say," Marcus Howard remarked.

"Would you rather Sarah have shot him? I noticed she was tapping the butt of her .44. The fat-ass chief's danger awareness was so bad, he never knew."

"If she had shot the pompous little prig, it would have done a service to the fine folks of Denver," Howard said.

"I'll keep it in mind for next time," Sarah said.

Howard turned to Pope, smiling, and asked "What's it like traveling with someone so dangerous?"

"I stay terrified all the time," Pope responded. Sarah said nothing but wondered if she did come off too quick to deal harm. She still felt badly about hitting Pope near a grievous wound. Sarah wondered if his laconic humor masked other more worrisome feelings.

If so, she knew, finding out would take all off her interrogatory training. Pope was a silent man, and it was hard to probe his real feelings.

"I wonder if Soapy Smith told the chief about the two we're after. Or maybe the printer who printed the wanted posters did?" Pope asked, generally in Howard's direction."

"Could be either. Lots of people want his favor. He has a long history of granting it to the most undeserving of them. This city needs to have its house cleaned, Pope, and sooner than later."

Towards the end of the day, a man who would be identified as a gambler anywhere in the West walked in. He spotted the two detectives and headed straight for them.

"Friend of mine said to give either of you this here paper," he said.

Sarah read it and nodded to Pope. Reading it upside down, he saw it was the wanted poster and a hotel address followed by Soapy Smith's signature was on the bottom.

Pope handed the man two-bits and he left.

"Know the address?" Pope asked Howard, showing him the poster.

"Yeah. It's just on the wrong side of town from the saloon where you found Soapy. He probably owns it. I don't know whether it's a brothel or hotel nowadays," Howard said. "Probably both," he added.

"Let's hit it tonight around midnight. I'm thinking we should offer to take a couple of city policemen with us and let them get the credit. Hume knows who's behind it. The publicity the two of us are getting is going to ruin our ability to properly do our jobs," Pope said. Sarah agreed.

Howard was dumfounded the detectives were going to share credit with the city police.

They had a quiet dinner at the hotel and walked over to the police department around ten o'clock.

They asked the desk sergeant for a senior detective and one appeared shortly.

"What can I do for you?" he asked. He was a large middle-aged man who looked like he could handle himself in a brawl. A brawl which did not last too long and did not require running.

Pope handed the wanted poster to the detective after identifying himself and Sarah.

"You can see what charges these two are facing. Hazeltine is sure to hang. Black will probably get twenty years hard time in Wyoming."

"Isn't this something for the US Marshal, being across state lines and all?" the local detective asked.

"Probably. But why don't you take the credit and then have the marshal take the prisoners off your hands after you get the newspaper coverage?"

"Are they both shooters?" he asked.

"We don't know for sure. We do know the evidence says Hazeltine killed one and shot two. I don't mind taking him. It's what I, or rather, we do," Pope said, nodding to Sarah.

"She shoots too?" the detective asked.

"She does. And fast and straight."

"Let me get a couple of my bulls to go along," the detective said, disappearing down the hall. He returned with two other detectives. Both were the size of a bull. They carried shotguns.

"Do we have warrants?" he asked the two from Wells Fargo.

"We don't. We can arrest based on the wanted poster. The sheriff of Laramie County Wyoming Territory is Seth Sharples. He worked with us capturing or killing the rest of the gang. He can have warrants wired here before you feed these two a delicious jail lunch. All we have to do is recover the money stolen from Wells Fargo and give you a receipt for it."

"How much?"

"They left northern Wyoming with eighteen thousand, five hundred. We don't know what they have spent on food, gambling or women since. We don't think much, because they only spent a few days running on the trail and it was real wilderness without even a trading post along the way."

"You all going to carry it all the way back to San Francisco?" the detective asked.

"No, we will turn it in to the office here. They will transfer it back by stage and train."

"So, we could just take the money to the Wells Fargo office here in Denver and get a receipt for it?"

"Yes. But the office is closed and we don't know where to get the agent in charge. His safe is probably on a time lock. So, it would have to be held until eight o'clock tomorrow morning when he gets in. The time locks probably don't expire until nine or so, but we have to count it a couple times anyway," Sarah said.

The department had a police carriage with seating for six and the detective, Sergeant Enos Purdue, elected to use it to get the five of them to the address. They could squeeze an extra two prisoners in, the size of the three Denver detectives notwithstanding.

Purdue arranged the timing to arrive at the address at midnight. The house had some activity. It appeared to be a cross between a rooming house and brothel, so people were arriving and departing more than normal for the time of day.

They parked the carriage around the corner and went in fast and hard.

"Older man with cigar and partner with strong hillbilly accent? What room? Murder warrants!" Pope said to the clerk.

"I can't," the clerk began. Purdue slapped the copy of the wanted poster on the desk and flashed his Denver badge.

"The damn room number now, or you get arrested for subverting justice!"

"First room top of the steps," the terrified man said.

The two big Denver detectives were already

climbing with surprising speed. Before Pope and Sarah topped the landing, they heard the door being crashed in.

"Denver Police! Don't move!"

Awakened from a deep sleep by giants with shot-guns, the two fugitives froze in their beds.

They were quickly manacled and moved aside, while the two Wells Fargo detectives searched the room. A carpet bag under Black's bed contained a large amount of cash and coins. There were some silver coins, but most were gold.

Pope removed a .45 Colt single action from under Hazeltine's pillow. He held it up for Sarah and the other detectives to see.

"Here's our murder weapon. We have a bullet removed from the body. I can ballistically tie it back to this gun," he said for the benefit of the Denver detectives. Pope knew the ballistic matching started by Hume was in its infancy, and few other agencies knew about it. Sara recovered a Colt Navy cap and ball revolver from under Black's pillow. Though technically obsolete, the percussion cap and cylinders loaded with loose powder model remained popular. Even Hickok carried two as late as the mid-1870's.

She noted its details and turned it over to the Denver detectives, it having no relevance to Wells Fargo's case.

Pope approached the night clerk.

"Does Soapy Smith own this place?" The man nodded.

"Get word to him to come by the Wells Fargo office after nine this morning and claim his reward," Pope said.

The seven with the fugitives luggage, climbed into the police carriage and drove to Denver Police Headquarters.

Sarah did the honors arresting the two. The arrest may or may not hold up in court after extradition to Wyoming, but it worked to get them held and extradited.

The chief was more receptive to the two Wells Fargo detectives once he saw the article in the Denver Republican, Daily Spur, and Weekly World newspapers. It credited his department with the arrest of two suspected murderers, train and stage robbers, and rustlers wanted in Wyoming. The only mention of Wells Fargo was "Detectives Pope and Watson of Wells Fargo assisted the Denver Police in locating the fugitives."

After multiple counts, they recovered eighteen thousand two hundred seventy-four dollars. Wells Fargo was out only four thousand seven hundred twenty-six plus the detectives' expenses. Hume would be happy to report the success of the case to his leadership.

Pope wired Sheriff Sharples in Cheyenne and

advised of the arrests and requested he have an extradition order sent to the Denver Police Department. He received a prompt congratulations and acknowledgement.

"I suspect the extradition of Black and Hazeltine will be pretty fast. Everybody who has to touch the case has lunch together daily at the Cheyenne Club. When Wyoming becomes a state, all they will have to do is make the Club the new state capital," Pope said to Sarah, somewhat tongue in cheek.

"Well, it surely helps us. One or both of us will have to testify at their trial and probably at the gang members trials, too. I am wondering if we need to secure rooms in Cheyenne for a while?" she asked.

"We'll see what Hume says, but I think you are right on the money."

They spent the next two days creating and handwriting a report on the entire case for the chief detective. It was seventeen pages upon completion. Parts could be used to jog memories during the upcoming trials.

They sent an executive case summary by encrypted telegram. Instead of US Mail, they elected to send the detailed written case summary via Wells Fargo express pouches. They were faster.

The following day, they received a coded telegram from James Hume.

It advised them to temporarily base in Cheyenne.

Due to the growth of population and financial impact, Wells Fargo needed a much larger office. They were to work with Byron McCarthy on the security aspects of the site selection. Once the site was selected, they were to assure proper security was built into the building. Security included safes, door locks and wire security for the telegraph equipment.

McCarthy received several sets of plans for offices in the new size range. Company Superintendent Pridham was the sender. The security drawings and specifications were included and were to be passed to the detectives for review and assistance.

The detective's part in the process was corroborated in his documents.

Hume sent the two detectives the security checklist he used on new offices, including the new San Francisco dock office. It had been replaced after being blown up. Pope, a San Francisco detective at the time, had solved the case.

This, Hume assured them, would fill in their time waiting for and testifying at the series of trials for the suspects they had apprehended.

CHAPTER 6

The prosecutor, sheriff, and judge met the next day. They scheduled individual trials for each gang member on stage, train, and cattle theft. Rufus Black was charged with the same in addition to accessory to attempted murder and accessory to capital murder. Cletus Hazeltine was charged with the same as the gang members, plus attempted murder and capital murder of one passenger during a robbery.

The prosecutor decided to seek three years for the first part of the gang which broke off due to violence. He sought five years in prison for the second set of gang members who stayed with Black and Hazeltine. For the two captured in Denver, he sought twenty-five years for Black and death by hanging for Hazeltine. All were to be jury trials.

A local attorney offered to represent the gang members *pro bono*. Black and Hazeltine hired a separate attorney.

The prosecutor subpoenaed Pope and Sarah to answer questions about the evidence which led them to the gang in its various iterations. He said they could expect to get questions about the members they shot, though neither would be charged. Pope would answer ballistic questions in Hazeltine's trial about the .32 and .45 bullets from the jehu and a robbery passenger tied back to Hazeltine's two revolvers. Sarah would testify about gaining possession of the .32, as would the gun store owner who took it in trade from Hazeltine.

The prosecutor assured the Wells Fargo detectives and sheriff the cases were sure wins for the Territory. Because of the questions about both detectives killing gang members, Wells Fargo retained counsel for both Pope and Sarah.

The trials were set to begin in a week. Though separate trials, the gang member series of trials would be preceded by the prosecutor setting the stage with time and crimes and the apprehensions. No individual gang member trial was anticipated to take more than half a day.

Pope hired a photographer to take cabinet card-type representations of the two guns and separate comparison photos of sample bullets fired in the presence of the sheriff and deputy with the bullets removed from the two victims.

The photographer said this type printed on card stock would be easier to pass among the jurists than ambrotypes or other media currently in use.

The charge for shooting the Wells Fargo train shotgun messenger would be based purely on his testimony identifying Hazeltine. His would was a pass-through and no bullet was recovered. Ballistics would prove Hazeltine's shooting of the Wells Fargo jehu with the .32 and murder of the passenger with the .45 Colt later.

The two detectives worked with McCarthy and a building coordinator from San Francisco to locate and obtain a site for the new Wells Fargo office.

As there was no lot available to build a new office, space was obtained on the ground floor of a three-story hotel. The space had been occupied by a large mercantile which had moved out of the immediate downtown area to a developing shopping area several blocks away.

The current office was now cluttered with plans and notes about walls being moved, a vault being installed, steel security doors on the vault room, and wiring for the telegraph.

This type work represented a welcome change to the detectives. They were used to frequent travel, danger and searching for clues. This was a part of Wells Fargo to which neither had been exposed.

Having run a county tax office, Sarah was accustomed to the administrative duties associated with inside work. Pope had been a cowboy and a policeman. He was not architecturally inclined, other than planning security measures. He admitted something frankly to Sarah after several days of looking at plans and talking with contractors. He admitted he found it extremely tedious.

The series of trials began, and each testified about the events, using their drawings of crime scenes. They spoke about the apprehensions and the resisting arrests which led to shooting.

Pope's first ballistics testimony was on the murder of Eb Carson. He convinced the jury the man who he had winged in the scalp at the ranch's gun was the gun used to murder the rancher.

Neither the prosecutor nor defense counsel made any effort to question the need for deadly force. Once the trials for the two sets of gang members finished, the attorney from Wells Fargo declared his responsibilities had been fulfilled. He chose to stay on to watch the two major trials and the ballistics testimony. The latter was something seen for the first time in Wyoming jurisprudence. Pope's use of the actual bullets and statements proving they came from Hazeltine's gun.

As recommended by the prosecutor, the first half of the robbers each received three years in prison. They were the ones who broke off to avoid violence. The half who stayed received five years in prison. These were considered light sentences for men who robbed trains and stages and who rustled cattle. Clemency was given for cooperation and later testimony in the Black and Hazeltine cases.

The exception was the man who killed Carson. He received a death verdict.

The clerk of the court called the case for Rufus Black the following week.

Pope was the first witness.

After being sworn and identifying himself to the court, he was asked a series of questions.

"Detective Pope, how did you come to identify the defendant as a suspect in the robberies?"

"When Detective Watson and I examined the scenes of the stage and the train robberies, we looked for clues. Ideally, we wanted to find the same clues at each scene to tie the robberies to specific people.

We consistently found these cigar butts at scenes. They had a distinctive tooth pattern. It was consistent with someone biting down on the end of the cigar on the right side of his mouth. There was a raised area between molar indentations. It showed the smoker had a missing molar. It was the second one back on the right. If you examine Mr. Black, you will find he is missing the molar I just described.

Further, the cigars are expensive and an odd brand out of Key West, Florida. Not popular cigars found at merchantiles. They were sold only in specialty stores.

We found where a man meeting Mr. Black's description bought a seventy-five dollar box of these same La Rosa Española cigars at Smith store in Laramie.

Mr. Smith did not have his name, but he gave us a description closely matching Mr. Black. And, he is here in court today to make a positive identification," Pope ended.

Black's attorney cried "Objection! It is not up to a witness to identify or predict the testimony of another witness, Your Honor!"

"Sustained. Prosecutor, do you have any more questions for the detective?" Getting a negative response, the judge turned to the defense attorney, who nodded in the affirmative.

"Detective Pope, are you schooled in dentistry?"

"No."

"Then, how is it you can look at a cigar butt and predict the dental situation of the man who smoked it?"

"Years of studying clues based on logic."

"How old are you?"

"Twenty-seven."

"How long have you been a detective?" the attorney asked.

"Six years. Five with San Francisco Police Department, one year studying under James Hume at Wells Fargo, one of the world's most respected detectives."

"And those years give you the ability to predict the teeth of a suspect?"

"In this case, yes," Pope said with confidence.

"I seriously doubt it!"

The prosecutor interjected.

"Objection! Your honor, the defense is defaming a highly respected detective taught by the best. As you will see from forthcoming ballistic testimony in the next case, Detective Pope is a top investigator with the newest technologies."

"Sustained. Counsel, do you have any more questions?" He did not.

Smith, the owner of the tobacco store was called next. He testified about selling the expensive box of cigars to Black and identified him in the defendant box.

When pressed about how people bite down on cigars, he gave expert testimony validating Pope's tooth mark claims.

Both wounded jehu Berenson and the wounded shotgun messenger identified Black at being present, but in the background of their respective robberies.

Several gang members were called to acknowledge Black was the leader of the robbery and rustling gang.

The Denver police sergeant was called and described the arrests of Black and Hazeltine in his city. He told about the officers finding over eighteen-thousand dollars in cash and gold coins under Black's bed.

At four o'clock in the afternoon, the jury was

sequestered to render a verdict. They returned after forty-five minutes with a guilty verdict. The judge had considered the sentencing well before this and sentenced Black to twenty-five years in the prison in Joliet, Illinois.

The trial of Cletus Hazeltine was scheduled to begin the following Monday at nine o'clock.

******

1882 Cheyenne was not unaccustomed to shots being fired in the middle of the night.

Shots in a snow covered streets at midnight were perhaps odd. But these shots were odder yet.

They were preceded by a dynamite blast.

Pope rolled his shoulder out from beneath Sarah's head as she stirred. He was already pulling on pants and shoes as she sat up in bed.

"What was the noise?" she asked groggily.

"An explosion of some sort. Then, shots."

"Which way?"

"I'm not really sure. But it seemed to have come from the direction of the courthouse and jail," he said.

"Damn!" she cursed.

"My thought exactly. I will investigate. No need for you to get up and get dressed. I'll be back soon."

"You sure?" Sarah asked.

"I'm sure, honey. Back shortly."

He ran down the stairs and onto the street. A few people were running down towards the courthouse.

Snow was falling. The streets had previously been covered. More was falling on the packed snow. Pope went as quickly as he could without slipping.

By the time he got to where people had congregated, his suspicions were confirmed. It was the courthouse. More specifically, it was the Laramie County jail which had been hit.

The Durant Steam Fire Company was in the same building and was already putting water on the small fire started by the explosion.

He saw Horatio Akin.

"Horatio! What happened?" he yelled from the crowd. The chief deputy turned angrily, but smiled relief once he saw who yelled.

"Pope! Jail break. I have one jailer down and two beat up. Hazeltine is gone, as well as a couple of drunks who were there and a chicken thief. The jailer is still deaf from the explosion. But he said some 'hillbilly' sounding guys, including an old one, blew their way in the door with dynamite. They seemed to target getting Hazeltine. He left with them. The others just ran out the opening and scattered."

Pope shoved his way over to Akin.

"They must have had horses," he began. Akin nodded affirmatively instantly.

"Any direction of travel?"

"Down 17th. I don't know anything else. Thank God we moved Rufus Black to prison this morning!"

"I'll get my gear and try to roust the livery for a horse. I will get on their trail while you round up a posse, alright?" Pope asked.

"Thanks. I'll be behind you as soon as I can. Not a great time for posse formation at midnight in the snow. Only people awake now are drunks in the saloons. They are the last people I want riding behind me armed," Akin said.

"It'll be dawn in four or five hours. Why not wait until then? I will try to leave markers about the direction along the way," Pope said.

Akin nodded and Pope left.

He knew his saddle and saddlebags and bedroll with tarp were at the livery. He went there first and woke the manager up.

"I have to track prisoners from the jailbreak," he said.

"What jailbreak?"

"The one the explosion allowed about thirty minutes ago. Put my gear on the strongest trail horse you have. I will be back in ten minutes with my rifle and some food, if I can find any." The man nodded.

Pope made his way and got the night clerk to go to the kitchen and put together whatever he could take for food. Then, he went to the room.

"Was it about Hazeltine?" were the first words

Sarah uttered.

"It was. I am going to try to do my specialty night tracking. The livery is preparing a horse. Akin will put together a posse at dawn. You should get some sleep, in case you want to ride with them. Get food from downstairs. Your saddlebags and bedroll are still at the livery. Ask for a tough horse. This is not very nice weather for what we have to do."

She reached out and drew him down.

"Be careful. I will see you on the trail. It's unlikely you will make contact with them tonight but be careful. Outside of town is virtually wilderness and it's cold and dark."

"I know. Love you!" he picked up his investigative bag with the Dietz lantern and bottle of oil in it and the .45-70 Marlin lever action in its scabbard and went out the door.

At the desk, he picked up a mystery bag of food. He did not have time to check it. He knew he had coffee and jerky in his saddlebags.

His horse was saddled and waiting. It was a big dun with a roman nose.

"I know he's ugly, Detective Pope. But he has the ability to run most horses into the ground."

"One like him is just what I need! Will you give me a bag of feed to hang off the saddle horn?" Pope asked. He got enough for a week, supplementing whatever browse was along the way.

Pope extracted the Dietz lantern and made sure he had a dry box of Lucifer's so he could light it. He knew it was already full of oil. He kept his lantern like his guns. Loaded and ready.

Pope rode off down 17th Street in the direction of travel Akin had indicated.

He was in his element. A cold night trail against an unknown number of outlaws. He tried not to be overly protective over Sarah. She was tough. But this was a trail most hardened cowboys would find punishing. He would rather have her in the company of Akin and a posse in a few hours.

After a mile, he began to see relatively fresh hoofprints. It was hard to tell with the wind blowing falling snow, but he thought there may be six sets. He smiled. He could handle six. Handle them just fine! They would not expect anyone to be trailing them tonight. They thought they had a six or seven hour head start on a posse. And he likely, with the .45-70, had power and range on them.

Pope rode on, content with his situation and enjoying being on the trail again.

From the spacing of the prints, they seemed to be at a fast trot. He likened the formation to a military one. If he was right, it may not be a good sign.

He periodically made an arrow out of branches for the posse or used his hatchet o make a blaze mark on a tree.

An hour later, he thought he had probably gained a bit on them. The last thing he wanted was to ride up on either them or any camp they would pitch.

Pope guessed the group he was trailing would stop for a quick camp to rest. Riding at a trot in blowing snow was hard on man and beast. He just did not know when they would decide to take their break.

Reckoning he had the advantage of surprise over them, he found a small grove of trees and stopped for a three or four hour rest.

Pope saved his Lucifer's and lit some kindling he found with the flame in the lantern.

He put the coffee pot on full of snow and melted it for the horse.

Putting the tepid water in the brim of his Boss of the Plains Stetson, he gave it to the horse. He sprinkled a little feed on the ground and hobbled the horse near it.

The next snow he melted was to replace canteen water he would use for his coffee.

Shortly, he had coffee brewing and water replaced in his canteen. He delved into the food bag and found four biscuits, some slices of beef and a chunk of cheese.

Not bad, he thought as he began to eat. He knew neither he nor the horse needed to eat yet. But his grandfather had taught him to eat and drink when he could on the trail.

"Boy, you never know when your next chance will

be!" the old former mountain man counseled.

He smiled at the thought of the man, who was not as old really as he imagined as a boy. He was young enough to have just courted and married a woman in her forties.

This was Israel Pope's kind of trail. He would relish this as much as his grandson did.

Pope checked on the horse. The big dun was fine.

He took the rifle out of its scabbard and put it in his blankets with him and rolled up in both the blankets and a small waterproof tarp.

He was relatively dry and warm and went to sleep quickly.

Pope automatically awoke an hour before dawn. He stoked the coals in the campfire and heated his coffee. He ate a now-stale biscuit with it.

He broke camp, saddled the dun and began trailing again. He chewed on a piece of beef jerky was he rode.

The sun told him the men were heading northwest. So did the increase in elevation as they approached the Laramie mountain range.

Pope came upon the horsemen soon. Too soon. They were in a military formation. The man at the front was in his sixties. Israel Pope's age. Pope knew better than to take him for granted. He was probably the military one. Maybe a Confederate officer. Maybe a guerilla. Or maybe just an old time Appalachian hunter.

While these thoughts were running through Pope's mind, the man sensed his presence two hundred yards behind them.

He turned and drew a rifle from his saddle scabbard just as Pope did.

"Damn!" It looked from a distance like a big Sharps or Ballard single shot buffalo gun. As much power as Pope had. Or maybe more power.

Pope snapped the Marlin to his shoulder, aimed at the man's head and pressed the trigger. He automatically levered another .45-70 cartridge into the chamber. The man fell from his horse, hit in the upper torso with Pope's Tennessee elevation.

His men began shooting at Pope with smaller carbines and revolvers. Pope rolled off the big horse and away to protect his mount.

From a prone position, he aimed at the man whose bullets were getting closer to him than others. Shortly, he would get his elevation right and hit the unprotected Pope.

Pope had to take him out of the fight.

He took in a long breath and let half of it out.

Front sight, on the man, he pressed the trigger slowly.

Usually men hit, even with a big round like the .45-70, crumple forwards.

This man flew backwards. The bullet hit him in the head, snapping his body back as it followed the direction of his head.

The other four, including Hazeltine, mounted.

Pope suspected there were others there, including the man he shot first who were also named Hazeltine. He was too far away to see resemblances, but this had every probability of a family job.

As the men rode away, Pope aimed carefully at Cletus Hazeltine. He picked a point three to four feet above where he wanted the bullet to go.

Hazeltine's horse veered to the right just as Pope fired.

Pope was using the newer five hundred grain bullet. It had better ballistic performance than the original army load of four hundred five grains.

His shot was from two hundred fifty yards. With the horse changing direction unexpectedly, the five hundred grain bullet hit Hazeltine in the leg and went on to kill the animal.

The horse fell and Hazeltine fell free without being pinned.

Pope mounted the dun and rode carefully towards the three downed men.

He rode with the big Marlin still shouldered and ready to fire.

A glance told him the first man was dead. The bullet hit him in the upper chest. His eyes were open and staring sightlessly.

The second man's condition gave even Pope a shiver. A buffalo gun round to the head is never pretty.

Hazeltine laid on the ground by his dead horse. He was moaning in pain. Soon, Pope knew, shock would set in and he would lose consciousness.

"Who are these men, Hazeltine?" Pope asked.

Through gritted teeth, Hazeltine cursed him for almost a minute then admitted "You killed my daddy and my brother!"

"I'm sorry about your mount. You are lucky your horse turned or you'd be in hell with them, Hazeltine. Or, maybe not so lucky. You are going to die hard, I'm afraid."

"You are sorry about the horse, but not my daddy or brother?" Hazeltine asked.

"They were a threat. The horse was just an innocent beast carrying an ass. You. Take your bandanna off and fold it into a pad. Push the pad against your leg to help with the bleeding."

"Ain't gonna do not good, Wells Fargo man. You have killed me for sure."

"Who used the dynamite?" Pope asked.

"Go to hell," Hazeltine responded.

"Just tell me for the record. It's not like either of them is going to hang for it."

"My daddy would not let me rot in jail!"

"So, you're saying he did it?"

Hazeltine passed out.

Pope wondered if the three who got away were

brothers or cousins. If so, they might double back and try to dry gulch him.

"But, then again, they were high-tailing it out of here, leaving their family behind in the dust. Not much loyalty there," he thought.

He was faced with a dilemma. He had two dead bodies and one which would die soon. He only had two horses in addition to his own.

Pope was damned if he was going to walk back to Cheyenne so dead outlaws could ride.

He disarmed Hazeltine and took the canteen off his brother's horse. He placed it by the man.

He also removed weapons from the father and brother. He put them in the now-depleted cloth food sack and slung it back on his saddle horn. No need for Hazeltine having a way to kill him if the outlaw miraculously got a pre-death flash of energy.

Pope rode over to a stand of cottonwoods a half mile away. He cut five straight pieces twelve feet long and three inches thick. He bundled them and dragged them back to where the bodies and one victim were.

He checked on Hazeltine. He was still alive, though not for long.

Pope, trained by a mountain man, set out to build a travois to transport the bodies back. If Hazeltine lived, he would ride on the travois. If not, he could go over one horse, while the other towed the travois with his father and brother.

Building the travois would be easy. Working out a harness to attach it to a saddle horse would be challenging.

He placed two full-length pieces in a point, then arranged them so the top half was three feet apart and the bottom half was six feet apart. Pope cut appropriate pieces of the lariat on Hazeltine's saddle and lashed them to provide a base every several feet on the travois. He used latigos from the dead men's and Hazeltine's saddles to lash the cross pieces.

Pope then took two small tarps from behind the saddles and tied them to the cross pieces. He placed the one piece of either side of the end of the travois into the stirrups on what appeared to be the strongest horse. Pope then lashed them tightly so they would not come loose as the horse pulled the body-laden travois over the prairie.

He dragged both bodies over. Taking the elder man's coat off, he used it to cover what had been his son's and Cletus Hazeltine's brother's head.

Pope then tied both bodies securely on the travois. He took a chance Cletus Hazeltine would not need emergency transport.

Pope was right. When he checked the wounded man, there was no pulse. He had bled to death from a bullet through his femoral artery.

He appreciated the term "dead weight" when he muscled Cletus onto his father's horse and tied Cletus' belt to the saddle horn. He tied the dead fugitive's his legs together under the horse's belly. The horse did not like the smell of blood but did not buck or try to dislodge the body.

Watching over his shoulder in case the other three turned around and came back after him, Pope headed to Cheyenne. He led both horses. It would be a long trip at a walk.

Before dark, he saw a group of riders coming towards him from the direction of Cheyenne. It had to be the posse. They also had a wagon, probably for supplies and sleeping gear.

He recognized Sharples, Akin and Sarah in the front.

She saw him and spurred her horse ahead at a full gallop.

"Are you alright?" she asked.

"Nary a scratch." She looked at the bodies on the horses and travois.

"He has to be Hazeltine's father. Looks just like him," she said.

"It is. The one with the covered head wound was a brother. Three got away. I think they were family. If they were, there was not much loyalty. They took off as soon as two fell."

The sheriff and chief deputy rode up, posse behind.

"Looks like you had a little set-to," Sharples said.

"Hazeltine's father saw me. I'm thinking from the

way he led them and his presence of mind on the trail he was former military. Anyway, he pulled a Sharps rifle. It's on the travois. I had to take him out. He probably had some range on me.

The others opened up with everything they had. I killed one and they ran, including Cletus Hazeltine. The piece of garbage left his father and brother lying dead. All he cared about was himself.

I took a shot at him from several hundred yards and hit him in the leg. It went through and killed his horse.

First aid did not stop his bleeding. It must have hit an artery. He went into shock. While in shock, he bled to death as I was building the travois to transport him on. Three took off and I have not seen them since.

He said his father was the one who used the dynamite."

"Well, the explosion and who engineered the jail-break is solved. It also saves Laramie County the time and cost of hanging Hazeltine. The prosecutor might want a brief posthumous trial to close the books.

I'm not worried about the three who got away. If they didn't have any more loyalty than they showed, they were probably just along for the ride. They'll likely get lost on the way back to wherever they came from.

I'm thinking we should take the gear out of the

wagon and put it on the two horses. We can make better time pulling the wagon with the bodies than the travois with the bodies," Sheriff Sharples finished.

Akin directed some possemen in transferring the bodies to the wagon.

They rode through the night and got back to Cheyenne before dinner the next day.

CHAPTER 7

The sheriff was correct about a posthumous trial.
Pope delivered his ballistics testimony and it was used
to find Cletus Hazeltine guilty of the murder of EB
Carson and the wounding of one of the two Wells
Fargo men posthumously. Perhaps more importantly,
the testimony and its exhibits showing the bullets and
the guns got wide coverage in the press. Hume was
as pleased about the ballistics coverage advancing in
the minds of prosecutors and citizens alike as he was
the treasure recovery.

The two detectives prepared an encrypted executive summary and a ten-page case closure on the
train and stage robberies and shootings and sent it
by express to Hume.

"Well, the world famous and feared partnership of
Watson and Pope has closed another one!" Pope said
at the hotel restaurant. They had Champagne with

dinner, on their own tab.

"We surely did, dear John. I still did not like you riding off like Don Quixote in the middle of a snow-storm though."

"Who?"

"Never mind. It does not matter. I realize there are some trails you can make better time on alone. I don't like it, but I accept it," she said.

"Look, Sarah. Nobody considers you more an equal than I do. But there are some things you'll always be better on. And somethings I will. It's what makes us such a good team. I will always be bigger and stronger. It's just the way it is. And, I have a lifetime on the trail. Just a fact," he said.

Then, smiling, he raised the Champagne flute and offered a toast.

"To windmills. They don't shoot back!"

"He continually surprises me," she thought, but said nothing as she smiled and touched glasses with a "clink."

Later she asked, "Think we can sleep through the night without an explosion or something equally disruptive?"

"Probably not. It's cold, snowing and approaching midnight. Why should everybody else be up and not us?" he asked.

"I need to know something. How in hell do you know anything about Spanish literature?"

"My grandfather made me read Don Quixote when I was learning Spanish. So, I read it in the original Castilian."

"Are you going to continue to surprise me?" she asked.

"Every single day for the next sixty or so years."

"Got any teasers for now?" she asked.

"Hmmm. Maybe. Did I ever tell you my grandfather is pretty versed on Indian religion?"

"I am assuming not Hindu," she said.

"All but Cheyenne the most. I don't know where he learned so much, but he promised to tell me one day. He said it was a story which would take time and emotion to tell."

"Mysterious."

"He was certainly mysterious, all right. Anyway, he believes we all have spirit animals to look over us and guide us. American Indians know about this. Most whites do not have a clue about it."

"How do spirit animals square with Christianity?" she asked.

"I asked him the same question. He said to think of them like the angel on your shoulder. Then, you would not have to worry about a conflict. Seemed reasonable to me," Pope said.

"Do you have a spirit animal then?" she asked.

"I do. A bald eagle. He appears when I am confused or in danger. Somehow, I get through it."

"Does this eagle tell you anything?"

"Not in words. More in feelings. Like he guides me."

"Does he ever bring bad news?" she asked.

"No."

"Have you seen him recently?"

"I have. When I was riding a few days ago," Pope said.

"So, you think the eagle boded well?"

"I do. He has not let me down yet," Pope said seriously.

"Do I have a spirit animal?" she asked.

"Yes, if you will allow yourself to acknowledge it."

"If I agree to have one, how will I know who or what he or she is?" Sarah asked.

"You will know. It will appear in a time and way you will recognize what it for what it is."

"You know something? You are as mysterious as your grandfather."

He smiled at her.

"Sarah, I will never be half the man he is, not if I live to be a hundred years old."

"He seems to think you already are."

"He just sets me on the top rail of the fence," Pope said.

"Me, too, cowboy."

She rolled over and nestled against his shoulder. Then, she decided snuggling was nowhere near enough. He absolutely agreed.

******

The next morning, they went to the office and met with McCarthy. They talked about the new office. Though it was in an existing building, the weather was still delaying arrival of the materials needed to make new rooms, for the vault a steel door into the vault room and new décor.

Pope had completed most of the security feature planning from Hume's checklist. Sarah had helped McCarthy with the layout and furnishings. It was now a matter of sit and wait for the weather to improve and materials to arrive. Trains were running on schedule, but the problem was getting items to the train from warehouses in Chicago, New York and other places as snowed in as Wyoming.

Pope and Sarah were assigned the Wells Fargo detective job they and all other detectives with the firm hated the most. They investigated fraudulent claims against Wells Fargo and lawsuits against it. These were not dangerous but were contentious and boring to investigate. The firm was conspicuously honest. The two knew any claim of wrongdoing against it was wrongfully made. At the very least, it would be found to have been caused by mitigating circumstances. But they had to investigate nonetheless.

While all twenty-three thousand dollars of treasure stolen by the Rufus Black gang had been returned—at a loss—by Wells Fargo, one shipper sued for interest lost on the money.

It claimed the loss of its money for the two weeks processing after a robbery caused "immense and unreconcilable damage to its business."

It was a coal mining company in Carbon County, approximately one hundred miles west. The company and its attorney were from a small town on the Platte River, but the suit was in the court in Cheyenne. Sarah and Pope traveled to Carbon. They separated before arriving in town and were not seen together publicly.

Using her real background as the tax collector of Yavapai County, Arizona Territory, Sarah got a part-time job as an accountant at the mining company. Wells Fargo's attorney subpoenaed financial records from the company. The records with which they responded showed a considerable loss. Sarah found the real records showing no loss. She slipped them into her bag before leaving one night and left the modified subpoenaed ones in their place.

The company treasurer was censured by the judge and the case dropped when the treasurer was called upon in court to substantiate any loss. Where and how the correct records came from never came to light. The treasurer was caught, and he knew it. Sarah, undercover, resigned suddenly from the mining company. She did not appear in court.

Pope had the treasurer sign an agreement to not

bring another claim against Wells Fargo regarding the matter. He signed and Pope and Sarah did another case closure report.

It was a colder than usual winter in Cheyenne and, indeed, all off the Territory of Wyoming. The area in the far western part of the territory, near the Wind River Range, was snowed in.

Days were bleak and nights cold. Snow, while it never got more than a few feet deep in the Cheyenne area, fell frequently.

There was no progress on the conversion of their new space due to continuing shipping delays.

Stores were open, but a lot of cowboys were out of work and drifted towards Laramie and Cheyenne to kill time. They mainly killed time by drinking. The drinking led to fighting. So, minor crime soared in the two cities.

The Cheyenne crime wave would have been a non-event between coverage by the local officers and the sheriff's department being headquartered there.

The problem was where to put lawbreakers, since the Hazeltine's had blown down a major support wall in the jail. The temporary wall, due to lack of construction materials, was wooden and largely insecure. Two jailers with shotguns had to guard it day and night. Resources were stretched at patrol officers from both departments were called in to stand watch.

The judge asked Pope and Sarah to ride up to

the Carson ranch and check on cowboys Willy and Roscoe. Descendants had not yet decided on the fate of the ranch.

They rode back to the Wells Fargo office and found it was in chaos.

******

Wells Fargo agent in charge McCarthy was in over his head. As good he was, he had more business than the small office could handle. The newspaper just reported Cheyenne to be the richest city per capita in the world. Yet, he did not even have a cashier. Just a telegrapher. He needed a cashier and one or two front desk people to handle simpler customer demands and a messenger.

McCarthy had been trying to hire an experienced cashier, but to no avail. Both Pope and Sarah had stepped in to assist, but it was not their job. And, they had to be gone on investigations too much to be serious help for him. The telegraph operator was at the key from open until after closing. He could not be cross-trained and help.

McCarthy was busy with the new office. However, he had customers all day. Most were business customers from hotels and retailers transferring money.

He knew such customers needed immediate service. Their livelihood depended on it.

There was a break in customers, then a man walked in. Byron McCarthy got a glimpse of him just before he pulled a kerchief over his face. The action was followed by him drawing a large revolver from his left topcoat pocket.

"It's a robbery! Let's go to where you keep the money!" he said.

McCarthy arose and led the man into the vault, which was in a corner of the open room. Only a temporary curtain blocked public view from an adjacent table where office funds and customer money, or treasure, was counted.

"I will open the vault. There's not much in it. The weather has delayed transfers in and shipments out by businesses. It's the wrong day of the month for payrolls," McCarthy told the man. His voice was shaking nervously.

"Just open the damn vault. Be fast about it!" the man ordered.

McCarthy opened it and the robber saw an office cash box and a smaller safe within. The small one contained customer money. It had not been opened for four days, except for the daily count.

"What's in there?" the man asked pointing his gun at the small safe.

"Our customer's money."

"Open it now!"

McCarthy did and the man saw a variety of banded

bills and stacks of gold coins.

He pulled out a flour sack and ordered McCarthy to fill it. The agent did.

"Now, dump the cash box in."

Again, McCarthy complied.

As they turned, a woman walked in the door. McCarthy hoped it was Sarah.

Instead, it was an employee from the bank coming to send a wire.

The robber panicked and fired his gun. He hit the woman in the upper chest, just below the throat. She died instantly and toppled onto the tile floor.

McCarthy grabbed the man and they wrestled for the gun. It went off and McCarthy fell ten feet from the woman.

The man rushed out of the door and ran down the street, still with his face covered and the money sack in one hand and the revolver in the other.

A town policeman saw him and drew his Iver Johnson .32.

Before he could bring it into play, the robber shot him in the chest and he fell. Men yelled at him. A woman nearby began to scream.

The robber disappeared down an alley.

The two Wells Fargo detectives immediately saw two people on the floor and civilians from the street checking them as they pulled their horses up in front of the office. They quickly tied the horses to the hitching posts out front and pushed through the crowd.

There was a female shooting victim just inside the door.

A woman was squatting on the floor beside McCarthy. She was doing nothing, frozen with panic. Telegrapher Lon Olson was kneeling, patting McCarthy's hand.

"Sarah, I've got him. Please check the woman near the door," Pope said.

He checked McCarthy for wounds and found one in his left chest, not far above the heart. It was similar to the one Pope had, but closer to the heart. Pope's was just now healing. Pope removed a clean folded handkerchief and pressed it on the wound and held it firmly.

"Lon, what did you see?" Pope asked.

"I walked in from the privy and saw Mr. McCarthy fighting with a man in a mask. Then, the gun went off. Mr. McCarthy fell and the man ran out the door and turned left on 17th."

"Describe him to me, please."

"Medium height. Maybe five-six or seven. He had on a heavy coat, but his face under the mask and his hands looked skinny. I couldn't see no hair, what with the bandana and his Stetson hat. His clothes were kind of worn, but not ragged."

"What was his voice like?" Pope asked.

"He didn't talk in front of me."

"How about his gun?"

"Long barrel. Blue or black. I don't know enough about guns to name the make or model. It was big though. Oh! He looked kinda bow legged. Maybe a cowboy," Olson said.

"Pope, it's the woman from the bank. Nobody can help her now," Sarah yelled.

Akin stuck his head in the door. He looked at the woman. Sarah looked up and shook her head.

"McCarthy?" he asked Pope.

"Bad wound. He needs to be transported to the hospital really fast. I've somewhat stopped the external bleeding, but I don't know what's going on inside."

"I've got a town policeman shot a block down 17th. I will go there, but you should try to find a carriage to take Byron to the hospital." He then turned and sprinted down the street to the fallen officer.

"I cannot let up on the pressure on Byron's wound. Will you see if anyone saw the shooter?" Pope asked his partner. She left the body and rushed to the crowd outside.

"Lon, you've done well! I need you to do one more thing. Find me a buckboard with a bed or a wagon or carriage. We have to get McCarthy to the Memorial Hospital. It's not far, but we can't carry him."

Sarah began canvasing the small crowd near the office door. Most arrived to see what was going on and stayed. One, however, had seen a young man in a dark brown topcoat wrestle with McCarthy after shooting the bank woman. He said the two men scuffled a bit, then the robber's gun went off, wounding McCarthy.

"I knew he was shorter than me because he damn near knocked me over going out the door. I saw over his head. I sure did!"

Sarah pressed him for more information.

"How tall are you?" she asked.

"I'm six foot one," he said, "so he was probably five foot seven or so."

"You're really helpful! What was he wearing?"

"He had on a dark brown sheepskin ranch coat and a matching wide brim hat."

"What kind of gun was he carrying?"

"A S&W Schofield. He waved it in my face when he shoved me aside. I thought I was going to die!"

"Did he still have a mask on?" she asked.

"Yes! A red bandana tied around his mouth and nose."

"Did he say anything?" Sarah asked.

"Nothing. I heard him yell at a man in his way when he was running down the street."

"What kind of a voice did he have? Did he have an accent?" Sarah asked.

"Regular voice. No accent. Sounds like from around here," the man said.

Five minutes later, Lon Olson came back, having commandeered a farmer and his buckboard for the quick trip to the hospital. Pope carefully picked McCarthy up in his arms and carried him outside.

"Lon, go get his coat so we can cover him up and keep him warm," Pope said.

The telegrapher brought the coat and covered his boss.

"Two more things, Lon. One make a "closed sign" and post it. Two, telegraph James Hume at Wells Fargo headquarters and tell him what has happened. Tell him the two detectives and you have the situation under control for now, alright?"

"Yessir, Detective Pope. I sure will," and he ran back inside where it was warm, but still had one bloody body on the floor. He keyed up his machine.

McCarthy came to briefly during the short trip to the hospital.

"Pope. Am I going to die?"

"One day for sure. But, not today as near as I can tell. I had a real similar gunshot some months ago. Same place. Hurt like hell. I just took off the sling some weeks ago. But I think you will be fine, Byron."

Pope thanked the farmer for the ride as they pulled up in front of the hospital. He offered to pay the man.

"Naw, I can't take no money for helping a man. It wouldn't be Christian. Lemme go inside and get some docs out here with a stretcher or something."

He was as good as his word and moments later, a doctor, nurse and several orderlies ran out with a gurney. They loaded the unconscious McCarthy on it and Pope followed them inside.

One of the doctors asked about the circumstances.

"You will find a large caliber revolver wound to the upper left chest between the shoulder and heart. I put a pad on it and kept pressure within minutes after it happened. The shooter killed one woman and shot a policeman in his escape. You'll know if the policeman lived soon enough, as he will be brought here."

"Anything else?" the doctor asked, in a hurry to prepare for surgery.

"Yes. It is important for me to get the bullet when you take it out."

"Souvenir for your friend?"

"No. I am a Wells Fargo detective. We have developed a way to compare bullets from victims with particular guns. It doesn't always work, but most of the time it's good enough evidence to put away a shooter. If you are the coroner too, I'll need the one from the woman dead on our office floor and the policeman. When we catch this shooter, he will hang for sure."

"I'll make sure you get them both. Where can I find you?"

"The Wells Fargo office. I will get you to sign a statement of where you obtained them."

"Fair enough. Gotta go!" and the doctor rushed off down the hall.

Pope went back to the office.

Akin was there talking to Sarah. Because of the relative lack of business due to the weather, she was able to verify the loss at twenty-four hundred dollars. Eighteen hundred had been money on account for customers, the rest office cash.

"How's McCarthy?" both asked simultaneously.

"Don't know. I survived a similar wound a few months ago. I hope he will, too."

"This poor lady and the constable weren't so lucky. We have to catch this man and hang him," Akin said.

"Between your questioning the telegrapher and Sarah, we have a good description. Sounds like a skinny, mid-twenties, probable cowboy. Slightly bow legged, no particular accent or voice description. Brown ranch coat and wide brimmed hat. Nothing on his hair or whether he has a mustache or beard. He was packing a Schofield with the standard military length barrel," Akin continued.

"Pope, could you or Sarah show me how you draw crime scenes. They make perfect sense to jog memories, whether for solving or testifying."

"How about watch us do it now?" Sarah asked. The chief deputy agreed.

"Is anybody coming to remove this poor lady?" Pope asked.

"Soon. I sent for the undertaker," Akin said.

"I made preliminary arrangements with the surgeon to get the bullets from all three victims.

We can do the ballistics analysis. It would be good if you follow up on it with the undertaker and the surgeon. We don't want bullet to slip through the cracks since people aren't trained to think about it yet," Pope said as he removed his sketch pad and pencil. He used a square and a ruler to lay out the room. He drew the position of the victims then used a tape measure to note the dimensions of the room and distance between where the two victims fell. Then, in a box on the lower right, he put his name, title and date. He gave Akin his pad and pencil and he drew his own version.

"Horatio, do you create a file for each crime you investigate?" Sarah asked.

"Not really. Should I?"

"It would probably keep you organized when things get hectic. It helps to have something weeks or months later to use for a referral before testifying in court. Whether it's in a notebook, or pages in a folder for larger cases, it helps keep an investigator on track. Having a closed, controlled file room at the sheriff's office would give you a place to keep case files and evidence, or property to be returned after a trial."

"Like?" he asked.

"Oh - how about a gun is held for a trial, then the defendant was found innocent?" she said.

"I see. We have a small, spare room. I'll talk with the sheriff about it. Will you all help me set it up?"

"Glad too," Pope said, entering the conversation. While Akin and Sarah were talking, he had finished his review of the crime scene. There was no evidence except for a lot of blood. They knew whose blood it was in both cases. Pope suspected blood would one day be a personal identifier. Technology just was not present yet, he lamented.

The undertaker arrived and removed the woman. Sarah obtained her name from Olson who had sent and received many wires for her on behalf of the bank. The bank manager had come while Pope was taking McCarthy to the hospital and stood struck with the needless violence perpetrated on his employee and a wife and mother of three.

"Has anyone notified her husband?" Pope asked the banker.

"Yes. The sheriff and I went by shortly after he told me she was shot and had not survived. Her husband is pretty broken up. They have three young children and no nearby family. He's already looking for a woman to come in and care for the young ones. He does not have the liberty to grieve until they are taken care of," the banker said.

"You know, Horatio, we in law enforcement have to see the other side of crimes. The suffering on part of victims and their families. Though a bit different from pure crimes, I know the impact. I saw my mother, father and baby sister killed in front of my eyes.

It was seventeen years ago and still as clear to me as a picture," Pope said. Sarah was shocked. Pope was not one to open up. He must think highly of Akin to pursue this line of thought.

"You must have been what, ten years old, John?" Akin asked.

"I was. When the raiding party came, Pa put my sister and me in the root cellar. We could hear the shooting and screaming. My little sister panicked and came out of the root cellar. She ran towards the action. The braves saw her, but thought she came from the house they had just torched. They shot her down and scalped her, Horatio. It was the worst thing I ever saw."

"What happened then?" Akin asked.

"I did what Pa had told me and laid low. They burned the house down after taking what they wanted and left. I went to the neighboring farm. It was about three miles and told them. They kept me until my grandfather arrived from California."

"What then?"

"We watched the tribe and saw another raiding party go out. I recognized some of the braves. We tracked them and caught them in the open. The two of us opened up with rifles and pistols. We killed every damn one of them and scalped them. The ones we killed were the only young men in this band. Grandpa and I rode into the camp we had watched.

He dropped their scalps at the feet of the old chief. I saw scalps hanging by his tent. My baby sister's was there. Grandpa saw me looking and knew what I was thinking. He looked at me and I read his approval."

"Approval, John?" Akin asked.

"I raised the 1866 Winchester Yellow Boy carbine Grandpa had given me and shot the chief between the eyes. I have not committed a cold-blooded murder before, nor will I ever again. But it was like my sister was watching and willing me to do it."

Sarah saw something she had never seen before. A tear forming in the corner of the big detective's eye.

"What you did as a boy wasn't cold blooded murder. It was payback to the man who sent the braves out. I'd like to think I would have done the same thing. Though I'm not sure I could have pulled it off at ten years old," Akin said softly and introspectively. It was as if he was speaking to himself and not them.

They were interrupted by a telegram being brought across the room to them. Pope knew it must be important for Olson to rush it over.

It was in code, so Pope went to his desk and sat down with the Wells Fargo Cipher book and quickly decoded it.

It was from Hume. The first thing it said was "Get robber." The second thing was a surprise. Hume said he had spoken with Wells Fargo Superintendent William Pridham. The legendary former Pony Express rider had authorized Sarah Watson to replace McCarthy as manager until he recovered. Hume told Pridham about her history, including being tax office manager for Yavapai County, Arizona Territory. Pope would have to track down and arrest the Wells Fargo robber and murderer without his partner. The case was named the highest priority case currently under investigation by the company. Even higher priority than Black Bart.

Sarah was looking over Pope's shoulder as he wrote the simple language version of the coded message.

He looked up at her wide eyes.

"Are you alright with the temporary assignment?" he asked.

"I have to be. It did not seem to be an option on my part."

"More like an expediency," he said.

"Think you can solve a crime without your brilliant and beautiful partner?" she asked.

"It will be difficult. Truly. But we have to do whatever is assigned. Do you think you need a manager from somewhere else like Marcus Howard in Denver to ride up for a day's orientation?" Pope asked.

"Yes. Definitely. Especially with him being a short train ride away. I'll compose an in-the-clear non-encrypted telegram to Hume. I guess he'll have to clear it with Superintendent Pridham," she said.

"Sounds like a good plan, Sarah. Horatio?" Pope

called to the chief deputy who was still there, now speaking with one of his deputies.

Akin walked over to Pope's desk. Pope showed him the translated telegram.

"Looks like you lost a pard for a while," he observed.

"Looks like it. Are you running with this one, or are you going to assign a deputy to manage your case?" Pope asked.

"I have several cases going and know you will bring this fella in with or without the Laramie Sheriff's Office. So, I may put a young deputy on it for experience. Maybe you and I both can look over his shoulder."

"Sure. Let me work out my investigative plan. Send him over and I'll share it. If I need to ride out and cut sign, I may do it alone and bring your man fully aboard later."

"Haha. 'Cut sign.' You are mountain man-trained for sure," Akin said chuckling.

"I sure am, brother! And I think it's going to pay off in this hunt."

Sarah opened the office for limited business. She organized during slack periods. After the office closed, she would do her daily cash counts and compare with the previous day's office cash and OPM or "other person's money." The count was done with one counting and another watching. They reverified the take from the robbery during the process. Both signed the cash register.

A deputy came in and motioned Akin aside. They spoke in low voices for a minute, then the deputy left. Pope looked questioningly at Akin.

"John, I have news. Good news!" Akin said.

"I have deputies and the remaining constable questioning everyone who might have been on the street around the time of the robbery. One found a witness who saw the robber, money bag and all, mount a gray gelding and head out of town at a full gallop."

"Which way?"

"He was high-tailing due south towards Colorado."

Pope looked at his pocket watch.

"He's got a two and a half hour head start. You can't put together a posse equipped for several days in the snow between now and dark. But night trails are my specialty. I'm on it," Pope said.

He donned his heavy coat and quickly walked over to the livery stable nearest the office. He inquired whether the big, Roman nosed dun was available for a few days. He liked the horse's endurance and power. The horse was available, and Pope reserved him starting immediately. He got the manager to add a small bag of feed. There was enough snow now to make finding browse difficult. He stepped into a tobacconist and picked up a box of good cigars.

When he returned, Akin was already gone. He could not kiss Sarah goodbye with Olson there, so he winked at her and blew a kiss with his back turned towards the telegrapher. He had stopped by both a mercantile and a restaurant on the way back from the livery. He kept his saddlebags, bedroll, and tarp in the office. He put them on the horse and attached the scabbard with the Marlin lever action.

He mounted and galloped out of town, heading south. It would be dark in less than two hours. Pope knew he was in for a cold camp. A real cold camp.

The big horse was named Caesar for his Roman nose. He seemed happy to be flexing his muscles in the cold air. Heavy and sixteen plus hands tall, Caesar had a comfortable smooth gait. Pope knew from experience the horse could put away miles effortlessly in any conditions.

Ten miles into his southward journey, Pope met a waggoneer coming north and hailed him.

"Howdy. I'm a lawman trailing a lean cowboy on a gray gelding. Might be wearing a brown ranch coat. He he's probably riding pretty fast," Pope said.

"I seen him a couple hours ago," the stocky driver said.

"He was cutting the gray towards the west. It was around Ft. Collins. Other than the village of Laporta, there's nothing west until you cross the Laramie River and go into Walden. Not much there either. There's a trail all the way though."

"It's pretty mountainous over there isn't it?" Pope asked.

"Yeah. Medicine Bow range first, then officially the Rocky Mountains start. Hope you got plenty of grub if you are heading all the way after him, lawman. 'Course you could kill a deer for some meat. I never thought squirrels or rabbits was worth the trouble," the man said.

"I agree," Pope said. He thanked the man and rode on.

He saw the turn off the wagon driver described to him and headed west on a trail which ran northwest to the village of Laporta. He rested Caesar and got a hot meal.

His suspect had stopped there for lunch and to buy provisions. He also got feed for his horse. There was no place to stay, so the suspect rode on.

Pope had his horse fed at a stable to save his bag of feed. He added more provisions to those he had quickly picked up leaving Cheyenne.

Pope rode on into the growing darkness. The trail began to straighten out. And, headed into the Medicine Bow range. Pope would rather camp in the mountains where there were trees, streams and woods than on the windy prairie.

He found a spot protected from the blowing snow. He felt secure in not hobbling Caesar. Pope did his usual long radius swing around his campsite. There was nobody in the area.

He gathered long branches from the ground and

cut them with his hatchet. He reckoned he had enough fire-wood for the night and for breakfast tomorrow.

Pope dug a pit and set his fire. He used a steel and scraped it along the top edge of the blade on his Bowie. The bright shower of sparks caught in the tinder. Soon he had a small, hot fire. Saving the limited supply of Lucifer matches seemed prudent. He built a lean-to with one of his two tarps to protect against the snow. It seemed to be falling faster.

While the fire was burning down to coals, he got out his coffee pot and melted snow for the horse and for his coffee. He added coffee beans to his and the coffee brewed as he selected some meat, cheese and cornbread from the restaurant. With coffee, he ate to his fill. Beans and roasted meat for trail food was fine when one had hours to simmer the beans and use a Dutch oven for the meat or combination. But, for a lawman tracking someone, it was quick or nothing.

It was getting colder and colder. Pope ate quickly and cleaned his utensils with snow to not attract coyotes or other varmints. He checked on Caesar and hand fed him some feed from the bag. He was starting to respect the horse more and more. He talked with him for a while before going back to the fire.

Pope lowered the height of the tarp lean-to in an effort to better keep the increasing volume of blowing snow out. He crawled in and leaned against his saddle. Fully dressed, even with his coat, he wrapped in both his wool blanket and the smaller, waxed tarp.

Despite his preparations, he was cold. He feared it was going to be a long miserable night. It was.

Before dawn, Pope built up the fire and melted more snow for coffee. Caesar stood butt to the wind and seemed to take the miserable weather without complaint. Pope fed and watered him while the fire was working on providing some heat.

Soon, he had coffee and ate a cold meal with it. He broke camp and headed in the same general direction as the tracks had led him to this point. The overnight accumulation of snow obliterated any remaining tracks.

Pope's only chance was to happen upon the out-law's morning trail and track him from it. Usually, he would have a potential town and a chance the fugitive would head towards it. In this case, he was headed into mountain wilderness. He was not sure even of a ranch out here.

He and Caesar walked slowly in the dark. By light, if one could call the miserable gray day light, he still had not encountered horse tracks.

His outlaw must have a greater lead on him than he thought. Still no camp from last night. Or perhaps he had missed it. He doubted he had. Pope's sense of smell for horses, coffee and wood smoke seldom failed him on the trail. The one benefit of the icy air was to heighten smell. But, so far, he had nothing.

By noon, the detective happened on something he did not expect to find. It was a ranch in the middle of nowhere.

"Hello, the ranch!" he called, to avoid surprising someone and being shot.

A man opened the door, a full-length Sharps buffalo gun in his hand. Pope had moved his badge to the lapel of his outer coat, and it glinted in what passed for light.

"Come on in, lawman," the older rancher called. "I got coffee on and the missus has come bacon and mush still warm from breakfast."

Pope slid off the big horse and petted it on the flank.

"Good boy. Wait out here," he said.

"You been on a cold trail, it looks like," the rancher offered.

"I have. I'm John Pope, detective for Wells Fargo. I'm after a thin, young cowboy who shot a woman and a policeman in cold blood after robbing the Wells Fargo office in Cheyenne."

"Shot a woman?"

"He did. For no reason at all. Left a husband and three small children behind."

"Not right detective, not right at all." Pope nodded.

"I'm going to take him in, mister. On the saddle or over it."

"He seemed like a nice young fella..." the man said,

catching Pope off guard.

"So, he was here?" Pope asked.

"He spent the night in my barn. We fed him and his horse. A nice gray gelding. A likeable young man, maybe twenty years old. He did wear his gun low and tied like a gunfighter though."

"Nobody got a look at his face because of the mask. Will you describe it for me?"

"Too young for much of a beard. Actually, he looked like he didn't need to shave at all. Light eyes, light brown shaggy hair. No scars or anything showing. Wore a brown ranch coat and a red plaid wool shirt. Brown or tannish canvas pants. Just looked like a cowpuncher. Except for the gun."

"Did you note what kind of gun he was packing?" Pope asked.

"A Smith & Wesson, it appeared."

"Well, the gun and description clinches it. Sounds exactly like my man."

By this time, they were into the house. The rancher introduced himself as William Brown. His wife offered Pope a tin mug of steaming coffee.

"Thank you, Mrs. Brown. This coffee is a lot better than the trail coffee I made before five o'clock this morning!" Pope said.

"I'm heating up some oatmeal mush, for you to warm your stomach, Detective Pope," she said.

"It would be most appreciated."

"Mr. and Mrs. Brown, did the man identify himself by name?" Pope asked.

"Never offered, so we never asked."

"Did he hint as to where he was going?"

"Said he had a friend up near the Continental Divide. Has a cabin or something. Kid said he was fearful the friend might have packed it in and left. If so, he did not have the supplies to winter there. I told him the old general store at Kremmling had some other buildings and was almost a town now. He could follow the Muddy River down from near here. Then, he could pick up the old Midland Trail and go east or west. He seemed to like it as an alternative. He left here going south. So, I figure he decided to head to Kremmling instead of his friend's cabin."

Pope enjoyed the oatmeal and coffee. Mrs. Brown packed him a bag with cooked bacon to heat and some cornpones.

"He's got a four-hour head start on you. But he didn't look like he was in a hurry. I guess he reckoned nobody would follow him through a snowstorm," Brown said.

"I'll catch him. I really lucked out at the livery stable. Old Caesar is like a buffalo. He's big, strong and has good endurance. And he rides like a big-wheel carriage. Thank you all for the information and the hospitality. I better hit the trail south," Pope said. Brown told him the way to reach the Muddy

River and how to follow it down to Kremmling. He said he heard there might even be a rooming house just built there.

Pope hoped so. There might be a chance the trail-weary murderer would try to get a night's sleep on a real bed.

"Oh! One more thing. Mrs. Brown, did you also give the fellow food to eat on the trail?"

"Yes, I did. Some bacon like you and cornpones. He will probably stop and build a fire to finish cooking the bacon. I reminded him half raw bacon would mess up his stomach. I figured you'd already know it."

"I sure do. Thanks, Mrs. Brown. You may have just bought me an hour. Longer if it warms up enough for him to have a nap after lunch."

He bid the Brown's adieu and rode south, warm for the first time in eighteen hours.

Snow had neither fallen nor melted since his fugitive left the Brown's ranch this morning, so Pope had a clear trail to follow. He even picked up and studied a couple of hoofprints in dirt. There was nothing distinctive, however.

It appeared his man was walking his gray. Pope urged Caesar up to a canter. The big horse seemed pleased to stretch his legs.

Pope found where the fugitive had stopped by the river for lunch and continued on, picking up a half hour or so by eating in the saddle.

He saw Kremmling beside the river in the distance. Stopping, he unpinned his badge and re-pinned it inside his coat lapel out of sight. He shifted both Colt's into his outside jacket pockets.

He rode into town, slowly and looking from side-to-side. He was looking for the fugitive from general description and also the gray gelding tied to a hitching rail. He did not see either.

The little village had the original settler's general store, a new thrown-together rooming house and a blacksmith shop. There were a few small cabins.

Pope figured if the railroad came through or ore was discovered, it might grow. If not, it might disappear. He tied Caesar at the general store and went in. In a place this size, news of most of the goings-on were available in the general store or livery stable.

"Howdy," he said to an older man who was probably the owner.

"I'm a Wells Fargo detective. Have you seen a young guy, clean shaven, early twenties come through today on a gray gelding?"

"Why are you looking for him?" the man asked.

"I aim to arrest him for murder of a woman and a policeman related to robbing a Wells Fargo office in Cheyenne."

"A woman? He killed a woman?" the man asked with shock and disgust.

"He did. For no reason at all. She left a husband

and small young ones behind. He shot down a town constable in cold blood, too."

"He ought to hang!" the man said.

"I suspect he will, assuming he gives up peaceably," Pope replied.

"Young fellow like him stopped in here an hour or two ago. Had a gray horse. Bought jerky, some horehound candy sticks, and some .38-40 cartridges. About busted my till when I had to break his gold piece."

"Probably from the robbery. Did he say where he was going?"

"He asked how long a ride it was to the train line. I told him Frisco or Breckenridge was probably the closest. He asked the distance. I told him almost a full day ride."

"How long a head start does he have on me? Two hours?" Pope asked, not knowing how long his suspect had actually spent in the village after arriving.

"I expect less. Mebbe more like an hour. He had some coffee and crackers. Didn't talk much."

"Did he mention his name?" Pope asked.

"Nope. So, I didn't ask."

"The trail by the river...is it the one to take to get to Breckinridge?"

"It will get you to the main road. Hang a right when you get to the first really big road you see. It will take you right to Frisco. There's a train stop there. It'll take you east to Denver or west to the Pacific, eventually."

"Thanks for your help. I'd better get Caesar on the trail."

The man looked out at the horse and said "He ain't pretty, but I bet he will ride when the other horses have called it a day!" Pope nodded at him and mounted up.

He reached the main road by four o'clock and Frisco half an hour later.

Pope went directly to the small train depot.

"Sorry, you just missed the westbound by an a few minutes." Pope had thought he heard a train whistle in the distance as he was coming down the river trail.

"Did a young fellow with a gray gelding board it?"

"He did. Put his horse on a stock car."

Pope identified himself and showed his badge.

"Where did his ticket go?"

"San Francisco, California," the agent said.

"When is the next train?"

"Tomorrow at four fifteen."

"Better give me a ticket for me and to transport my horse the full way," Pope said.

He bought the ticket and inquired about a telegraph in town. He knew there was not a Wells Fargo office yet.

"It's on the opposite side of this building."

He walked over and sent Sarah a telegram saying where he was and asking her to do two things. First, was to have Hume send a couple detectives to arrest the fugitive when he arrived in San Francisco and advise him Pope was on the next train. The second thing was to try to buy Caesar from the livery stable. It would not only be less expensive than having him sent back to Cheyenne circuitously, but Pope had taken a real liking to the big horse.

Telegraph lines paralleled the intercontinental rail tracks and were becoming increasingly important in train operations. But it was not possible to send and receive from trains yet. Pope could communicate with Sarah at the Cheyenne office and with Hume from any station along his route.

Pope checked back at the train depot after checking into a small hotel. He found he had received telegrams from Sarah and Hume.

Sarah said he was the proud owner of Caesar for sixty dollars. She said he owed her the money when he saw her. She sent her "best feelings of congeniality." It was her way of signaling the love they could not yet publicly admit.

Hume said congratulations. He agreed to have several detectives meet the train.

The chief detective also sent some new information. A man meeting the description was on a wanted poster out of New Mexico. His name was John Henry Randolph, AKA Kid Taos. He was wanted dead or alive with a five-hundred-dollar reward. His description was virtually identical to the shooter in Cheyenne, down to his horse. He was supposedly a cold-blooded killer with five deaths attributed. He was also a known gunfighter and fast draw.

"Well, Kid, let's call it seven deaths. The last two, at least were not very noble. And let's see how damn fast you are," Pope thought to himself as he read.

During his trip, Pope checked on the big horse travelling with several other horses in a cattle car modified with horse stalls. He made sure the water was pure and Caesar was getting decent feed. He spoke to the horse each time the train stopped and could tell the horse was glad to see him. He reckoned it proved to Caesar he had not been abandoned.

His grandpa, Israel Pope, taught him well.

"Animals have feelings just like people do. Treat all living things fairly boy, unless they are trying to kill you," he said. "If they are, kill fast and clean, whether man or beast. Try not to make anything suffer. If you wound something, track it down fast and end its misery."

He stepped off the train at Salt Lake City. While he was looking for a telegraph office, he saw the familiar blue uniform of a Wells Fargo office manager.

The man walked towards him.

"Are you Detective Pope?" he asked.

"I am."

"You look just like Mr. Hume described you. I

have an urgent telegram from him. It was sent without encryption."

He handed the piece of paper to Pope. It was short and sweet.

"Randolph got off train somewhere before San Fran. Stop. Come office to formulate next actions. Stop. Hume"

"Thanks. I have the gist of it. You can have it back for your files if you like," Pope said, initialing it.

For a major station, the stop in Salt Lake City was short, because the conductor was calling "All Aboard!" before they could introduce themselves. Pop shook the man's hand and turned and walked briskly to the train and resumed his seat. The next major stop was Elko.

The conductor told him it was approximately seven-hundred fifty miles to San Francisco. He said they would arrive in about twelve hours.

He went back to his seat and began to study his map of the Western United States. "Where could Randolph have gotten off? Why? There's very little between here and San Francisco but desert or mountains," Pope pondered. The map stared back at him and offered no obvious conclusions.

The next day, he arrived and claimed Caesar. He rode the big horse to the office and left him and his tack at a livery he often used.

Pope went up to Hume's office and presented himself to the chief detective's secretary.

"He's in and alone. Just tap on the door."

"Enter!" came the order from within.

"Well, John! How was Wyoming?"

"Beautiful, but cold, boss."

"Did you get my telegram? Randolph was not on the train when it arrived here. I have several detectives checking with the railroad to try to determine where he exited. I looked at the map and could not come up with a logical place between Cheyenne and San Francisco," Hume said.

"I arrived at the same conclusion after I received your message in Elko, Nevada," Pope said.

"I've been thinking. What if we did our own wanted poster and sent ten copies to every office we have in the West. Maybe just 'wanted' instead of adding 'dead or alive.' I was thinking equaling the five hundred dollars. 'For information leading to the arrest of' language. Let's multiply our search capability by whatever the number is off every badge toter west of the Mississippi," Pope said.

"I must have taught you well," Hume began. "I ordered the printing and distribution of such a poster yesterday. Why don't you stay here a day and see what happens. If nothing, head back to Cheyenne. Sarah is going to need some help learning to run the office. Having you there for the rest of the winter is not a bad idea. We don't want to have some idiot wannabe come in with a gun. I've seen too many copycat robberies."

"Yessir. I think it's a good idea. I somehow don't think our man came all the way to the coast. Cheyenne has good rail connections, so if someone sees him or picks him up, I can jump a train and get there pretty fast. After checking mail here, I'll go back to my room and ready the shotgun to travel back with me. And get some warmer socks."

"You went to Cheyenne without a long gun?" Hume asked.

"I took a new Marlin lever action .45-70. It did well for me in a couple of long shots against revolver caliber carbines."

"What's your impression of Cheyenne?" Hume asked.

"It's an enigma in many ways, boss. A small city on the prairie, it's the richest per capita city in the world. The reasons are mining interests and rich Europeans who want to be cowboys and have brought big spreads. The Cheyenne Club has to be the equal of anything here, or New York or even London. They have a nice hospital, library, opera house.

And, they have fully stocked tobacconists," he said handing a box of Hume's favorite cigars to him.

"Are you trying for a promotion, son? This might work," Hume said, pleased with the gift of his favorite expensive cigars.

"No sir. I have the job I want. Just saw these and

thought of you." Hume arose and shook hands in appreciation.

"Figure on lunch with Morse and me tomorrow," Hume said. "You can get tickets back for the next day. Unless we hear something about Randolph."

Harry Morse was the owner of the Harry Morse Detective Agency. Like Hume, he was a former California sheriff known for his investigative abilities and fast gun. He often worked as a paid contractor for the chief detective. The two were not only best friends, they were also two of the three most famous detectives anywhere. The third now relied more on reputation than continuing action. He was Allan Pinkerton, now in rapidly failing health in Chicago.

"I'll wait for the location and time," Pope said grinning at his boss and mentor.

He went to his desk and began to read the large number of wanted posters, letters and telegrams awaiting him.

The top piece of paper on his stack was Hume's wanted poster for John Henry Randolph, AKA Kid Taos. A note across the top, in Hume's familiar scrawl, stated it had been sent to every sheriff, police department and US Marshal in the West. Pope was pleased with the wording and coverage. He knew this was not Hume's first roundup, so would have expected no less.

Pope wanted to see his grandfather this trip, but time only allowed for a letter. He was not sure if Israel

Pope was at his cabin in Marin County or his ranch in Alameda County. He sent duplicate short letters and plowed back into Wells Fargo work.

At the end of the day, he left his saddlebags and rifle at the office and went by a restaurant for dinner.

He found his room cold and stoked the stove quickly to burn off the dampness. It felt strangely empty without Sarah Watson. She lit it up. He wished there was a quicker way to tell her than a letter which took a week to arrive. He would see her before the letter was in her hands. Pope knew a telegram was not secure enough, even encrypted, for a love note.

The next morning, he bought tickets for himself and Caesar for the trip back to Cheyenne.

The lunch with Hume and Morse was informative. They brought him up-to-date on the years search for stage robber Black Bart. The two admitted they were no closer to him than three years ago.

"Do you all think the wanted poster for Randolph will bear fruit?" Pope asked.

"Most have an effect. Nothing Harry and I have done to catch Black Bart has after years of trying so far, though. It certainly can't hurt, especially with Randolph covering so much territory. Far more than our California and Oregon stage robber. Thacker and I have never been able to find so much as a hoof print in seven years. We have no idea how he even gets to a robbery site. It's like he is scared of horses," Hume said.

"When you get him, it will be one of the most significant arrests in history, though he has never fired a shot. The most he has done is leave poems and steal a lot of money," Pope said.

"All true. We will get him. One day," Harry Morse said.

Hume told him about having dinner with Pope's recovered kidnap victim a week ago.

"I had dinner with the Lane's," Hume began. "Mattie asked about her 'hero.' She told me she looked after you in the hospital for a couple of nights. She thinks you and Sarah are pretty special, John."

"She and her sister are both fine young ladies who took the night watch together. They've been raised right, sir," Pope replied. He omitted one fact.

Mattie, now seventeen and blossomed into a beautiful young woman, sent him love letters on a weekly basis. Sarah laughed at them. Pope was sure the laughter covered irritation. Pope certainly did nothing to encourage her. Nor, to stop her. She was a bright, interesting young woman whose letters were always enjoyable, romance aside.

He moved the conversation to a safer subject.

"I guess you know my grandfather just married the Lane's lovely cook and housekeeper recently?"

"I heard such a rumor. Good for them!" Hume said with Morse nodding.

Both detectives had seen Israel Pope in action

during the kidnap investigation and privately noted to the grandson the mountain man more than lived up to his reputation. Morse was more familiar with Israel Pope since he had been sheriff of the county where Pope's ranch was located.

"Was a double wedding considered?" Morse asked. He and Hume were among the only two people Pope was aware who knew he and Sarah were more than partners assigned to work together.

"It wasn't, Harry. Maybe one day, when one of us gets tired of the constant travel and settles down to run an office or something. I don't see such a situation happening anytime soon," Pope said.

"Sarah has been sending Superintendent Pridham and me daily telegrams about McCarthy's condition. I don't know if you have heard, but McCarthy has developed lead poisoning. The doctor is worried he may not make it," Hume said.

"I wasn't aware and it worries me a lot, boss. Byron McCarthy is a friend in addition to a fellow Wells Fargo employee. I have been moving around so much since the robbery, I have not had a chance to communicate with Sarah," Pope said.

"Well, John, pray for him. I fear he needs it badly at the point in his recovery."

"Yessir. I will go see him as soon as I get back to Cheyenne."

"Do you leave tomorrow morning?" Morse asked.

"I do. I have to get in early to have Caesar loaded on the train. He's a livery horse I could not get back to Cheyenne, so I bought him. Then, I brought him here with me. I reckoned I'd need a horse to track Randolph. The more time I spent with him, the more I liked him."

Both men had spent their early careers as county sheriffs on horseback.

"What kind of horse caused this immediate affection?" Hume asked seriously.

"A big dun, over sixteen hands high. He has a crooked Roman nose. The nose is how he got his name. He has the endurance of a buffalo. He likes nothing better than to trot along after a miscreant all day, no matter the weather. I swear he's smiling all the way down the trail."

"Do you talk to him?" Hume asked.

"Yessir. I've talked to all the horses I ever owned."

"Me, too, John. I think all real horsemen do," Hume said, and Morse nodded.

Hume and Pope walked back to Wells Fargo. Morse walked back to his office at the corner of California and Kearny.

Pope thought a lot about his current circumstances staring at the ceiling later. He was happy with Sarah, with his job, and he liked Cheyenne. Though tracking anyone on the lonesome prairie was tough, the weather was better than many more mountainous places. Or places further north. He had met Sarah in Prescott, Arizona Territory. They both liked Prescott and spoke about settling there if the opportunity arose. Once she had some experience running a Wells Fargo office, maybe it would be time to discuss future plans.

Having come to such a conclusion, he rolled over and went to sleep. He slept badly, turning, waking. He had grown used to the long black hair of his lovely partner splayed across him at night. If not with Sarah, he could sleep better alone on the trail.

CHAPTER 8

Sarah and the telegraph operator spent two days running the Cheyenne office by logic more than experience. The third day, Marcus Howard from the Denver office took the train to Cheyenne for a rapid one-day orientation.

The first thing he impressed upon Sarah is the immediate need for a cashier to help her and handle the money and much of the customer contact work. He also urged hiring a messenger.

She knew the positions were approved and McCarthy had begun searching for the right people. He had no luck. The only people out of work in Cheyenne in the middle of the winter was a bunch of cowpunchers. And one of them robbed the office.

Howard helped her write a request to Superintendent Pridham to inquire within the company for an assistant cashier or a full cashier who might like to relocate to Cheyenne. The inquiry was more successful than the local search. A young man was on the train from the Los Angeles office two days after Howard returned to Denver.

While he was there, Howard instructed her in the formalized opening and closing procedures, the cash control procedures and the security related to wiring money and the telegraph in general.

She got the office organized to the point McCarthy had before being shot, if not more organized.

Sarah walked over to the city's high school, now operating for almost fourteen years.

She sat with the vice principal and outlined her need for a messenger. The job required diligence, energy and strength lifting a variety of items. The man had a boy in mind. He met all off the requirements. He was unable to graduate because his father passed away several weeks ago and he now had to serve as the primary provider for his mother and several siblings. The salary Sarah mentioned was more than he might reasonably expect working at a saloon, retail store, or working cattle or sheep.

The vice principal offered to contact the young man through a letter home by a sister attending the high school. The man showed up the following day, was hired, and a couple of uniforms and messenger cap were ordered from San Francisco.

The following day, the new cashier arrived. He was

in his early twenties.

The man, Chester Lyon, served as assistant cashier of the larger Los Angeles office for three years. The cashier was only several years older than Lyon, had a home and family and was unable to move on. Chester was happy to move to an expanding office and already knew the job.

Sarah visited McCarthy daily at the hospital. She was saddened to see the effect the lead poisoning had on his body and constitution. She tried to keep him up to date with office matters, but he simply was not able to focus on them.

By the time Pope arrived back in Cheyenne the office was fully staffed and running smoothly.

They went over to the hospital together to visit Byron McCarthy. He recognized them, but little more. They sat with him speaking softly with him in a one-way conversation. Both felt he knew they were there. After their visit, the two detectives returned to the office. Both were saddened from the visit and very worried about their friend.

McCarthy succumbed to his gunshot wound later in the evening.

When they got the word, Pope stamped around the closed office and cursed, something Sarah knew he seldom did.

"I will track down this Kid Taos, if it's the last thing I ever do. And I will bring him to the hangman or administer justice to him on the spot. His call! But he's going to die. By rope or bullet or my bare hands!"

Sarah had called Pope a stone-cold killer in the past. Sometimes in jest, sometimes seriously. Now, she knew she was right. The grown up who hunted down braves twice his age when he was ten years old, killed and scalped them. He would find this killer. And justice would be done. She shivered, but not in revulsion. Her love and respect would never waiver. But Pope was a very scary human being, deep beneath his surface.

"Thank God he is my scary human being," she thought.

Pope spoke, now calmly and logically.

"You know, there's something I've been thinking about," he said.

"What darling?"

"In casual conversation, we have assumed Randolph would not go anywhere near Taos. He chose it as his nickname. He must be known and wanted there.

What if we are totally wrong? What if he's from there, but has no warrants there and is not known by Kid Taos in Taos, New Mexico? What if he is just circling around, leading us on a long wild goose chase and is heading home to hide in plain sight.

Just like in Poe's 'The Purloined Letter.'"

Once again, the literary knowledge of a mountain man instructing a little boy astounded Sarah.

"I think you might be on to something! What do we do about it?"

"I think we send a telegram to the US Marshal for New Mexico Territory and the Sheriff of Taos County. Ask about the name of John Henry Randolph. Give a description in case it is an alias."

"Do we need clearance from Hume to send it?" Sarah asked.

"No, it's our case. We run it within reason like we want."

He sat at his desk and started writing on a telegram pad.

"US Marshal NM Terr Santa Fe and Sheriff Taos County Taos Stop. Request info on John Henry Randolph AKA Kid Taos Stop Early twenties Five seven Clean shaven Stop. Wanted for killing Wells Fargo agent Woman and Policeman Stop. Send any info to Wells Fargo Cheyenne Wyoming Terr Stop. Det John Pope End."

Sarah read it and had nothing to add. She walked it over to Olson who keyed it into his telegraph.

"Now, we hurry up and wait," Pope commented.

Sarah noticed a line forming at the front. Chester had fit into the operation smoothly and was assisting a banker from a new bank in town. He had several retailers waiting. She quickly moved in and began helping the first in line.

With some trepidation, a new feeling for him, Pope

followed her suit and waited on the third customer.

It was the beginning of an afternoon of one customer after another. At the end of the day, Chester felt he accomplished a lot. Sarah was ambivalent. Pope knew once and for all customer service was not his cup of tea.

Sarah initiated a new procedure of having a brief debriefing meeting with all employees following cash settlement.

"Honey, your sense of organization is astounding to me. Your intelligence is obvious, but you have turned this office around. I am so proud of you," Pope told her once the doors had been locked for an hour and they were alone.

"I enjoy making something run smoothly. Allan wanted me to take over the female detective division. He saw it in me. I would have done it, but for my stupid choice to follow the wrong man to Arizona Territory."

"Yes, but it brought you to the *right* man," Pope reminded her.

"Our cashier and new messenger are going to have to hold the fort alone tomorrow while we attend Byron's funeral, John."

"I have not attended many funerals," he said. "I have caused a few though," he added.

"We have to go. He was our friend and our Wells Fargo associate. We have planned the funeral. We have to be there to pay for it, also. The company is not paying," Sarah said.

"I know, honey. When I was out late this morning, I was speaking with the preacher, telling him about Byron. His character, his orphan life as a child here in Cheyenne, and the like. He seems to be ready to conduct the service," he said.

"I attended the funerals of the bank lady and the constable. Both were very sad," Sarah said. "The gray, snowy days made both even more depressing. They are why I liked Prescott better than Chicago"

Pope nodded appreciatively.

"Do you think the Superintendent will ask you to stay as agent in charge of the new, larger Cheyenne office, Sarah?" Pope asked.

"What would you think about it?" she countered.

"Two big if's. If you wanted to and if they would allow me to work out of this office. The good news is we would no longer how to hide our relationship. We could even get married."

"The only definite is the last part. We could. It would be very nice, wouldn't it?" she said.

"Yes. It would be very nice. We'd stay partners, too. Just not investigating together officially. I'd be able to pick your brain on every case," he said.

"Oh, my. How on earth did you ever get along before me?" she asked.

"Blind luck, I suspect. Awfully far from my grandfather, though. He's not getting any younger. Though, getting married may add to his years."

"Or shorten them if he tries to perform like a twenty-year old," she said.

"I had not thought about it in those terms. However, if you keep those type of thoughts in your mind, I will buy you dinner and take you back to the hotel to continue them in reality."

"You, have a deal, partner!"

They checked the office one last time and relocked the door on the way out.

It was snowing lightly as they walked back towards the hotel and its restaurant.

"We could forget dinner," Pope suggested.

"Hold your horses, cowboy. I'm hungry," Sarah said.

******

The funeral was attended by many office patrons. McCarthy was well-liked and respected. Pope did not think anything could further harden his resolve to bring Randolph to justice. The funeral did.

A freight wagon for which Wells Fargo was waiting made it to Cheyenne two days later. It had some of the construction materials necessary for modifying the new space to company requirements. Carpenters started working immediately.

Tile, paint, paneling and some new furniture followed. Before Christmas, the space was beginning to look useable. Only the steel vault door for the brick walled safe room and the safe itself delayed opening.

Pope received a letter from his grandfather saying he and his new wife, Millie, were coming to Cheyenne to spend Christmas with Sarah and him. Both were thrilled at the news and reserved a suite for them at the Western Hotel.

One night, Sarah and Pope returned from the hotel after a day of work to find it decorated for Christmas. The Opera House had a holiday concert just after Israel and Millie's arrival and Pope bought four tickets.

Three days before Christmas, Pope received a letter in response to his telegram to the US Marshal for New Mexico. The marshal said John Henry Randolph was born in Taos and his parents still lived near there. He said his deputy in Taos went by the farm several times and never saw Randolph. No one in the area was familiar with the Kid Taos name.

"Not much, but a clue we need to follow up on," Pope said.

With Hume's concurrence, Pope boarded a south-bound train which took him through Denver. He transferred to the Atchison, Topeka and Santa Fe for the final part of the four-hundred-mile trip.

Pope got directions to the Randolph ranch from the sheriff's office. His livery stable horse was not up to the standards Caesar set, but the ride was short.

He wore a suit and heavy coat, with a Colt in each outer pocket. He carried his Marlin carbine in its saddle scabbard.

Arriving at the ranch mid-day, he sat in a copse of trees for a while waiting for some sign of life at the ranch. He drank some water and munched on a piece of jerky.

Finally, an old man came out and picked up some firewood and took it into the house. Pope thought a twenty-year old son might have gotten the wood, but could not be certain of the logic. Anyone who would shoot down a lady for no reason would not necessarily help his father with firewood.

After a half hour, he decided to approach the house and try to obtain information on Randolph.

"Hello, the house," Pope yelled in a stentorian, but not threatening voice. Presently, the old man opened the door. His hands were empty, but Pope knew he might well have a ten-gauge stashed just out of sight. Drawing his Colt from a jacket pocket was nowhere near as fast as a holster. He compromised by keeping both hands in his jacket pockets as if he was cold. Which he was anyway.

"Help you?" the old man said without positive or negative emphasis.

"Are you Mr. Randolph?"

"Who's asking?"

"I'm John Pope, with the Wells Fargo Company,"

Pope said.

"What can I do for you?" the man asked. Up close, Pope could see he was only in his fifties. He was tanned, wrinkled and weatherworn. A typical rancher or farmer, used to being outside working all the time.

"I would like to speak with your son, Mr. Randolph."

"Why on earth would Wells Fargo want to talk with my no-account son?"

"I am a detective with Wells Fargo, Mr. Randolph," Pope said, removing his hands slowly from his jacket pockets and flipping his left lapel to flash his badge.

"We had an armed robbery of an office up in Cheyenne. The robber matched your son's description. If he's innocent, I would like to eliminate him from my inquiries."

"You tell me about the robbery and I'll tell you about my son, young fella. You may as well come in where it's warm. Let me warn Ma a stranger is coming in." Randolph turned his back and walked away, giving Pope time to quickly unbutton his coat and transfer his revolvers back to their holsters.

"We are ready to talk with you now. Ma put on some coffee."

"Thank you, sir."

Randolph pointed towards a table. The three sat, Pope nodded at the wife, who remained silent.

"A week ago, a young man who appeared to be in his twenties walked into our Cheyenne, Wyoming

Territory office. He pulled a gun and ordered the agent in charge to open the safe. He did and the young man put several thousand dollars in a flour sack or something like it."

"Did he hurt anyone?" the woman asked, speaking for the first time.

"I'm afraid so, Ma'am."

"Who?" she asked.

"A woman who walked in the door at the wrong time. And, the manager, who tried to stop him. The robber left, ran down the street in a snowstorm and shot a city constable before escaping."

"How are the people?" the father asked.

"Mr. Randolph, none of them survived their wounds," Pope said, knowing this is where the communication would turn. One way or the other.

There was silence in the small ranch house.

"How did you get John's name?" Randolph asked.

"Our San Francisco office located a wanted poster of someone meeting the description and style of robbery. To possibly eliminate your son, I'd like to ask you some questions about him," Pope said. Both nodded, hesitatingly.

"What is his age?" Pope asked, his leather notebook and a pencil in hand.

"He's twenty-one"

"His height and build?"

"About five and a half feet. Skinny as a rail."

"Eye color?"

"Green."

"What hand is his primary use hand?"

"He's right-handed."

"When you last saw him, what kind of horse was he riding?"

"He stole my gray gelding when he left outta here a year ago."

"Do you remember exactly when he left with your horse?"

"Thanksgiving day," Mrs. Randolph said quickly. Pope nodded his thanks.

"What kind of gun or guns does he carry, Mr. Randolph?"

"A .44 Smith & Wesson and a .44 Winchester carbine, last I know."

"Did he give you trouble as a youth? Skirmishes with the law? Fights? Harm animals?"

Pope watched as the color drained from the wife's face. He knew he had hit on something.

"Mrs. Randolph, did he harm animals?" Pope asked specifically.

"Johnny liked to hurt things then kill them. Whether it was a cat, stray dog, anything. We couldn't get him to stop," she said. "He fell out of his crib when he was just able to pull himself up to standing. Still has the dent in his skull where he landed. We thought he was dead. He was out for an hour, at least. Randolph and I always reckoned the fall made him ... different." she added.

"This one's a crazy killer," Pope thought to himself, saying nothing and keeping a stone face.

"Which side is the dent on?" he asked.

"Very back, towards the top."

Pope drew a sketch and marked where the skull dent would be. It might be decisive in identifying him. Dead or alive.

"Did he ever use the alias Kid Taos?" Pope asked.

"Not around here, he didn't detective. Listen, I want to ask you something. You say this person killed three people in Cheyenne. How do the answers to your questions square with what you already knew?"

"Real close, Mr. Randolph."

"Will you take him alive?" the woman asked.

"Well, arresting someone is always my objective, Ma'am. However, the person I am arresting usually makes the decision about what happens. Your son has warrants from a number of locations unrelated to our robbery. I cannot say what other lawmen might do.

Thank you for answering my questions. I fear I have not improved your Christmas this year. But I will promise you this: I will do my best to bring your son in unharmed. But it's gonna be his call."

"It's cold for a father to say, detective, but sometimes I think a bullet would be preferable to sitting in jail waiting for a noose. No disrespect to your Wells

Fargo man, but it appears Johnny also killed a woman and a policeman. It's killing the woman what makes me sick in my stomach. They are all hanging offenses but killing her is worse to me."

Pope reached out and shook the man's hand. These appeared to be good people. Heartbroken over a mean, crazy son. A son destined for death at the hand of a lawman or hangman.

He was reminded how much he would have liked another Christmas with his own family. He hoped they would be proud of him now. He knew his grandfather was.

Pope turned the livery horse back towards Taos. His mood, this day before Christmas Eve, was strangely sad. He was pretty sure he would go up against Kid Taos. And kill him, despite the best of intentions. He had never worried about such a thing in his life. He did now, though.

He arrived back home, for Cheyenne was home for now, on the morning of Christmas Eve. Israel Pope and Millie were at the Wells Fargo office when he trudged in. His mood immediately soared as he hugged his two-favorite people in the world and his new step grandmother. He was almost knocked over by his excited blue tick hound, Scout.

"Ha! My boy! Coming home from a business trip carrying his rifle and two guns. You got a Bowie, I hope, sonny?"

Pope reached behind his coat and withdrew a Sheffield Bowie with a ten-inch blade.

"Well, It's almost a real Bowie. I guess a real fourteen-inch blade Bowie would not hide under your suit, huh?"

"No sir. I don't think it would." Pope turned to Millie.

"Has he got you packing a Bowie yet?" Pope asked, already knowing the answer.

"No, John, but I'm expecting him to any day!" Pope smiled.

"I am going to take the afternoon off. Our three young men will run the office and settle it. They will close at four in the afternoon. Millie and I are going shopping," Sarah said.

"Grandpa and I are, too. I have to write up my trip and get a telegram to Hume first. Grandpa, do you want to stay here or go with the ladies?"

"If I go with them, can you find us?"

"I'll cut your sign. Usually, I can find about anyone. Now, I have this Randolph fellow whose mother asked me not to kill him. I cannot seem to find him. But I will."

"I will go with the women. You know my prints. Wonder how they'll take on sidewalks?"

"Not well. First thing we'll do when I break out of here and meet you is go to the stable and you can look over Caesar. I've been gone and he needs some attention," Pope said.

"John, tell me the short version. Did the parents confirm our man is actually Randolph?" Sarah asked.

"Almost definitely. And, I have an identifier if we catch or kill him."

He got an idea from Sarah where she planned on taking Millie and started on his formal report. The detailed one took an hour to write out in longhand. The six-line telegram summary confirmed new information proving the Wells Fargo robber was Randolph.

Pope donned his suit and heavy coat and headed out in search of his family.

He found them at a large mercantile store. It reminded him of Goldwater's in Prescott, but smaller.

The men went past a grocers and Pope picked up a carrot for Caesar. Israel Pope was an equine expert, though much of his early travel through the West had been by foot. He appreciated the horse's characteristics but whispered to his grandson "He shore ain't pretty though."

Pope took him to a tobacconist and bought him a large tin of his choice of pipe tobacco. He bought a matched pair of .38 Smith & Wesson Double Action Perfected revolvers and two boxes of ammunition. One was for his grandfather as a backup to his long barrel Colt, the other was for Millie. Both were nickel plated and had stag grips. He had also gotten a small, six-inch blade Bowie for Millie earlier. He knew his grandfather's affinity for Bowies and reckoned his new wife ought to have one.

Pope stopped by their rooms and picked up one of the rings Sarah wore on her left ring finger and took it with them. With help from his grandfather, he chose an emerald ring for her for Christmas. The ring was carefully checked by the jeweler to make sure it was the same size as her original ring. Israel got Millie a cameo and a winter scarf, primarily for wear while they were in colder Wyoming.

They met at the Western Hotel and went to Ramsey's Restaurant for Christmas Eve dinner. Dinner was followed by the Christmas show at the Opera House.

The day proved to be a family Christmas Eve unlike any the two Pope men had ever experienced. They found the hotel restaurant would be open for limited hours during Christmas to feed guests and reserved a late breakfast. They returned to the suite reserved for the senior Popes to exchange gifts.

Israel and Millie left for California on the train the next afternoon.

"This is the best Christmas I ever had," Pope told Sarah.

"I love my ring. John, what does it signify? You were a little vague about it when you gave it to me a few hours ago."

"It signifies as much as you wish it to, Sarah. From

Christmas gift to engagement to wedding band."

"If we let it be engagement, can we leave the date open? We still don't know what our employment outlook is. I am half expecting the superintendent to ask me to take over the Cheyenne office on a permanent basis. I don't know what I'll say. Even if the chief detective says you can work out of here. I don't see why not. Cheyenne has good transportation and you can get more places quicker than from San Francisco. We could even get married. If you want to, of course."

"Silly, you know you have a standing offer on marriage. All you have to do is say 'when,'" Pope said.

"Perhaps the bigger question is, are you ready to take a management job and stop detecting. You missed being a detective when you were in Prescott."

"I did. I also like covering your back on the trail. It scares me to think of you out there facing people like this killer, Randolph, alone."

"I did it before I met you."

"Before you met me doesn't count. Not for a damn thing, John Pope!" she said.

"You still have not answered my question," he reminded her.

"Because I don't know the answer. I have argued it both ways in my mind. I am fifty-fifty, John."

"Well, let's call the ring an engagement ring to ourselves. Something tells me circumstances will provide an answer before we can," he said.

She looked at him with a skeptical and almost accusatory look.

"You haven't seen your eagle recently have you?"

He grinned at her.

"The eagle on this one may be Kid Taos. Or Kid Hume. Or, maybe, Kid Pridham."

"Well. I surely hope one of them flies in soon. I really wouldn't mind being married to you."

"A 'yes?' I presume?" he asked.

"Of course. There has never been any question about if I wanted to marry you. I decided on it the day we met in the tax office. There was no question in my mind. It's always been about when we could. When we can depends on some things we cannot determine for ourselves unless one or both of us gives up Wells Fargo."

"Or, has a title change."

"Like me becoming a manager?" she asked.

"Or me."

"John Pope. I am a good detective. As are you. I am a pretty good gunsel. Didn't you know you are known around the headquarters as the gun for Wells Fargo? Your fame has spread beyond our massive company, too. There was some truth in the joshing about being a Ned Buntline character in dime novels."

"Those dime novel are all crazy stuff. I don't put any stock in it at all," he said.

She had made her point but decided not to press it

more than she had already. Her partner was a lot of things. "Stubborn" was high on the list.

"It's a good thing I'm not stubborn," she thought to herself and dropped the subject.

******

The period between Christmas and mid-spring proved relatively uneventful for crime against Wells Fargo interests.

The vault door and safe arrived and Sarah opened the new office with virtually no fanfare. Pridham left her as interim agent in charge without offering her the position formally.

"John, I'm relieved I have not heard anything from the superintendent about making this my permanent assignment. I still have not decided whether I want it.

At the same time, I am somewhat irritated. It's like he is either taking me for granted or saving the company money. This new office ranks in the large office category. I am sure the salary for the manager is higher than the one for a detective."

"I understand how you feel at both extremes," Pope said.

"You have done a wonderful job taking over, staffing, and moving to this beautiful new location. I would have thought a letter of appreciation or a visit to your grand opening by Pridham or someone high up in the company was in order. But I guess not," he said.

"It's not as if we need the money on an immediate basis. We are still on travel here, so our bills for hotel and meals are able to be expensed. But we should be building a nest egg for a small ranch wherever we land."

"Don't forget, we have a small ranch on some pretty prime real estate across the Bay from San Francisco," Pope said.

"Yes, but your grandfather is younger than I had envisioned. I agree with you. Millie will add years to his life."

"He told me privately the ranch was getting to be too much to handle without a cowboy. Since he just had a few horses and was not raising any sort of livestock, he could not afford a ranch hand. He said he and Millie like the cabin up in Marin County more. They are just waiting for us, he said.

"John, isn't the ranch 'way too far to commute to the office in San Francisco from?" Sarah asked.

"It is for sure. Moving there would mean resigning from Wells Fargo."

"You could run for sheriff," she suggested.

"I know and like the sheriff there. So, does everybody in the county. There's no way I could win at this time. He does not have an undersheriff and I believe would take me on. But it would be a serious cut in income. Especially with you being a ranch wife."

"Reality is not always a good thing, is it?" she said, not really expecting an answer.

"On another subject, it is March 10, 1883."

"I know. Your point is?"

"We have heard nothing in almost five months from or about Kid Taos."

"You are right! I have almost forgotten about him!" Sarah said.

"Sarah, I believe either he is dead or has just hunkered down for the winter. He's a crazy one. He kills spontaneously. If we don't hear from him in the next month or so, as it warms up, I am going to be convinced his bones are beside a trail somewhere."

"Makes sense."

"In the meantime, I have composed a telegram to Hume to get one of our junior detectives to study the Western newspapers the firm gets and archives.

I want him to search for any mention of Randolph or someone operating like him but not identified.

Then, I will take a map and number the sightings, starting with Cheyenne being number one. I'd like to create a map of his travels and see if we can predict where he may be headed. And I can wait there for him."

"Have you sent the telegram?" Sarah asked.

"Not yet, I have been holding off for a sighting."

"Perhaps send it. Randolph, maybe unnamed, could have been shooting or robbing somewhere and nobody has picked up on it at headquarters. Have them start looking, John."

"I am glad you agree. I will send it right now." Since she was in the new detectives office with a secure door, she reached over and kissed him on the lips. Sarah then returned to the customer area and sat at her temporary desk and began paperwork.

"JHume Stop Request junior detective study Western papers November until now Stop Look for anyone who could be Randolph and send to me Stop JPope"

He received a telegram back from Jim Hume an hour later.

"JPope Stop Assigned Stop JHume." It was laconic Hume at his best.

******

It was new detective Jake Bell who caught the Kid Taos assignment. Things had even been slow over the winter in San Francisco. He was glad to take on something new, especially with the detective who was known as "the gun for Wells Fargo," or "the gunfighter." He would be surprised to learn Pope was barely five years older than he was.

Bell went down into the archives to gather papers from as many Western states as he could find. The archivist primarily filed case files, legal records, contracts and construction documents, such as building plans. He checked his national file of the newspapers the firm received daily or weekly and came up with thirty fitting search parameters.

Detective Bell set a date range from the first of September, 1882 to the current day in 1883. He sought mention of John Henry Randolph, Kid Taos, or any unnamed robber or gunsel in his early twenties. He eliminated known entities such as William Bonny AKA Billy the Kid.

The archivist recommended looking only at the first three pages on his initial pass.

Seven months of the dailies and weeklies of thirty newspapers gave Bell a stack of two hundred ten newspapers. The light was not good in the archives. He took roughly twenty-five papers at a time up to the detectives bull pen.

Without the chief detective giving specific instructions, Bell suspected Pope would want to track the outlaw geographically by date. He laid out his notes with date, state, town, incident type columns and delved in.

Bell's very nature was detailed. It was his attention to detail as a very young Los Angeles detective which attracted Hume's attention to him on a case.

He did not attempt to set a pony express speed record and read the papers as if he was preparing for a test at school.

By five days, he had his report. Each of the forty entries on his sheet where a specific or different name was mentioned instead of Randolph's had a footnote.

Jake Bell went to his boss' secretary and asked for an appointment.

He was bidden to sit, albeit nervously, at the chief detective's desk while the older man carefully studied his work.

"A very nice piece of work, Detective Bell," Hume said.

He took two draft approvals from his desk and a MacKinnon & Cross Stylographic ink pen and began to scribble furiously on them.

"Here's a draft voucher for some travel money and one for travel. This is a big case for us. The man killed a Wells Fargo manager. Pope is a top detective but has hit a dead end. His partner, Detective Sarah Watson, is busy managing the new, large Cheyenne office. I want you to go out to Cheyenne as soon as you can and give them a hand."

"Yes sir. Is tomorrow morning soon enough?" Bell asked.

"Absolutely. If you don't have a long gun, check a shotgun or a carbine out from the armory today. Be sure to get a scabbard for it."

"Yessir, I will."

"Have you taken a train trip before?"

"Only up here from Los Angeles when you hired

me, sir," he said.

"This will be a lot longer. You can eat on the dining car of the train, but I would advise taking some water and things to nibble on also."

"Yessir."

As he was wont to do, Hume stood and proffered his hand to the young detective. They shook.

"Be safe, Detective Bell. This Kid person is a wild murderer and apparently good with his revolver. Pope will take the lead. Just cover his back." Bell nodded and left, trying to hide the big grin on his face.

Hume withdrew his cipher book and composed a message to Pope. He did not put in the stops. His telegrapher could worry about such things.

"Pope. Det. Jake Bell on way with your requested info. Keep him as long as you need him. Things quiet here. Show him the ropes. Hume"

An hour later, Pope walked out to the manager's desk.

"News from Hume. He has my historical sightings of Randolph done and is sending them by a Detective Jake Bell. Said to keep Bell as long as we need him."

"I wonder if Hume knows something about my assignment? Maybe Bell is your new partner. He's a nice kid. I met him at the office while you were recovering. Los Angeles detective, I think," Sarah said.

"I doubt it. We don't have partners. You and I kind of evolved into partners. We are the exception, not the rule. I think the boss is taking advantage of a slow period to get him out of the office and get a little field training. Nothing more. Hume must think he is worth the effort."

"You are probably right. He seemed bright. Nice kid, but with an underlying toughness. Kind of like you five years ago, I bet."

"I'm a tough kid?" Pope asked.

"Honey, you haven't been a kid since you were ten. Tough ... yes. Tough as hell. Kid? Nope."

She punched him in the shoulder. He did not grimace with pain this time. All of his recent bullet wounds were healed.

The telegrapher, new cashier and new messenger did not bat an eye at this. She had punched them, too. Hard, but never in anger and always smiling. All three would take a bunch of punches for her smile. They figured Pope would too. Gunfighter or not. They also knew she had killed at least two men. All three were convinced the decedents had deserved it. They had no idea how right they were.

******

Detective Jake Bell boarded the northeast bound Santa Fe train. He carried his bag and a scabbard with a short-barreled Colt model 1878 twelve-gauge shotgun inside. He carried two boxes of double-ought buckshot and his personal S&W model 1 double action revolver like Sarah carried. It was a favorite of detectives because of its 44 Russian caliber power and its concealability.

He had risen quickly at the Los Angeles Police Department because of both aptitude and education. Bell was a bit above average height and of muscular, wiry build. He had boxed and won many matches during his two years in college.

Bell found his seat and settled in for a long trip, including the Rockies and crossing the Continental Divide. He searched his bag, pushing his cipher book and US maps book aside in favor of Sir Walter Scott's Rob Roy and The Heart of Midlothian, told in one volume. He picked up a coffee and began to read.

He got into Cheyenne around nine the next morning, filled with Scottish history and ready to investigate.

He got off the train with his book under his arm and the shotgun cased. It would be a short wait for his checked bag and investigative kit.

Three thugs approached him.

"Well, a dandy! You come from New York City of somewhere in the bowler hat and pretty little suit." At twenty-two years old, Jake looked sixteen.

"I don't want any trouble, so just back off," he said in a well-cultivated copper voice.

The three were listening with their eyes, not their

ears and missed the authoritative tone.

"I think I want your hat. I bet you got a gold watch, too." The smallest of the men said. The speaker was about Jake Bell's size. Taller than average for a grown man in the 1880's.

He stepped forward and reached. The former college boxer struck out and connected with the point of his chin. He hit the platform unconscious as the large man, over six feet and two hundred pounds moved forward. A left-right combination put him down.

The third man drew a wicked looking blade. Jake thought it might be an Arkansas toothpick. If so, it was the competitor to the Bowie knife and just as long.

The man never knew what hit him as Pope's black-jack slammed down on his head. He, too, collapsed in the growing heap. Pope kicked the knife away as he heard the whistle of a town constable. The policeman was running towards them and summoning his partner.

Pope flipped his gold badge outside so the policeman could see it. He turned to Bell.

"Welcome to Cheyenne, Detective Bell. Hope you had a nice train ride," Pope said and grinned at the young detective. Bell grinned back. This was fun already and he had just arrived.

Bell's bags arrived. The constables used both handcuffs. Two were handcuffed together and the third, still not fully conscious, was cuffed behind the back.

Pope knew he hit him hard but was not worried.

"He pulled a big knife on someone. Deadly force was justified. There were plenty of witnesses," Pope explained to Bell. The two town constables nodded. Nothing more would come of it before trial unless the third man died. The two constables left. The two handcuffed prisoners were made to drag their semi-conscious friend along like a drunk, toes dragging.

They went to the office first.

"Detective Sarah Watson, say hello to Detective Jake Bell."

"Oh, Jake and I know each other from headquarters while you were off licking your most recent couple of bullet wounds."

"How often does a Wells Fargo detective get shot?" Bell asked.

"Almost never," Sarah said. "But this one attracts bullets like a magnet. Especially when he's saving his partner's life."

"Was it the gunfight in San Francisco against the kidnappers?"

"I received two holes there," Pope confirmed.

"I would never have guessed Cheyenne would have street crime like today," Bell said, causing a quizzical look on Sarah's face.

"Three knuckleheads tried to strong arm Jake at the train depot. I'm guessing they were hanging in there to get warm. Anyway, he knocked two unconscious. Then, one pulled a long knife. By the way, Jake, you need to report it in a telegram to Chief Detective Hume."

"John. You seem to have left something out. Did you shoot someone else?" Sarah asked.

"No. I just gave him a tap on the head. No big deal. It will be good enough if Jake includes it in his telegram. Just put both our names at the end, Jake," Pope said.

"We both really want to sit down with you and review your findings on where our boy the Taos Kid has been since he visited Cheyenne. But, first let me walk you over to the Western Hotel. We have a room booked for you. It will be direct billed to the office. You should move in and we'll meet you for dinner at seven after Sarah closes here. There's a good restaurant in the hotel. You can leave your shotgun here or take it to the hotel."

"Where's yours?" Bell asked.

"Hotel for my .45-70. I believe Sarah has her ten-gauge at her room," he said looking at Sarah and getting her confirmation.

"I'll take it then. Boy, Sarah! You can handle the kick of a ten-gauge?"

"In a fight, I don't notice it. If I were just shooting it at a tin can or something, I would probably be terrified to pull the trigger," she responded.

They left and walked the several blocks in the light

snow. Though it had been a snowy winter in Cheyenne, there was little accumulation.

"What do you think?" Sarah asked Pope when he
returned alone.

"My initial opinion is good. He handled the thugs
well. The only reason I tapped the knife wielder
on the head was to keep Bell from shooting him.
He already had his coat open to reach his shoulder
holster. Packing a S&W like your bigger one, near
as I could tell."

"Well, then. I approve of him already," Sarah said.
Pope just shook his head.

Dropping her voice so nobody else in the office
could hear, Sarah said "what floor is he on?"

"Two floors down and far end of the hall from our
rooms." With her back to the other three employees
and five customers, she pursed her lips in a silent
kiss. She received and imperceptible eye movement
on Pope's part. She read his body language like a
book. Thank God any person facing him in a gunfight could not.

The next day, Bell spread out his sheet of sightings
of either the verified or suspected Kid Taos. They
were in date order. It was a wild scattering across
the Western US. There seemed to be no coherent
reasoning behind his travels. He did not seem to
choose his stops for robberies well and often the take
was little or nothing. His largest score to date was

the Cheyenne Wells Fargo office. He was reported to have escaped on a gray horse in many of the reports.

They concluded, logically, he was transporting the horse on the train. His train trip from Cheyenne to the next few close dates was highly erratic and made no sense.

Fully two thirds of his reported sightings were due to shootings and not robberies.

Whether Kid Taos planned it or not, he established a name as a fast gun and killer. A lot of the reports were just reports of shootings instead of crimes. Some shootings appeared to be self-defense, though the details as to whether he prompted the shootings were unclear.

Pope carefully transferred the tabular data onto a Western US map pinned on the wall. It was his embryonic version of a murder board.

While the first month or two of Randolph's travel seemed just random meandering, a later pattern appeared to be evolving on the map.

"It looks like he wintered in Round Rock, Texas," Bell said.

"Round Rock was where outlaw Sam Bass was killed in a gunfight with Texas Rangers five years ago," Pope said.

"Guess who else was there?" he asked Sarah.

When she did not reply, he said "Our old friend Soapy Smith was at the gunfight. I don't know if he was a posse man or just an eye-witness. He was not arrested, so I am thinking he was not part of Sam Bass' gang."

"Small world, for so many miles of wilderness," Sarah observed.

Pope took a few minutes and explained their recent brush with Soapy Smith and how he got his name.

"How did you know he was there in 1878?" Bell asked.

"Jake, Pope just knows stuff. I don't know how, but he does. And he's always right, no matter how obscure or tiny the fact is. He just has a lot of stuff rolling around in his head," Sarah explained. Pope did not see any need to elaborate on her observation.

"Your last post was here," Pope said, pointing to near Bowie, Texas. "He looks like he is moving up the Chisholm Trail in a northerly direction. This is the kind of thing I wanted your research to show us," Pope said.

"The Denver & Fort Worth Railway just opened into Bowie last year. We can connect to it and be there by tomorrow. Let's get our trail gear. You will need to buy saddlebags, canteen, blanket and a small tarp for a bedroll. I will get food and retrieve my horse Caesar from the livery and get one for you. How about I meet you at the train depot in an hour?"

"Sounds good, John. See you then," Jake Bell responded and put on his coat and hat and left.

"He's pretty excited to be on the trail with you!" Sarah said.

"Oh, he's just excited to be on the trail in general. Maybe I can show him how to cut sign."

"I doubt it on the Chisholm Trail. Unless it's sign of thousands of cows," Sarah said.

"Spoil sport. I'm heading to pick up gear and get my good-looking horse from the livery. Damn, I like old Caesar. I've had prettier and faster, but none who could stick to a trail in the worst situations and plow onward smiling."

"Well, I hope you and Caesar will be very happy together. I will sit here, Miss Efficiency, and do my thing where it's nice and warm."

"You and the boys be safe. I will see you in a couple days," he said.

"Be careful, John. I don't want any new partner," Sarah said.

"Me either, Sarah."

He walked out of the door without turning around. He rode off the same way. Sarah knew it was a Western characteristic. It bothered her, however.

Pope's saddlebags, canteen and rifle were in his wardrobe in the hotel. He grabbed them and headed to the livery stable.

Pope stopped at the café and bought a dozen corn pones, plenty of jerky and some cheese sandwiches wrapped for the trail and some beef sandwiches for the train. He also picked up several bottles of carbonated soda water.

He retrieved Caesar and a bag of feed to carry, though he suspected browse would be widely available.

Bell was at the depot when Pope arrived and went with him to settle Caesar in a stock car for the trip to Bowie, Texas. They checked their bags and long guns. Pope kept the sack with the train food, bottled water and trail food with him.

They ate lunch in their seats. Dinner would be in the dining car, as breakfast would be.

"John, what do you think our chances of encountering Randolph on the trail or in a town?"

"It's real hard to tell. We have done everything logically. The problem with Kid Taos is he's crazy. We cannot depend on him to do what a normal person would do. Look at how he skipped around until he apparently wintered in Round Rock. It made no sense at all. It's a shame, Jake. His parents seemed like fine folks. His mother told me to try not to kill her boy."

"Nothing like a little pressure, huh?" Jake said.

"His father understood the son would make the call. If we come to a face down, I want you to step aside. Your shoulder holster makes sense for a detective. I wear two sometimes myself. However, a good gunsel can always outdraw a shoulder holster from a Buscadero holster on his belt.

He could be fast, Jake. Maybe faster than me. But,

let me take the lead, alright?" Pope asked. Jake knew it was more of an order than a request.

"You are the boss. And the Gun for Wells Fargo. I will watch your back and learn."

"If he gets lucky and drops me, which I doubt, give him a couple barrels of buckshot in the torso," Pope said.

"I will do it, John. I promise. If not buckshot, certainly .44 Russian slugs."

"Jake, I have used a revolver in fights a lot. But, when it comes down to it, remember your pistol is what you use to fight your way to your long gun."

"Hmm ... a new rule for me. Make sense, especially coming from someone who's been there and done it."

"Changing the subject, these carbonated waters are good. In San Francisco, they have started putting flavored syrup in them. I don't care much for them. Too sweet!"

"I had one of those too. I agree completely," Pope said.

"When did you stop wearing your bowler or derby hat, John?" the younger detective asked.

"I wore it the first six months. Still do in a big city. But the Stetson blends better and is much better on the trail. I understand the requirement to represent the company well by wearing dark suits. I also know it is damn tough to blend in a lot of places when you look like a banker. When I can, I wear cow puncher clothes on the trail. Better to chop wood in and camp in. Do you have any informal pants, shirt and vest with you?" Pope asked.

"I'm afraid not," Bell said.

"Maybe we should pick some up at Bowie. We don't know how long we will be on the trail. I've been thinking about horses. If we hire a livery horse for you in Bowie, the good Lord knows where we will end up with it. Those are the circumstances of how I bought Caesar. It was cheaper to buy him than pay to ship him back to where I rented him. You should pick out a horse and saddle in Bowie. Expense it. You might have to dig into your own money if the boss does not approve the voucher, but it's not a bad thing chasing miscreants with a horse you know you can depend on, Jake."

"I agree. I have to get a livery horse often even back in San Francisco. Where do you keep yours when you are in town?"

"I keep Caesar in the livery down the street from headquarters. I recommend it. He takes good care of Caesar and can have him saddled and a bag of feed in the winter with short notice. I rely on natural browse most of the warm months unless I will be crossing desert."

Detective Jake Bell was absorbing the reality of Wells Fargo detective work with every sentence Pope spoke. He knew he was a good detective, but a city one. The wide-open spaces, tracking, camping and moving hundreds of miles pursuing a fugitive were all new to him. He could not wait to get started.

They arrived in Bowie the next day. Their first move was to get a hotel to stow their gear. They then did a walk through in the small town to look for a gray horse or its fugitive rider.

Bell spotted a gray gelding tied to the hitching post of a saloon.

"Follow my lead," Pope reminded him as they entered the saloon, coats open and guns ready for action. They moved to opposite corners and scanned for Randolph. There was nobody there meeting his description.

The two official-looking young men in dark suits caught a lot of attention. The barkeep asked "You gentlemen appear to be looking for somebody. Care to share who?"

Pope nodded to Bell to take it.

"We are Wells Fargo detectives. We're looking for a man named Randolph. Goes by Kid Taos. He rides a gray horse like hitched out front," Bell said in his best policeman voice.

"My gray is the one out front," a tall, lanky cowboy said. He clearly was not Kid Taos. Bell nodded as Pope continued to monitor the crowd in the saloon.

"Why don't you boys sidle up to the bar and talk about some drinks," the barkeep said. Pope detected an eye movement suggesting he had more to say without yelling across the saloon.

Keeping his right hand loose and free, he walked up to the bar. Bell followed.

"Two beers," Pope said.

"Your man could have been here yesterday. Medium height fellow, bow-legged and kept his hand near his gun. Looked like he wanted to use it. Drank a beer, gave dirty looks to everyone. Nobody bit. He downed his beer and left. I figure he was disappointed because he didn't kill anybody. He had real strange eyes."

"Thanks for telling us. He shot down a woman. Mother of three. No reason at all. Was at the Cheyenne Wells Fargo office. Killed our manager and then a policeman as he was escaping. He's a crazy killer with at least five other shootings to his discredit.

Killing a woman and my friend was his big mistake. I won't rest easy until he feels rope around his neck or my bullet enter his chest," Pope said.

"You are the gunfighter fella from Wells Fargo, aren't you?" the barkeep asked.

"He's been known to respond to threats in the line of duty," Bell said. The barkeep just nodded, remembering some news articles he had read.

"Did he happen to ride a gray horse?" Bell asked.

"Didn't see his horse. I just wanted him out of here before bullets started flying."

"Do you have any idea where he might have been

heading when he left here?" Pope asked.

"One of the boys said he was going out towards the road to Wichita Falls. It's northwest."

"About what time of day was this?" Bell asked.

The barkeep stopped and thought a minute and said "Late in the day. Maybe four o'clock. Takes a good five hours riding the average horse without running from a posse or something."

"Anywhere he could get a room along the way, or would he have to camp?" Bell asked.

"Only burg of any size would be Henrietta. He could not make it there until several hours after dark. I'd say he slept in the dirt under a tree."

"Thanks for your help. Jake, I think we should give up those rooms, get you a horse and ride all night. Maybe we can catch up with him in Wichita Falls. Otherwise, I bet he crosses the Red River into Oklahoma and Indian Territory."

The nearest livery had a cowpony for sale. It was a pretty little black and white pinto. The livery owner said it had heart and endurance. Bell bought it and a used saddle, tack and saddlebags for a fair price. They loaded their gear on their horses, checked out of the rooms they never slept in and hit the trail.

Pope took out his Dietz police lantern and was glad to see Bell had one also. The road was wide and well-marked, so they did not use the lanterns but once.

The two detectives hit some storms and did not

reach Wichita Falls until midnight. They found a livery for their horses and two rooms in the downtown area. Despite waxed canvas dusters, they were soaked to the skin from the hard rain. Both had changes. Pope changed to cow puncher clothes. Bell put on a suit until he could get to a store and buy a trail outfit. They had a breakfast sufficient to make up for missing dinner.

While Bell went shopping, Pope went to the sheriff's office and the town marshal's office looking for word on Randolph. Nobody in law enforcement had any useful information. He reckoned any worthwhile bits might come from a saloon.

As soon as Bell got back looking less like a young banker and more like a Texas Ranger, they hit the saloons.

"Want to split up?" Bell asked.

"No, we should stay together. He could be in a crowd and start shooting before we see him. We have a better chance of taking him down together," Pope said.

He was not at nor was there any information on him from any of the saloons. They tried liveries and hotels. Nothing there, either.

"He must have gone past here and directly to Lawton. So, we have to head there next," Pope said.

They officially decided they had lost him by Lawton, in the Indian Territory. They turned south and sought the quickest train home, their horses in stock cars.

"Is it always this frustrating?" Bell asked Pope.

"More than we'd like to admit. When you are a city detective or even a county deputy investigating a crime, you are not traveling a thousand miles. It's the nature of what we do though. We, or somebody, will get this gunsel. I'd like for us to put the nippers on him just because he killed one of us and robbed a Wells Fargo office. But, either way, he'll get his due. I am confident of it. In the meantime, we keep plugging along as logical as we can and doing our job."

"Do you think we will ever have regional detectives?"

"We have a few now. One day, maybe real soon, Sarah will become a full-time manager. If so, Hume has said I can base wherever she is." Pope's response answered a question he and others had about the pair. They were truly partners in all respects as he suspected.

They stopped at a depot along the train trip back to Cheyenne and telegraphed Hume.

They were due in Cheyenne by noon the next day.

They got an immediate response from the chief detective in San Francisco.

"Kid Taos shot two Denver today. Stop. Headed Cheyenne. Stop. Return Apprehend. Stop. Hume"

It was a quick stop and the conductor was calling "All Aboard." Pope told the telegraph operator to send a return with two words "Warn Sarah."

He jumped on the train in the nick of time, as it began to slowly move away from the platform.

"Jake, he's going back to Cheyenne and gonna rob the office again!" Pope exclaimed.

"Why would he rob it again?" Bell asked.

"I guess it was his big haul of money. It's hard to tell when you are dealing with a crazy person. I am convinced he has major mental problems. I sent Sarah a warning just now. I just hope he's riding and we can beat him there. We are due in at noon tomorrow. If he rides all the way through, he might get there tonight. What I really hope is Sarah advises our friend the chief deputy and he or some of his deputies stake out the office."

The train steamed on through the night. The detective next to Pope slept. Pope did not. He was mortally terrified for Sarah.

The next day, when the train pulled into the depot at Cheyenne, Pope asked Bell to have someone deliver their gear. He also asked Bell to claim both horses, then meet him at the office as soon as possible.

Pope left his long canvas duster on his gear and sprinted the several blocks to the office. He stopped about three minutes out and looked around the area.

CHAPTER 9

Sarah received the warning Pope asked Hume to send. She sent the messenger with a note to Chief Deputy Akin about Pope's concerns. He returned shortly, having left the note for Akin.

She also placed her sawed-off shotgun under her desk. Sarah warned the staff to not become involved if something happened unless asked to do something by her, Pope, or a deputy. She did not want any untrained heroics by someone popping off with a .32 revolver from Sears Roebuck.

The messenger found Akin was in court but was expected back momentarily. He waited at the sheriff's office to give Akin the note as soon as he returned.

Detective Sarah Watson was as ready as she could be under the circumstances.

******

Kid Taos, as he liked to call himself, had ridden into Cheyenne in the late morning. He was hungry and stopped for a breakfast of coffee, steak, and eggs.

The robbery in Cheyenne was the height of his career as a famous gunman and robber. He knew he could pull it off again. They did not have guards in the office.

The policeman he shot was under-armed. And, slow. He had been no match for a real gunfighter. This would be easy, like it was before.

He felt like a drink or two before robbing the Wells Fargo and high-tailing it out of town once again. He never saw a posse on his trail last time, he reminded himself trying desperately to organize his thinking.

Of course, it was snowing during his first robbery. Maybe posse's did not ride in the snow. He knew it would take a while to form a posse. By then, his gray would be in the next county.

Two rot-gut whiskeys later and feeling more in control, he rode past the Wells Fargo office. He tied the gray about a hundred yards down the street. He used a hitching post in front of a store. He went in to buy some candy to eat on the ride out of town. It would be like a lunch, he thought.

He walked the distance to the entrance to Wells Fargo.

This would be the one. The robbery and shootout which would cause Ned Buntline or Prentiss Ingraham to start writing Kid Taos dime novels. The thought thrilled Randolph. A big smile appeared on his face.

Three men and two women walked in the door.

He quietly followed them, gun still holstered.

******

Pope stopped and scanned the office and the street around it. He saw a gray hitched to the rail in front of a general merchandise store. It was pretty far from the office.

He checked the Colt's. They were free and loose in their holsters. He was wearing a vest and pants. There was no coat to interfere with his draw. He did not usually walk around a town with his guns showing. Today was different. Besides, his gold badge was pinned on the left lapel of his vest.

Pope walked slowly up to the office door. He peered in. He saw movement reflected and turned his head. Somehow, Bell had gotten their gear and put it on the horses and was riding one and leading the other.

Pope held up his arm in a signal. It had no meaning beyond "I know you are here. Be silent."

He looked in the glass door. He saw a bow-legged cowboy facing Sarah. She looked both scared and defiant. Pope wished she would just be compliant and not make the crazy killer mad.

He saw the cashier, messenger and the telegrapher. Both were standing facing Sarah and the gunman. All three had their hands raised.

Three men and two women were with them. They looked terrified and had their hands up also.

Pope heard Jake Bell ease up behind him.

He whispered "Ready?" not expecting an answer.

Pope eased the door open.

John Henry Randolph did not hear the door. He did see a change in the pupils of Sarah's eyes.

He quickly slipped around her and pointed his gun to her head.

Sarah Watson was now a hostage.

He put an arm around her and grasped a breast in his non-gun hand. His head and most of his skinny body were blocked by his captive. He was so close to her, he had to hold the gun at an awkward angle to get the long barrel against her temple.

Kid Taos saw two serious men in cowboy garb. Both had badges. Two at a time! He knew he could take them. The fame of killing two lawdogs in a gunfight would be worthy of the dime novels he dreamed so much about.

"Mr. Randolph, drop your gun. We can deal with this without anybody getting hurt," Pope said in an uncharacteristically soft voice.

"Who the hell are you?" Randolph asked.

"I am John Pope. I work here. I think we can come to a peaceful conclusion. All you have to do is stop pointing the gun at the lady."

"You don't look like no Wells Fargo man. You look like a cowboy."

"Check out the badges my friend and I are wearing. Now, take the gun off her head."

"What if I don't? Are you going to draw?" Randolph asked.

"It would not be very smart of me to draw on a man who already has a gun in his hand, would it?" Pope asked.

"What if we just gave you five thousand dollars and let you slip out the back door?" Pope tried.

Kid Taos got a pensive look on his face and hesitated.

Pope saw him get an even crazier look in his eyes. "He's going to do something stupid!" Pope thought to himself.

Pope drew faster than anyone present could imagine. It was probably his fastest draw ever. He was indexed in such a position, he did not have to raise his Colt to eye level. As soon as he cleared the holster, he cocked the hammer and pressed the trigger. It was a trick he had perfected during his recovery last year. He aimed close range shots with his body. Usually he used it for a mid-torso shot. This time, he was sure Randolph was getting ready to kill Sarah. There was no time for anything but stopping him instantly from pulling the trigger on the S&W.

Pope noticed something which gave him an extra split second. Randolph had just begun to cock his gun. With the speed of the detective's draw, it probably did not matter.

The .44-40 bullet hit Randolph in the wrist from seven feet.

Randolph screamed as the bullet tore through skin, cartilage and bone and rendered his right hand worthless, probably for the short time remaining in his life. As the gun fell to the floor, Sarah spun away and moved against the counter. She pulled her own revolver and levelled it at Randolph.

Pope shook his head almost unperceptively and she read his signal and held her fire.

Randolph looked at the blood spurting from his ruined wrist.

His legs lost their strength and he leaned against the counter behind him. The would-be dime novel hero's back slid down the counter and he landed on his butt on the floor.

He sat there soiling the new tile floor with crimson.

Pope and Bell moved in fast. Pope kicked Randolph's gun aside and cashier Chester Lyon picked it up and moved back by Sarah.

Pope ripped Randolph's bandanna off his neck and made a tourniquet. He tied it just below the right elbow and some of the blood flow began to abate. He frisked him for a hideaway gun or knife. He did not find one.

"Messenger, go and get the sheriff or chief deputy. Tell whoever you find at the sheriff's department we have Kid Taos. Tell them he needs to go to the hospital right away, or he will die before they can hang him." The new young man ran out the door.

"Watch him?" Pope asked Bell, who already had his .44 pointed at the wounded man. Pope went to Sarah and held her tightly in his arms.

"You okay?" She nodded, not yet ready to speak. He just held her as a constable and a couple deputies entered in response to the gunfire.

"Hey, John?" Bell called.

"Yeah, Jake."

"The way he was holding the gun on Sarah? You shot off his left ear lobe, too."

"Probably won't matter on the scaffold when they hang him."

Pope let go of Sarah and walked back to the robber, who was wailing and moaning in the floor.

Pope watched Randolph for a few minutes. The tourniquet seemed to be working.

He waited another five minutes for the robber to stabilize before addressing him.

"John Henry Randolph, I am arresting you for murder of a Wells Fargo manager, an innocent lady, a

Cheyenne constable, robbing a Wells Fargo office, and aggravated assault against this Wells Fargo manager. Other charges may be forthcoming."

Randolph was still moaning. Pope poked him in the shoulder and asked, "Did you hear me?"

Randolph answered "Yes, damn it, now get me some help." Pope stood up and started to kick him in the ribs as hard as he could but restrained the impulse as Chief Deputy Horatio Akin walked into the office.

"Pope? He's still alive. Have you ever just winged anybody before?"

"No, but he was holding a gun to Sarah's head. His head was mostly behind hers, so I could not take a head shot. I had to disable the gun hand. If I shot him anywhere else I could see, he might have pulled the trigger on her. It was my only option."

"You arrested him yet?" Akin asked.

"Yes. For killing Byron, the lady, the constable, robbing this office, and aggravated assault against Sarah."

"We have a bunch of other warrants on him, but your first three will guarantee his neck stretches."

He bent down and put his face inches from the injured robber's.

"You little piece of dung. You thank your lucky stars you didn't try to draw on this man who shot you. You would have been dead before your gun cleared leather.

You see, the thing is, he's a real gunfighter. You are just a half-ass wannabe gunfighter. As it is, his shot today will go down in Wyoming history. But, you won't live to read about it."

Randolph spat at Akin. Like Pope, Akin showed great restraint and just stood and stepped out of range of another spit.

A doctor and several orderlies from the hospital arrived with a large wheel gurney. They loaded Randolph aboard. They certainly could not put nippers on his right wrist. It was a pulpy mess.

They removed the makeshift tourniquet and put a proper one on. Once Randolph was on the gurney, the doctor wrapped a gauze bandage around his head to put pressure on the bleeding stub of ear lobe.

"Once the sawbones say it's alright, Detective Bell and I need to question him," Pope told Akin.

"Not Sarah?"

"No, she's a victim this time. Just doesn't seem like it would be right."

"I see your point. Mind if I sit in?" Akin asked.

"No, I'd want you to."

"I'll follow the gurney to the hospital," Akin said.

"Mind if Jake Bell goes with you. I would, but I want to make sure Sarah is fine."

"No, not at all. Hey, Bell? C'mon with me to the hospital for the medical portion of your report. It's historical. Usually your man Pope has to get reports for the coroner. This will be on a live body."

Bell grinned and grabbed his coat off the new horse on the way past, then caught up with the chief deputy and the hospital people wheeling Randolph down the middle of the street.

Pope got the names and addresses of the three men and two women who were witnesses. All were local. He decided to interview each the next day and asked they come in on half-hour intervals starting at nine in the morning. He would let Akin know so the sheriff's office could participate for their reports.

"Let's close early, Sarah," he said. She nodded. She had not said a word yet.

"Chester, would you get the messenger and get the blood cleaned up. Lon, stand by for a short report telegram to Chief Detective Hume."

Pope sat at his desk, cipher book open and converted the following to code.

"J Hume. Stop. Kid Taos attempted robbery Cheyenne WF office. Stopped. Took manager hostage. Stop. Wounded by J Pope. Stop. Case closed except for reports trial and hanging. Stop. Pope"

Lon Olson keyed the message. An hour later, he brought a reply over to Pope and Sarah.

"J Pope. Stop. Wounded Question Mark. Stop. Practice more. Stop. J Hume."

"I never thought of the boss as a smart Alec," Pope remarked.

"He's not, honey. He is just relieved you saved his prettiest detective and captured one of the most wanted men in the West. Even though the wanted man is a crazy one. He could, with any kind of half decent lawyer, be found guilty by reason of insanity," Sarah said.

"I'd actually like guilty by reason of insanity. I promised his mother I'd do my best to not kill him. Insane asylums are worse than prisons. He really is crazy. He needs to be kept in one instead of walking down the street."

"Did your promise to his mother come into play at all when you wounded him while he was holding me hostage?"

Pope just looked her directly in the eyes for a long time, then got up and walked out the door without saying a word.

He untied Caesar's reins from the hitching rail and mounted his horse and rode silently to the livery. He unsaddled Caesar and left with his saddlebags and rifle. He walked past the office and on to the hotel.

Pope put his gear in the wardrobe and took off his hat, vest and boots.

He laid across the bed and stared at the ceiling. Sarah heard him explain to Akin why he took the shot he did to save her life. She had no business asking him what she asked.

The detective fell asleep on the top of his blankets.

The ceiling had no answer for his thoughts or emotions. He tossed and turned until he was awakened by a knock on his door.

He got up in shirt, vest, pants and sock feet and went to the door. As always, he had a Colt in his hand.

Standing to the side of the closed door, he said "Yes?"

"It's me, darling. Your stupid fiancé."

He opened the door to a tear-streaked Sarah.

"I am here to beg your forgiveness," she said.

"For what?"

"For questioning your choice of the best action to save my life. Nobody could have done what you did. So fast. So accurately. I was not thinking when I blurted out about your conversation with Randolph's mother influencing the action you took. It was stupid of me. Damn stupid, John.

Jake and the guys saw how upset I was. I was shocked when you walked out and asked Jake why you might have done such a thing. He told me you probably felt pretty let down by what I said. He lectured me on how you explained to Horatio why you took the action you did by shooting Randolph in the wrist. He said it's the only thing possible to save me and probably nobody else in the world could have pulled it off. He said you probably thought I had no faith in you. I can see why!"

After her long admission, she broke down in tears. He just stood there and watched her. She dropped to her knees in the doorway and sobbed uncontrollably, something he could never envision her doing.

Finally, he lifted her up and guided her into the room. Pope closed the door.

"Will you ever forgive me for questioning your honor and skill?" she asked.

"Sarah, a man's honor is about all he has," he said.

"No, it's not!" she almost screamed to him. "If he's lucky, he has a woman who loves him as much as I love you!"

She embraced him and buried her face in his vest, still sobbing.

"If you are going to soak my vest and shirt, I better take them off."

She started ripping at them and did not stop there. Then, she did the same to her own apparel. Soon she was laying, head on his shoulder, still crying softly.

Pope had never wondered whether she would play on his emotions. Primarily because he never thought about emotions. And, he had virtually no experience with women.

One of the things he was exceptionally good at however, was reading people. He always had been, but honed it sharp as a San Francisco officer, then as a detective.

He did not question Sarah's sincerity. Perhaps her reaction was caused by the trauma of thinking she was going to die. Of thinking he was powerless to stop it. He knew he loved her and could forgive her anything. And this was not so very much to forgive under the circumstances.

Pope gently turned her head to face him.

"I took a chance, Sarah. It was the only thing possible to save you. I watched his thumb begin to cock the hammer. It was then or never. The shot was a calculated risk. Shooting inches away from the head of a person you love more than life itself always is a risk. I knew I could do it. But it had to be right then. The clock had run stopped.

Sarah Elaine Watson, I would die for you. I will and have killed for you. I will love you through my dying breath and take my love to wherever I go when I leave this earth. I will take a smile into the hereafter because I spent time on earth with you. Do you know these words are true?"

"I do know, John. And I feel the same way. I think Wells Fargo is going to make me manager here and station you here as a regional detective. As soon as we hear, we need to go to California to your grandfather and Millie. There's a wedding in our immediate future if you will still have me."

"I will. Let's consummate our pact now."

She smiled and her smile was far less than angelic.

******

By morning, things were more than back to normal. They were better than normal.

Jake Bell returned from the hospital mid-morning.

"Jake, what's new with our friend Kid Taos?" Pope asked.

"They had to amputate his right arm just below his elbow. The doc said it would be a week or so before you can interrogate him."

"Not bad. It will give you, Horatio and me some time to plan our investigative strategy."

"John, I heard you and Horatio talking, but couldn't hear everything. I take it Sarah will not participate in the questioning?"

"I don't think it would be appropriate. I will check with the district attorney who will prosecute, but as a victim, her job will be to testify what he did relative to her. I will ask her if there are any questions she might have after reviewing our list this week. She always has good ideas."

Pope and Bell went out and bought take-out lunch for everyone in the office. Sarah had employees eat in shifts to ensure customers would be served appropriately. The two-armed robberies with shootings and a hostage had not helped business.

She and Pope sat across from each other at his desk in the detective office.

"You know, after last night, I am leaning towards the manager job. I know I will intellectually continue helping with cases, but I suspect the money is better and more importantly, it will allow us to get married. If you are not ready for marriage, we can at least acknowledge our relationship without fear of it ruining our chances at Wells Fargo," she said.

"You really think I'm not ready to marry you, Sarah?"

"No. Just trying not to be too assuming. You taught me on cases never to assume anything."

"It's okay on this case," he responded. "Are you sure you can give up the trails, the excitement, the death defying deeds?" he asked.

"I liked the job at Prescott, actually. What I didn't like is not having someone like you coming home to me."

"You are a talented organizer and people manager. I cannot imagine William Pridham not giving you the position here. My only fear is you will be so good, we will get transferred back East or something."

"I wonder what happens to your career if you turn down a promotion?" she asked.

"I don't know. Either you stay here forever or get fired I guess."

"Well, it's not like I can stay home with the children."

"You'd go crazy staying home anyway," he said.

"Either way, we will have to stay here until Randolph's trial is over."

"Do you think he will hang or plead insanity?"

"I think it depends on the lawyer he ends up getting. It's going to be a big case. Horatio was telling me if there's a hanging, it will draw in a big crowd and the restaurants, saloons, and hotels will be full. It will bring thousands of dollars into an already rich city. As a big case, it would not surprise me if some lawyer offers to represent Randolph for free. I think it's called *pro bono*. The lawyer's business and reputation would benefit from being on such a big case."

"John, do you think he is crazy?"

"He is able to travel, have his horse travel in a stock car on the train, make basic living decisions. I don't know if an insane person can take care of himself like he does. You refer to me as a stone-cold killer. He's more a stone-cold murderer. I really want to question him and find out if he felt anything at all about mowing the poor woman down. It will be real telling, I think.

When an escaping robber shoots a policeman it's terrible, but it happens. It's them against us. The game has always been played according to those rules. But a woman walking in the door? Does meanness and lack of conscience prove insanity? I really don't know for sure. But I think the answer is no. He may be slow, but mainly, he just is mean and has no conscience."

"I don't think it would be right for a victim to be one of the detectives questioning him. But I sure would like to be a fly on the wall," Sarah said.

"Maybe it can be arranged. It will give me the opportunity to get your ideas during the questioning by you passing notes, too. I will go over to the sheriff's office after we finish lunch. If the room we will use has a window, maybe it can be opened but blocked with a curtain. At least you could hear," he said.

"Or, maybe put a chair outside and keep the door cracked," she suggested.

Pope went over to the sheriff's office and met with Horatio after lunch.

"Good idea! I bet the sheriff would like to listen in and maybe suggest a line of questioning, too. Let's go look at the room and see what we can do," the chief deputy said.

They walked over to the room and it was a ten by ten-foot room with a single door and no window. The wall was not hardened and just frame with plaster. Akin sent for the man responsible for maintenance at the large courthouse building and he arrived shortly.

"What do you think of a standard sized window about here? One which would slide open, so we could hear," Horatio said, pointing to the location he and Pope discussed. "I could have the blacksmith make a rack of bars you could put on the hallway side. We could put curtains on the inside and outside to hide the window from the person being questioned. When we had an audience, we could open the outside curtains and listen."

"My men could do build what you are describing. Let us talk with the blacksmith. We deal with him all the time about things for the jail. Give me about three days, Chief," the maintenance manager said.

"I wish there was such a thing as thing as one-way glass," Pope said, not knowing he was twenty years away from the invention of "transparent mirrors."

"Ha! Dream on detective," Akin said.

******

Pope went back to the office and worked with Bell on the case report. They had recovered seventy-three percent of the take from the fall robbery. Nothing else in Randolph's possessions was of any interest. Pope threw away some horehound candy stick which had gotten broken and dirty. They gave him an idea, however.

He went to the nearest mercantile and bought some more. His next trip was his first to visit Randolph at the hospital. Only a day had passed since the shooting.

Randolph was sitting up in bed. A deputy sat in a wooden ladder-back chair in the hall outside his room.

The outlaw's right arm was heavily bandaged from just above to just below the elbow. It ended there.

"You come to apologize to me?" Randolph asked as Pope entered. Insane or just mean, the man had an awful personality.

"I asked you to put the gun down and you didn't. I could have killed you, but I promised your ma I'd try not to," Pope said, stretching the truth a bit.

"I wish you had. Now, I gotta sit in a cell and watch and listen while they build a scaffold outside the window."

"Maybe not, Randolph. You have not even been tried yet. Changing the subject, your candy sticks were pretty broken up and dirty in your belongings, so I bought you some more," Pope said as he handed a small brown paper sack to the man.

Randolph took them without saying anything. His next words were conversational and surprised Pope.

"How many men you killed?"

Pope's plan was to befriend him and try to determine as much about his mental and moral state as he could. This was a surprise, so he had to handle it carefully.

"Well, my grandpa and I took on a war party when I was little. They killed my folks and baby sister. I guess about ten or twelve there. Grandpa killed at least half."

"How about as a policeman?" Randolph asked as if he was having a conversation with his best friend. Pope knew his demeanor could change in an instant. The detective wanted to keep it like this to learn more.

"I never counted. Probably the same number, I guess."

"You notch your guns?" Randolph asked, leaning

forward, but favoring the painful stump which used to be his arm.

"No. I like nice stag grips on my revolvers. Notches would harm the value. They cost a fair penny," Pope said. The truth was he thought notches were like bragging and were asking for trouble. He did not relish killing anyone. When Pope killed someone, it was because the person threatened his life or the life of someone he was protecting.

"I carve notches."

"I saw them on your Schofield," Pope said. "I did not see any on your Winchester," he added.

"Naw. I think they look funny on a rifle. Besides, I never killed anybody with it. Where's the sport if you can't outdraw them?" Randolph asked.

"Yep. Makes sense to me. What do you want me to call you? John? Henry?" Pope asked.

"Kid is good enough," the young man answered.

"Kid it is. Did you hear the other famous Kid was gunned down by his former friend last year?" Pope asked, again playing into the man's ego.

"I did. Damn lawdog turned on his gambling pard. Not right. Not right at all. Must have been for the reward."

"I heard the government refused to pay. Some town folks raised some money to give to Garrett," Pope said.

"Yeah, I heard such. I also heard it was a put-up

deal and he didn't really kill Billy the Kid."

"Really? I have not heard it was faked," Pope said truthfully.

"Either way, you are now the only Kid who is a gunfighter, huh?" Pope added.

"I shore am. I'm figuring one of the dime novel writers will show up here any day. Is my capture in the papers yet?"

"It's in the Cheyenne paper. I have not seen any others. But, given the number of wanted posters out on you, I would bet it's spreading far and wide."

"Well, the papers clinch the deal. The writers will be here fighting over who's going to write about me for sure."

Pope thought about bringing the local paper to him, but the article did not reflect well upon Randolph.

"Do you read and do ciphers?" Pope asked.

"I read and recognize my name. Not much more. I didn't hang around school long enough to get into adding and subtracting. Not the multiplication table either."

"I'll bring you any papers I can locate with articles about you," Pope said.

"It would be real good to see them, detective."

"Alright. I'll see you soon. Either here or when we have to do the official interview with you," Pope said.

"What's the official interview?"

"It's the one which is done after anybody is arrested. It verifies who you are, whether we have the right person, the proper way to spell your name."

"Before you go, detective—has anybody let my ma and pa know where I am?"

"Yes, Kid. Chief Deputy Akin sent a telegram to the sheriff over in Bowie. He sent a deputy over to let them know."

Randolph looked pleased with the information, so Pope left while things were still positive.

He stopped by the sheriff's office and found his friend in.

"Well, Pope. Is our boy crazy?"

"I don't know. I think I made some good progress getting him to feel comfortable talking with me. He now knows there will be an official police questioning. I think his ego is looking forward to it.

Horatio, his ego seems to drive everything he says or does. We will have to play on it to learn whatever is floating around in his head. This is a case where good policeman and bad policeman may not be the best approach.

I'd like to determine the way he acts when he's telling the truth. Then, when he varies from it, we should start suspecting he is lying. I'm not real sure he is going to lie at all."

"You are kidding, John!"

"No, I think he lives in a world surrounded by a misguided sense of how great he is. There may not be any reason in his mind to lie."

"Amazing! I actually look forward to this!" the chief deputy said.

"I do, too. There are some red flags we can watch for. One is when he switches from 'I or me' to 'it or them.' Those transitions often signal a lie beginning."

"Interesting. I might ask you to do some training for our deputies when this is all over."

"Glad to. Assuming I am still in Wyoming. With Wells Fargo, you don't know where you will be from week to week if you are a detective."

"Do you think Sarah will stay as manager?" Akin asked.

"I think there's a good chance. Funny thing is we have not heard one way or the other. Both of us were kind of expecting word before now. It's almost to the point of being a bit odd," Pope said.

"Let me know as soon as either of you hears."

"Sure will. I am going to head back to the office and see if anything has come in from the boss. When you work for the number one detective anywhere, the bar is set pretty high."

"Is Hume above Pinkerton?"

"Now, for sure. Sarah corresponds with her old boss periodically. He is failing fast after a stroke. Sad. I learned a lot from reading his books. If he's not still the greatest, he surely was once," Pope said.

Pope left and took his time walking back to the

office. The spring weather was appealing after an exceptionally cold winter in the area. It was a winter during which he spent a lot of time on the trail.

He could smell springtime. There was something else in the air. He could not define it. But it smelled like trouble.

******

Five days later and Pope nor Sarah had any news from Wells Fargo headquarters. Neither Hume nor Pridham had contacted them about staying, returning, sending Bell back or anything.

"They just moved Randolph back to the jail," Bell said to Pope and Sarah. "I saw Akin and he said we should plan on beginning our interrogation tomorrow morning. Maybe around nine o'clock."

"We'll be ready. We can spend some time today talking about the approach. With this individual, I want to take it slow and easy. Not like the old big city detective way."

"No punches or slams with a city directory?"

"I don't think so. Unless he goes crazy and attacks us," Pope said.

"He only has one fist."

"Yes, but he has two elbows, feet and teeth and a head for butting. So, we have to keep our guard up and our wits about us. This may be the most interesting interview any of us have done to date."

The two made notes the rest of the day. Bell had met a young lady at the grocers and invited her to dinner.

Sarah and Pope had the chance for a quiet dinner together.

"What do you think we should do if Hume just moves us back to headquarters and our old jobs?" Sarah asked.

"I have given it a lot of thought."

"And?"

"I have no idea. None whatsoever. Nothing."

"You're a big help, cowboy."

"Well, cowboy is always our backup position," Pope noted.

"You mean run your grandfather's ranch in Alameda County?" she asked.

"It will be mine sooner than later. Grandpa and Millie seem to spend most of their time in Marin County at the cabin even now."

"Being a ranch wife is not something I have given much thought to."

"I keep having this feeling all of this will be answered for us by something we didn't see coming," Pope said.

"Has your spirit animal, the eagle, visited you with some message?" she asked.

"Not quite as obvious as a visit. Just a strong feeling."

"Anything about the feeling foreboding?"

"No, not at all. Strong, but not bad."

"I am braced. This is where you usually punch me lovingly hard in a wounded shoulder," he added.

"Like this?" she punched him in the deltoid hard enough to rock him to the side.

"You know, Sarah, you are really going to have to break your punching habit."

"You're serious, aren't you?"

He just looked at her with a poker face.

"What are you, six foot two and a hundred eighty pounds? I am five foot six and a hundred twenty..." he looked at her and cracked a smile. "A hundred and thirty pounds, smartass. There is no way I can hurt you without a knife or gun or knee!"

"You are playing with me like I'm a little doll, aren't you?" she asked.

"Well, it's appropriate. You are my little doll. A dangerous one, but doll nonetheless."

"Now we've gotten the punching behind us, we are still faced with plans," she said.

"Sometimes, dear Sarah, things cannot be planned ahead of time. I think we have to wait a while and see what falls on our plate. When we get word, we can either do something, or do nothing."

"Alright. Let's attack something we can plan. Apple or cherry pie?" she asked.

"Hundred and what?" earned him a solid punch to the shoulder. He chose cherry anyway.

The rest of their evening decided nothing but was

far less violent. She hoped they would always tease and laugh as they did tonight. When he was eighty, she would not hit him as hard on the shoulder. She would be eighty-three and probably wouldn't throw as hard a punch as she did at thirty anyway.

The next day, the cashier was put in charge of the office and Pope, Sarah, and Bell walked over to the sheriff's office.

Randolph was sitting glumly in a chair at the table in the middle of the interview room. He faced a new window with its curtains drawn. On the side of the window facing the hall, another set of curtains were drawn. Before the interview started, a jail bailiff brought two chairs down the hall and placed them before the window. Sheriff Seth Sharples seated Sarah and took his place in the second chair. The bailiff quietly opened the curtains to a window whose top sash was elevated sufficiently to allow those outside to hear what was being said inside. Pope still thought his non-existent dream of one-way glass was better. However, this would work.

"Hello, Kid," Pope said as he walked in and sat down. He opened his notebook, as did Akin and Bell.

"Kid Taos, this is Chief Deputy Horatio Akin and you met Wells Fargo Detective Jake Bell on the occasion of the incident at the Wells Fargo office a week or so ago.

As I mentioned to you during the hospital visit,

this is a standard procedure. Police always interview people after a crime. The purpose is to get your side of the story, fill in any blanks we have and make sure the charges are fair and just. Do you have any questions?" Pope asked.

"Nope. You ask the questions and I'll answer what I want," Randolph said.

"Let's get going then. We will take notes so we can prepare your statement for the record. First, please state your full name and permanent address for me," Pope requested.

"It's easy question. John Henry Randolph. I live at my folk's farm just outside of Taos, New Mexico."

Smiling and speaking in a low, friendly manner, Pope asked another twenty questions he knew should elicit truthful answers. Questions to which he already knew the answer. This provided his baseline for Randolph the truthful person.

Pope studied his suspect as Randolph answered. He watched for body language, facial changes, perspiration, inability to look him in the eye, and other "tells." As he had briefed Akin and Bell, tells were not always dependable. Anyone being questioned by the police for a serious crime will be nervous and exhibit many of the same characteristics as a liar.

"Kid, why did you choose Wells Fargo for the first robbery?"

"Dumb question. Everybody knows it's where

the money is."

"Isn't there more money in a bank?" Pope asked.

"Yeah, but they got guards with guns. Wells Fargo doesn't."

"So, you wanted to avoid a potentially violent situation?"

"On the first robbery ever, I did. After, I knew I could outdraw anybody," he said, ego moving to the forefront.

"I see. When the lady walked in the door, what happened?"

"I saw her. The gun went off and she fell. The bullet killed her." Transference from "me" to an inanimate object. A normal sign of lying.

"How did you feel about her dying?"

"She shouldn't have come in!" Transference of responsibility from the shooter to the victim. Now, it was her fault.

"Did you worry about it later? Feel guilty?"

"No. Why would I?"

Pope looked at Akin and nodded.

"Kid, tell us about the manager, Mr. McCarthy," Akin asked.

"The fool grabbed me. It was just wrong to grab me!"

"What happened then?" Akin asked.

"We wrestled and the gun went off. He fell down wounded."

"Do you know what happened with him?"

"I guess he went to the hospital."

"Actually, he went to the morgue. He died from the gunshot wound," Akin said.

"He got what was coming to him for grabbing me."

Bell took over, using the same, quiet voice as his predecessors.

"Kid, you said you are twenty-two. So am I. You seem to have gone to a lot of places before you wintered. How did you pick them?"

"I didn't. They just happened. I was on a roll. I needed to fight some people. My reputation had to be built so the dime novel writers would come begging to me." He turned to Pope.

"Are any in town yet?" he asked.

"I think they are probably waiting for the trial. More fanfare makes for a more exciting story." Randolph nodded, pleased with the answer.

Bell picked up again.

"Kid, how much money did you get from the Wells Fargo robbery?"

"A lot."

"Do you know exactly how much?"

"No. Just a lot."

"You didn't seem to spend much in your travels. No whiskey, no wild women, no Champagne?"

"What's Champagne?"

"It's an expensive type of alcoholic drink. Sometimes people order it to celebrate good fortune. How about whisky or women?"

"They are the devil's tools!" He screamed out for the first time. Pope reentered the questioning.

"Then, we won't have to talk about them. Kid, why did you decide to rob the same Wells Fargo office again, months later," Pope asked.

"I did good there the first time, so I reckoned I would again."

Following the same reasoning on their questions and presentation of questions, the three lawmen spoke with him another hour. They stopped when he fell asleep in the middle of a question.

They summoned the bailiff from outside and he took Randolph back to a cell.

The sheriff motioned the three and Sarah to his office. He had sufficient chairs for all.

"Folks, I have seen a lot of interrogations in my time behind the badge. I have done a lot. I gotta tell you, this one beats all. You all were darn patient. I'd have wanted to slap him a couple of times. But you got a lot of information. I know you have not had time to gather your thoughts, but I'd like your quick and dirty summary. Detective Pope?" the sheriff said.

"First off, I do not believe he lied to us once. It's a first for me. Here's what he did do.

He refused to take blame for much of anything. He aimed the gun, the gun went off. All by itself, I guess. Byron McCarthy had it coming to him, because he wrestled with Randolph. Randolph had no idea he had killed Byron. When he found out, he didn't blink. I do not believe the man has a bit of conscience in his body. He blithely goes through life, people die at his hand and he keeps on going, never feeling guilt or compassion.

He is uneducated. He had no idea of how much money he stole. He looked for places to have gunfights. Gunfights he was sure he could win. He was cocking his Smith & Wesson to kill Sarah. I drew and shot him before he could finish cocking it. He is not much of a gunfighter. I suspect if we follow up on the fights he had, they were against drunks.

I believe he robbed Wells Fargo to stake his travels around the West to become a known fast gun and achieve his ultimate goal of being a dime novel hero. Dime novel hero is at the center of everything he seems to care about," Pope said.

"Is he insane?" the sheriff asked.

"Sheriff, It's a matter of what defines insane. I don't know enough about the subject to say. He appears to have no conscience. He fixates on things. He refuses to take responsibility for anything wrong he did. His folks told me he tortured and killed small animals as a boy. He's naturally mean. The blow-up about whiskey and women was interesting. It told us he has been exposed to Scriptures, probably at home.

It would be fascinating to know for sure what

prompted it, but I doubt it's germane to our case. I have my suspicions and I suspect each of you does, too.

If any or all of those traits fit the definition of insane, then he is. If they are just unacceptable character traits, he isn't. I suspect he is. Whether he spends his life in a strait jacket or whether he swings by the neck until dead for killing our friend and the poor lady and constable does not matter to me. I believe justice will be done either way."

The sheriff was thoughtful for a moment. Then, he looked at Pope.

"If he had not have had Sarah as a hostage, what would you have done?"

"I'd have sent him straight to hell before he cleared leather. Then, I would have turned and walked out the door and had a nice meal."

"Wouldn't he have done the same, if he was fast enough?" Sharples asked.

"I suspect so, Sheriff. Maybe the difference came out in a conversation Sarah and I had. She believes I am a stone-cold killer. I believe he is a stone-cold *murderer*."

Sheriff Seth Sharples nodded his head. He understood. The West needed men like Pope who could and would kill. Kill when necessary. Kill murderers who threatened them or others. Kill predators like Kid Taos.

He and his chief deputy went back to their offices.

There was a report to write, based on the past hour and a half.

Sarah went to the office to see what needed to be done. Bell returned to transcribe his large number of notes for Pope to review before both signed and sent a report to James Hume.

Detective John Pope took a long walk. It was a nice spring day in Cheyenne. He doffed his Stetson at ladies, nodded at men on the street and came back to the office just like what the day was. Just another day for a Wells Fargo detective.

CHAPTER 10

The initial trial for John Henry Randolph was to be held in Cheyenne for Wyoming Territory in a week. They had possession of the fugitive and first shot at him for jurisprudence. Any other extraditions came later. But it was unlikely there would be anyone left to extradite after Wyoming Territory got through.

The prosecutor met with the sheriff, chief deputy and the three Wells Fargo detectives. His prosecutorial plan was for the sheriff to list the Wyoming charges of three counts of murder in the first degree, one count of an aggravated assault against Sarah, one count of robbery, one of attempted robbery, and fleeing to avoid prosecution. He would not be allowed to mention the other warrants outstanding in Western states. The prosecutor planned to list those in his opening.

As Pope predicted, a prominent young attorney in

Cheyenne offered to represent Randolph for no fee.

Once the papers in the region mentioned the trial date, hotels in Cheyenne booked to capacity.

The local law enforcement witnesses and the Wells Fargo people did not have any preparations to make for the trial. Witnesses who had observed the shooting of the lady, McCarthy and the constable were called for examination. Witnesses inside the office when Sarah was taken were summoned.

Finally, the prosecutor reserved the right to cross examine Randolph at his option. His attorney, having spoken with the outlaw several times, raised objections which were overruled.

It had come down to a matter of hurry up and wait.

Neither Hume nor Superintendent Pridham contacted any of the three detectives in Cheyenne. On the part of the two senior detectives, it caused more angst than the upcoming trial.

Hume sent Pope a case where a customer was suing Wells Fargo in civil court for claimed losses due to the late arrival of funds, or "treasure," sent to its Douglas location.

Pope went to the clerk's office in the courthouse. He had financial records reflecting the alleged losses subpoenaed. Pope and Bell rode up to the un-platted town formerly called "Tent City" to deliver them and investigate.

The ride up was in good weather. The alleged

losses occurred during snow season.

Pope wanted to speak with the jehu and the shotgun messenger on the route for Wells Fargo. They were due into Douglas about an hour after the detectives' arrival.

The detectives waited and interviewed the driver and guard. They found out what happened.

Pope and Bell rode up to the company site. It was the beginning of a mining operation. No ore deposits had been found yet.

The local supervisor was a man named Becker. He provided duplicates of the subpoenaed materials. Bell reviewed the copies and originals for accuracy.

"Mr. Becker, we see the papers showing monies on hand and invoices for bills. In your own words, tell us how this caused you claimed loss of five hundred dollars," Pope asked.

The man began in his strong German accent.

"Well, it was snowing. The men wanted to go home, but it was payday. The stage was late. It was no fault of my own. I had to pay my men so they could leave. It cleaned out my cash box. I had other immediate bills and no money. The stage never came during the day with my money. People we owed charged penalties. I figured two-fifty would cover my losses and troubles."

Pope and Bell exchanged looks. Both thought "a very weak case," and knew the other's mind on the matter.

"Mr. Becker, do you have notices from your creditors charging you for the penalties?"

The man hesitated and had the wide-eyed look of the dog stealing his dinner off the family table.

"Not exactly."

"Let me offer you a solution. Detective Bell and I feel it's going to cost you will have lawyer and fees in court, even if you win. The stage was delayed by sliding off the road into a ditch. They spent a cold night with the shotgun messenger riding a team horse bareback to a station and getting help. It took much longer to right the stage and replace a broken axle. Our driver will testify to the incident and note it was an act of God.

We are not so sure you will win your case. But Wells Fargo is a fair company. One which values you as a customer.

I propose we give you one hundred dollars right now for your troubles and the case be dropped. I think it's a very fair deal for all concerned, don't you?"

Becker thought for a moment, then nodded.

"If you will write on your subpoena you are dropping your case in favor of a cash settlement received and get one of your employees to witness it, we will pay you the money and hit the trail," Bell said.

"I will do it."

Becker took his copy of the subpoena and wrote out the words Pope dictated to him. He signed it in front of one of his men, who then witnessed it. Pope counted out one hundred dollars in gold coins and handed it to Becker.

Hands were shaken all around and the two detectives mounted up and rode back towards Cheyenne.

They stopped after an hour and a half and made a quick camp for coffee and sandwiches along the trail.

"A good settlement, Jake. If we lost, it would have cost us five hundred and whatever fees and attorney costs. If we won, it would have still cost the attorney and court fees, plus your and my time wasted. Now, everybody is happy and the reputation of the company is not negatively affected. I'd say, overall, we won."

"This type of approach and logic is a good lesson, John. I came into the job thinking it would be kind of like being a LA detective, but with a lesser badge and more money.

I am finding it is nothing like it. I am also finding the power of the badge is what we make it. This was my first nuisance case. Are these our bread and butter cases between big ones like your kidnapping and the upcoming Randolph case?" Bell asked.

"They are. There are more of these pain-in-the-butt matters to investigate than the ones hitting the newspapers. These are not exciting. They are, however, most of what we are paid for. Our costs net out much higher attorney costs. Most companies hire attorneys who hire their own private detectives to do the work we do. Then, they bill us several times what they have to pay the private detectives."

"Are such cases how Detective Morse makes his income," Bell asked.

"More like how his more junior detectives do. He personally only handles big cases. Big for us when we hire him and big for him when others do. Murders of famous people. Kidnappings. Nationally famous robbers like Black Bart. He always gets them. Give yourself another year at Wells Fargo and he'd hire you in an instant. The work would be essentially the same. It would just be a job if you found you needed it."

"What could cause me needing a new job?"

"I don't know. Say James Hume had a heart attack and stepped down. Say they picked some jerk to run the detective division of the company and you could not stand him."

"I see. Wouldn't Thacker or you get the nod, though?"

"Who knows? It's a big company and well-run. But there are always politics. The governor's son who may be a SF police detective sergeant or something."

"What would you do?"

"Maybe run my grandfather's little ranch. Maybe go to work for Harry Morse. Maybe open my own firm or run for sheriff. Maybe do like a friend, JA McLaughlin, and take a ship to Hawaii and live in Paradise."

"Who's JA McLaughlin?"

"A fellow who lived near my grandfather's cabin in Marin County. He got tired of the protracted Reconstruction in Virginia and working on the family's failing tobacco and sweet potato farm. So, he did like Horace Greely said and 'went West young man,' in his teens. He's been in Hawaii for a while I guess. No stage coaches carrying the mail there. Just clipper ships. He sent a letter a while back. Said they had the most beautiful women he ever saw. They wear a scarf around the waist and a flower in their hair. Which side the flower is on tells you if they are married or available."

"You didn't mention them wearing anything else, John."

"They don't wear anything else. I guess the darn missionaries will change the way they live. Just like they are forcing Indians to give up their lifestyle and religions to accept ours. I don't think it's right."

"And, after what they did to your family, you have cause to hate Indians," Bell said.

"But, I don't. There are bad or misguided people everywhere. What they did was wrong and they paid for it with their lives and scalps," Pope said.

"You scalped them?" Bell said incredulously.

"My mentor, my grandfather, was a mountain man. Their ways were his ways," was Pope's only response. Bell thought for a minute, saying nothing. Pope was the most dangerous man he could imagine. The best friend. The worst enemy.

They continued munching on ham and cheese sandwiches and drinking coffee brewed on a small fire. Bell noticed Pope sparked the fire with a ferro rod and the top edge of his wicked Bowie knife. He did not use a Lucifer match. Just one stroke of the rod against his blade and a shower of sparks hit a nest of tender and the fire was going.

Somehow, Bell imagined Pope could light a fire in a snowstorm.

The office was already closed by the time they made it back to Cheyenne and stabled the horses.

They walked to the hotel and went to their rooms, agreeing to meet shortly for dinner downstairs.

Sarah was in her room waiting. She was ready for dinner. Pope gave her the short version of settling the lawsuit in Douglas. She agreed it was a fair settlement for all.

He would send a quick telegram to Hume in the morning, followed by posting a detailed report.

Pope suspected Becker would pocket the hundred dollars. The suit was dropped, and the settlement was clean. What Becker did with the money was between him and his company, as far as Pope was concerned. His last name was a trick of bloodline. It was not indicative of any sort of Papal responsibility or turpitude.

The only one tired at dinner was Sarah. She had

gone non-stop at the office, dealing with customer issues and deadlines. The ride to Douglas and
return had been a nice trot in delightful weather.
It had been a nice day on the trail which was for a
successful venture with no danger. Though Pope
referred to it as what they were paid to do, the lack
of threat was singular in their work. Yet, if any
of the three detectives were pressed, they would
admit the threat was what made them get up in the
morning and strap their guns on.

******

Cheyenne's big trial started on time. The witness
waiting room was full. There were more witnesses
than anyone associated with jurisprudence in the
district could remember.

The district attorney himself served as prosecutor.
As a politician who stood for law and order, he could
not turn down the publicity of a big case ending in a
hanging. He was convinced "hanged by the neck until
dead" would be the verdict.

The prosecutor and defense counsel made their
opening statements.

Pope was called an hour before the probable lunch
break.

"Detective Pope, state your name and make a brief
statement of your experience as an investigator."

"My name is John Pope. I serve as a detective with the Wells Fargo company. I have served in this capacity for about a year. Prior to Wells Fargo, I was a police officer, then detective with the San Francisco Police Department. I was there for eight years.

I was sent to Wyoming with my partner, Detective Sarah Watson, formerly of Pinkerton's. We were charged with investigating a series of stage and train robberies in the area. We did so and brought the robbers to justice. Then, before we returned, the office here was robbed. The manager, a female customer, and a town constable were killed by the robber."

"Objection!" the defense attorney yelled. "My client has not been found guilty of those shootings."

"Detective Pope, upon what do you base your conclusion the defendant committed those crimes?" the judge asked.

"I base them on the admissions of the defendant during questioning. The admission of all the murders was witnessed by the sheriff, chief deputy, Wells Fargo Detective Jake Bell, and Detective Watson."

"Continue your statement," the judge ordered.

"Detective Watson was named interim manager and I began to track down leads. We developed the chief suspect to be the defendant. I followed his trail for days during the late fall and winter and lost it when he started using trains. His travels were erratic. I even later went to Bowie, Texas and interviewed his parents. I was convinced we had the right suspect."

"How did you close in on your suspect, detective?" the prosecutor asked.

"I requested our main office construct a list of places he was seen after leaving here. Detective Jake Bell did the sheet listing sightings by name, Kid Taos, or someone with a similar method of operation. We found he had numerous murder and other warrants from other states and territories. Detective Bell arrived in Cheyenne with his sheet and we posted sightings in date order on a map of the Western United States.

While we were following up a lead, he was spotted in Denver. The informant said he was headed north. Cheyenne was the logical place. Based on the mental profile we had established we were pretty certain he was coming back to rob Wells Fargo again.

We raced him here and apprehended him robbing the office and holding Detective Watson hostage."

"How did you apprehend him during the robbery, detective?" the prosecutor asked.

"I tried negotiating with him to release Detective Watson and surrender. I watched his hand on his gun. He began to cock the hammer of a single action Smith & Wesson Schofield held to Detective Watson's head. I drew and shot him in the wrist. I then sent for medical help, put a tourniquet on his arm and took him into custody."

"You mentioned a mental profile. Kindly tell the court what you meant," the prosecutor asked.

"The suspect we were looking for shot down an innocent wife and mother for the crime of walking in the door. Now, managers, whether bank, Wells Fargo or whatever, get shot in robberies. So, do policemen like the one killed during the escape. But, killing a young woman who did not represent a threat indicated to me we were dealing with a cold murderer. The answers we received to questions asked during his interview gave the profile of a person who killed with no hesitation and no remorse. He was a man able to travel, buy railroad tickets, plan a route. But he had no sense of conscience about killing or lying."

"Objection!"

"Counselor, you will have your time in a minute," the judge said.

"Detective Pope, are you convinced we have the right man for the crimes occurring in Laramie County?"

"Yessir. I was convinced when we were looking for him, when he turned up here again and when he confessed to all three murders related to Wells Fargo robberies."

"Your honor, I have no further questions of Detective Pope."

The defense counsel approached the witness stand.

"Mr. Pope, and I will address you as 'mister' since you do not work for a bonafide police department anymore, you mentioned a mental profile. Let me ask you. Do you have a medical degree?"

"No sir."

"Then what in God's name qualifies you to develop a so-called mental profile?"

"Training and experience in listing characteristics of people who commit unspeakable acts of violence for no reason," Pope said quietly.

"Your honor and gentlemen of the jury, I propose to you this private so-called detective, has no more ability to do mental profiles than my pet hound!"

A few people in the courtroom chuckled until the judge slammed his gavel down.

"Mr. Pope. Did you not pull your gun and shoot near the head of your partner, Miss Watson?"

"I did."

"Don't you think such an act is awfully risky?"

"I absolutely do. However, I saw him cocking his firearm to shoot her in the head from inches away. The only way I could stop the gun from going off was to shoot him in the wrist. Had I shot his gun, a ricochet may have hit Detective Watson. It was this or she would have died on the spot."

"Mr. Pope, is it true your associates call you the 'Gun for Wells Fargo?' and you are a hired gun paid to fix things for your company?"

Pope waited a second for an "objection," and when none was uttered, spoke.

"None of my friends or associates at Wells Fargo refer to me by the name you mentioned, so I don't know the answer. As to being a hired gun? I work for one of the most respected, honorable firms in America. I am a hired investigator. My work is dangerous, so I go armed. It is my training, experience and investigative abilities for which I am hired. Not my gun, sir!"

"Moving on, how did you coerce my client into admitting to several murders? Beat him?"

Again, the prosecutor allowed Pope to answer without objecting.

"I did not threaten him or lay a hand on him. You have four other witnesses on your list to cross-examine who saw every second of the interview. I asked Mr. Randolph questions without raising my voice and he answered them the same way. Ask them."

"In your great realm of knowledge about mental matters, Mr. Pope, do you think my client is insane?"

"He has some characteristics of insane people and yet is fully capable of taking care of himself. As you noted, I don't have medical training sufficient to render an answer about his sanity. I know he is too dangerous a person to allow back on the streets."

"No further questions, your honor."

"This court will take an hour recess for lunch. We

will promptly reconvene at one o'clock," the judge said as he struck his gavel against its base.

"All rise," Sheriff Sharples said.

******

Court reconvened at the appointed time. The sheriff and chief deputy were questioned about the interview and validated Pope's report. Witnesses to the first robbery, the shooting of the constable, and the people inside for the second robbery all testified. To a person, their remarks were damning to Randolph's case.

Sarah was called and questioned about being a hostage.

The prosecutor and defense attorney gave their closing arguments, and the judge charged the jury with its responsibilities.

The jury left to discuss what they had heard and develop a finding of guilt or innocence.

Everyone left the courtroom. Most left for the streets and saloons, knowing the word would spread like wildfire when the jury returned.

The district attorney, sheriff, chief deputy, Wells Fargo detectives and mayor adjourned to the district attorney's office to wait.

"I am pretty much convinced they will return three capital murder convictions, as well as the other charges," the district attorney said, confident in his prosecution and the convincing testimony of all witnesses."

"Detective Pope," he continued, "you've been around enough to know the defense counsel was just doing his job. Nothing against you."

"I know. It was irritating, but anticipated, sir."

"Were you surprised the defense counsel didn't call Randolph up to testify?" Akin asked the district attorney.

"Not really. I think Mr. Randolph is a loose cannon and his lawyer knew it."

Like people winding down after a funeral, they joked and tried to relieve the anxiousness which accompanies a trial where people have died, and the defendant's life depended on the finding.

Thirty minutes later, the clerk called them back to the courtroom.

The foreman was told to read their findings.

"On count one, shooting Mr. McCarthy, guilty

Count two, shooting Mrs. Paulson, guilty

Count three, shooting Constable Hopper, guilty

Count four, aggravated assault against Detective Watson, guilty

Count five, robbery of the Wells Fargo office, guilty.

The judge nodded to the sheriff, who said "The defendant will rise." When Randolph did not, he walked over and assisted him almost gently.

The judge spoke again.

"Mr. Randolph. I have to decide your sentence and I am going to do it right now. There is no use in delaying. I must tell you, I have wrestled in my mind with putting you in an insane asylum for the rest of your life. I think, as the detective hinted, part of you is bent. But you seem to get by like normal people until it comes to killing someone.

The jury has found you guilty on three capital murders. I have no option but to sentence you to hang by the neck until you are dead."

The courtroom was silent, except for Mrs. Randolph fainting and luckily being caught by her husband. People filed out behind the news reporters who ran out.

The sheriff and Akin led Randolph back to a cell.

Pope, Sarah, and Bell walked out. Pope sought the Randolph's.

"Mr. and Mrs. Randolph, I am sorry how this went down," he said.

Mrs. Randolph, still tearful, looked at him a long time, then at Sarah.

"You said you'd try to take him alive and you did," she said. Then she addressed Sarah.

"I'm sorry my boy threatened you and the other detective had to wound him," she said.

Sarah hugged her and whispered in her ear "Mrs. Randolph, the other detective is my fiancé. I am sure you can understand the pressure he was under."

"I guess keeping his word was real hard, young lady." Sarah nodded. She learned from Pope a good nod beats saying the wrong thing.

Mr. Randolph shook hands with each.

"Go see your boy in the jail. The chief deputy is named Horatio Akin. He will arrange it," Bell suggested as he shook the older man's hand.

After they parted, Bell said "I think I need a drink, anyone else?"

"No, Jake. Not in the mood. I think I'll take a walk.

"Care for some company, cowboy?"

"I would love some company. Jake, see you later."

They walked down the street. A reporter asked for a statement and Pope denied him.

"How do you feel about this, John?"

"Mixed, honey. Justice was served. He killed people and almost killed one of the only two people I ever loved. At the same time, he was not right in the head. I almost wish he went to an asylum for life. But the district attorney said they are horrible. Worse than dying. He said the hangman was doing Randolph a favor over an asylum.

Maybe one day, there'll be a better way. I don't expect it anytime soon though."

She squeezed his hand.

"Every time I think I've got you figured out, you surprise me, cowboy. But, every time, it makes me love you even more. I didn't think three minutes ago I could. But now I do."

"'I do' sounds good coming out of your sweet lips. Keep practicing it."

"No need. I have it down really well. I can say it in my sleep."

"Good."

They walked on. As they passed the Wells Fargo office, they looked in. Cashier Chester Lyon looked up from where he was manning Sarah's desk and grinned and waved.

Pope gently turned her around and guided her in the door. He picked up a telegraph message pad from Olson.

"JHume. Stop. Kid Taos sentenced to hang. Stop. Case close docs on way. Stop. JPope SWatson JBell."

"Let's finish our walk," Pope suggested as he guided her out the door.

His first stop was the grocer where he bought two apples. They gave one to Caesar and one to Bell's paint. After visiting for a while with the two horses, they continued on.

CHAPTER 11

The day after Kid Taos was hung, the awaited telegram arrived. It was typically laconic, as was James Hume's fashion.

"Pope and Watson. Stop. Return SFO immediately. Stop. Bring all gear. Stop. JHume"

"Well, this telegram could mean anything. Almost sounds like we are being fired. But we've done nothing but clear the toughest cases in Wells Fargo history, so I doubt firing is the reason. You'd think he or Pridham would have the decency to let you know something about the office here, instead of just ordering us back with no explanation," Pope said.

"James Hume is an honorable man, John. You know it as well as anyone. He must have good reason. We should not second guess what it is. We will find out in about three days. It's too late to leave today."

The following day, an assistant manager from a

very large office arrived and introduced himself as the interim manager. Sarah gave him a solid orientation about the office, its staff and the type customers it has. They went by the sheriff's office for a quick goodbye.

Late in the afternoon, they boarded a train after getting Caesar settled in a stock car with the guarantee of plenty of feed and water.

The train whistle blew and the wheels began to turn, taking them to their next adventure. An adventure about which they had no idea.

"John, in the six months in Cheyenne, we have largely lived off expenses. We have saved hundreds of dollars! More than enough for a nice honeymoon!"

"Yes. Or, to buy food if we are out of work. Caesar eats more than both of us."

"I think things will be alright, honey," she said.

After the quick run to Denver, they turned west and crossed the Continental Divide, the Rocky Mountains and several desserts. It was a good trip. They arrived in San Francisco in the morning. They hailed a hansom cab for Sarah and their luggage and gear. Pope knew Caesar needed some exercise and rode along with the cab to their rooms. He tied the big horse outside as they moved back into the now-musty rooms.

"I'll ride Caesar back to the livery by the office and put him up. Then, I will drop by and let the boss know we are back."

Pope rode to the livery and checked Caesar in to a stall. He then walked the block to the headquarters and up the steps to the bull pen. He checked in with Hume's secretary. The man told Pope the boss was on the executive floor in an important meeting. He promised to tell Hume they were back when he returned.

After six months absence, most of the paperwork on Pope's desk was out-of-date junk. It took him a very short time to review and discard all of them.

He waited for Hume to show up. Towards the end of the day, the secretary brought him a handwritten note from the chief detective.

He took it out of the envelope and read it as the secretary waited for his answer.

"Pope and Watson, welcome home. Get out best suits and meet me at rear door of Bohemian Club at noon tomorrow. Highly secret meeting. Share with nobody. Do not come into office first. Hume"

"Tell him we will see him as requested," Pope said.

When he got back to their rooming house, Sarah had aired out both of their rooms and moved them back in.

"What did you learn?" she asked.

"Nothing, really. We have a luncheon date tomorrow at the Bohemian Club with Hume and I suspect someone else. Hume does okay, but he does not swing the kind of money necessary to be a club member. He said wear out best suits. Think we need to do some shopping?"

"I don't know. We can take a look at our wardrobe and decide then. This is very interesting. They would not take us to lunch at some sort of club to fire us."

"The Bohemian Club is the most ritzy club in San Francisco. I have never been there but it's top drawer," Pope said.

"This all means we are meeting with someone *real* important. I wonder who and why?" Sarah said.

"As we detectives say 'I don't have a clue."

"Can I even go into this club since I'm a woman?"

"We are meeting Hume at the rear door. I guess whoever we are seeing is not rich enough to get you in the front," Pope said bracing for the inevitable shoulder punch. It did not come this time.

"Or he is rich or powerful enough and this is really, really secret," she said instead.

"We will just go and see what it's all about. It may be something we will have to talk about privately before accepting."

"I have a strong suspicion you are correct about talking privately," she agreed.

They did not have food in the cabinets of the kitchen in Sarah's larger apartment, so they went to a formerly favorite café and had dinner. On the way out, they bought some baked items for breakfast.

Towards eleven o'clock, Sarah came in with a robe

and nothing else but her .44 Smith & Wesson. She put it on the bedside table on her side. A .44 Colt was already on his side.

She snuggled in beside him and sighed.

"I think we are about to embark on a really big adventure. One more exciting and demanding than managing an office or tracking down some poor deluded fellow. What do you think, my love?" she asked.

"I think there is a bald eagle circling up there somewhere in the night sky. He just has not decided to give me a message yet. And I'm getting pretty damn tired of waiting for it."

"We waited a long time for the wire about our future and it came," she reminded him.

"Umm," he said without conviction.

******

The next morning after coffee and pastries, they took a clothing inventory and decided with a little brushing and hanging by the open window, they would be ready.

At eleven-thirty, Pope hailed a hansom cab and they headed towards Union Square and the Bohemian Club. Sarah was in a maroon silk dress which showed her shiny black locks to good advantage. Pope wore his original Wells Fargo uniform of black suit and vest, white shirt and derby hat. He wore a single shoulder holster.

Pope bade the driver stop a block over from the club. It was part of his tradecraft.

They walked and took up a position behind a tree, out of sight from the street.

Within a few minutes, another cab rolled up and stopped near the rear door.

James Hume stepped out and also took a watchful position.

Pope looked at his beautiful partner. She winked and they circled and walked up to the rear of the club and quietly nodded at their boss.

Hume broke into a large smile and appeared generally glad to see them.

"Good! You both look wonderful. I will be proud to introduce you to the man with whom we are having lunch. More about him once we get inside."

He led them into the back of the building and they climbed one set of steps and went down a hall to a private dining room. It was opulent, though hardly more than the Cheyenne Club where they lunched with the judge, sheriff and Akin at the beginning of their stay in Wyoming.

They were seated and Hume began speaking once the door was closed.

"This is a totally secret meeting. You will be offered an assignment with stipulations. You may turn it down. Either way, it will be the toughest, most dangerous undercover case you have ever had, or likely ever will. It will also be the most important one.

It will possibly be lengthy. You will have to relocate back East for the duration. You will be on loan to the United States government and not reporting to Wells Fargo. I promise you will both be paid handsomely, though I don't know what the amount will be. Nor does the man who will be joining us shortly.

It was he who was approached for lending our two best detectives for a special investigation. And he wanted to be the one to ask you himself. I know you have questions. I can only address what I have said so far."

"Stipulations, boss?" Sarah asked.

"The first one is big. We are a moral company and the man coming shortly is among the most moral. Since you will be undercover in society as husband and wife, marrying is a stipulation. Whether you divorce after is up to you," Hume said.

"If we accept and see this through, will being married harm our careers as detectives?" Pope asked.

"No, it will not. We will make whatever accommodations are required."

"Mr. Hume," Sarah asked, "I kind of expected Mr. Pridham to offer me the manager position at Cheyenne. It looks like it's off the table now."

"Sarah, if you and John pull this off, I daresay you can choose whatever available positions you want at

Wells Fargo."

The door opened and a kindly looking man walked in. He exuded he confidence of power but appeared too grandfatherly to abuse it. He was bald, portly and his hair and goatee were white. He did not wear a mustache.

Hume stood and Sarah and Pope followed suit.

"Detectives Sarah Watson and John Pope allow me to introduce Mr. Leon Tevis. Mr. Tevis is the president of Wells Fargo and virtually all of our associated companies."

They shook and Tevis motioned for everyone to sit.

"Perhaps we should order. As I am sure, James has told you the matter I wish to discuss is highly confidential. We do not want to be chatting about it when waiters or others are about."

"Miss or rather Detective Watson, will you lead us off?" Tevis asked.

She and Pope ordered conservatively, though there were no prices on the menu.

Hume and Tevis were less conservative and both ordered filet mignons.

No alcohol was offered during the meal, which did not bother either guest at all.

After the table was cleared, Tevis spoke.

"What I am going to tell you is the most secret thing any of us at the table have ever heard. I will offer you a case. It will have stipulations. If they are too severe for you, you can turn it down without career prejudice. I am aware you recovered young Mattie Lane, solved the port office explosion, and apprehended this man recently who murdered our manager in Wyoming and others. Your invaluable service is what brought you to mind when this matter arose.

Before I begin, has James explained the marital stipulation to you?"

"He has Mr. Tevis. The marital part is not a problem for us at all," Sarah said. He looked at Pope, who nodded in support.

"The genesis of this case arose last week when I was at an industrialists meeting at the White House. I was called aside and asked for some help," Tevis said.

"Your country needs you most urgently, detectives. Let me tell you why, and how you can serve her."

NOTE

Be sure to watch Wolfpack and Amazon for Gun for Wells Fargo 3, Shooting for Justice. Release in print and Kindle eBook is anticipated in early 2021—The Detectives Pope go undercover on their toughest case. There is a very real risk neither will survive the conspiracy they will face.

A LOOK AT: SHOOTING FOR JUSTICE (GUN FOR WELLS FARGO 3)

STRAP IN FOR A WILD RIDE!

Wells Fargo detectives John Pope and Sarah Watson are on loan to the Secretary of War and the Attorney General. There is a conspiracy against the President, and no one knows who to trust, so they hired outside for the best.

Guns blaze and knives flash as the two develop and follow leads in Washington and around the country. They find sedition and assassination are very different from solving stage robberies.

Will the two detectives be left standing when the last shot is fired?

AVAILABLE MAY 2021

ABOUT THE AUTHOR

G. Wayne Tilman is a full-time author. He retired from the Federal Bureau of Investigation several years ago. Prior to the FBI, he was a Marine, bank security director, deputy sheriff, investigator, and security contractor.

He holds baccalaureate and master's degrees from the University of Richmond and has been an adjunct faculty member there, as well as the University of Phoenix, St. Petersburg College and Florida Metropolitan University.

Some of his law enforcement subject matter expertise includes threat assessment, continuity of operations, security and executive protection, counter intelligence, international terrorism, and small arms. He has been an instructor in those subjects in a number of training academies, conferences and seminars. Mr. Tilman holds the internationally-recognized

Certified Protection Professional board certification, generally accepted as the highest in the security profession. He also earned a US Coast Guard 50 Ton Inspected Vessel Master Captain's license.

G. Wayne Tilman's primary interests are family and writing. His avocations are bushcraft (survival/primitive camping), hiking, boating, kayaking, shooting sports, and travel.

He wrote his first novel over thirty years ago and has now written thirteen novels. Genres include espionage thrillers, mysteries, and Westerns.

G. Wayne Tilman's impetus to write in those genres comes from both personal experience and heritage.

A direct ancestor was a sheriff in Virginia Colony in 1680. Another ancestor was the lawman who brought in outlaw Bill Doolin singlehandedly and helped to decimate the infamous Doolin-Dalton outlaw gang, sometimes known as the Oklahombres. Bill Doolin was the Desperado of song fame. Closer to home, his mother was a counterintelligence agent for what is now the Defense Intelligence Agency or DIA.